Her Dream Wedding
(Cherry Blossom Garden)

A
Historic Christian Romance
Novel

Volume 1, 2nd Edition
A Multicultural Special Edition
Of
The Jenson Bridal Series

Author

Desiree' Evans

Her Divine Destiny
Copyright © 2011 Desiree' Evans

Published under: Create Space Imprint
An Amazon.com Company
7290 B. Investment Dr.
Charleston, South Carolina 29418

This is a work of fiction. Names characters, places, and incidents are either the product of the authors' imagination. Any resemblance to actual persons, living or dead, business establishments or events, or locations is entirely coincidental.

Library of Congress Catalog-in-Publication
Evans, Desiree'
Her Divine Destiny/ Desiree' Evans
LCCN: 2012906398

ISBN: 978-1475086157- Paperback
ISBN: 1475086156- eBook
ISBN: B008F79XNO- KINDLE-eBook

2nd Edition; Volume 1
Edited by: E.J. Wilson
Written and Formatted by: Desiree Evans
Cover by: Create Space Cover Creator
Printed by: Create Space
Charleston, South Carolina, USA
Visit author website @: www.devansauthor.net

Dedication

This novel is written, and dedicated to my late dearly beloved mother; a woman of strong and devout faith, who died of breast cancer at the age of [43]. She was survived by seven [7] young children, and our father. She loved reading the bible & novels. When I was a teen, my mother would often talk to me about the pitfalls of life that trap lovely young women every day. I didn't begin to understand until long after she had went home to glory. She had taught me how to overcome life's trials and tribulations by prayer, and strong faith in Jesus Christ.

This novel is also dedicated to every woman who has searched for her true love, and true purpose in her life. It is also dedicated to every hard-working Mom who only wants the best in life for her children, and encourages them to reach for the stars, because with God, nothing is impossible if you believe. It is also my prayer, that "Her Divine Destiny," will be a blessing, and inspire woman of every age and ethnicity.

Desiree' Evans,
Christian Author/Novelist

Acknowledgements

Giving honor to God the Father's grace in writing this novel; his precious son, my Lord & Savior Jesus Christ; and his Divine Holy Spirit.

My late Dearly Beloved Parents
Lonnie and Viola
I will always love you both; Mother and Daddy.

My Wonderful Husband
I love you sweetheart for always being so supportive.
My Children
Joseph (JoJo), Dione Monique, Eugenie Patryce
My Grandchildren
Patrick, Khamri, Antonio, Andrew, Ryan, Rydell
My Siblings
*Gregory, Darryl Keith, Brett Travis, Patryce Simone

Special Acknowledgements
Pastor Jeremiah Hosford and Lisa Hosford
Abundant Life Jackson
Dr. Gloria D. Pavageau
Lydia Carol Jenkins
Laney M. Moses
Betty Videau
Ann Carter-Catia
Mrs. Lillian Anderson
Gertie *(wife)

Evangelist Evelyn Randolph
God used you as a vessel in 2002 to prophecy that I was pre-destined to write a book someday.
My ninth grade English Teacher
She was first to recognize that I was a writer; when I didn't even know it myself.

Author Preface

There is absolutely nothing we ourselves can ever do, to earn the "gift of salvation;" except to surrender our lives to *Jesus Christ*, for whom be the glory. For, he has already paid the price for our sins; so we have but to walk in his loving grace.

For by grace are ye saved through faith, and that not of yourselves: it is the gift of God; not of works, lest any man should boast: (Ephesians 2:8, 9)[1]

This is the grace that he has given unto each of us, as his children, by sending his only begotten son, *Jesus Christ* to die on the cross for our sins, who is now seated at the right hand of the Father making intercession for us. So therefore, let us never forget, that whatever success we achieve in this life, we achieve by the grace and mercy of Almighty *God*; and that we are here, and were created by *God* for one purpose, and that is to give all the glory to *God* the Father; his precious son, our Lord and Savior *Jesus Christ;* and the Comforter his Divine *Holy Spirit*. May the Lord bless you and keep you.

Desiree' Evans, Author

Table of Contents

Introduction

Azalea Stevens, was a beautiful young American born woman; who was a descendant of Creole-multi-cultural heritage. Azalea's life began in a modest little white country style cottage; with green shutters, and window box planters filled with colorful perennials, that sat under each front window. The cottage had a cozy little front porch, that lead to a cobblestone walkway, trimmed with beautiful perennials on each side, whose trail led to a little white picket fence. Azalea grew up in a small southern town called Sapphire Blue; located just over four miles north of the City of Cherry Blossom, Georgia. Cherry Blossom was a beautiful picturesque city where streets were lined with cherry blossom trees. Located near the entrance of the city, was the famous tourist attraction known as, The Garden of Cherry Blossoms Trees. The city of Cherry Blossom was located near the coast of Georgia. This was where some of Azalea's ancestors had once been servants, and some of their beautiful multi-cultural Creole daughters, were taught the finer points of etiquette by fine rich ladies of Southern Aristocracy. It is believed that this was where Azalea's dreams of living a rich high-society cultural life had come from.

Azalea began life as a sweet and naive country girl, born and raised in Georgia, but she had big *dreams* of becoming a woman of statue, and prominence in the world of fashion designing. Azalea was determined to venture away from, the religious legacy of her ancestral background. Azalea wanted to escape the life she'd often heard about from her Aunt Mae, of attending church every Sunday, prayer meetings, and monthly revivals. Although Azalea was an ambitious young woman who craved success, her Papa was the catalyst in her life to keep her humbled. Besides Papa, there was another person in Azalea's life who was determined to keep Azalea grounded; her best friend Shelia. Shelia; was a constant reminder ever present of where Azalea had begun her search for purpose, and true fulfillment in life.

Azalea's *desires* led her to seek love with the wrong men. The first of these men was named Winston Sanders. Winston was selfish in nature, and very self-centered. He had no set goals in life, which really disturbed Azalea. His desires in life were limited to his immediate wants and needs. He was not able to recognize the special qualities that Azalea possessed, because of his narcissistic personality. The second of these men was named, Jacque Marquette. Jacque Marquette possessed all the outward characteristics that would attract any young woman. Jacque was a dashing young man, who was handsome, suave; as well as debonair. Jacque had a reputation for dressing impeccably. Although, Jacque had feelings for Azalea, his lust for money, and his quest to inherit his family's wealth, dominated his emotions.

Azalea's *passions* would finally lead her to the man of her dreams; her knight in shining armor; Lane Jenson. Azalea would marry Lane and live a life of prominence and privilege she had always longed for; but she would soon discover; that no matter how perfect it may seem in the beginning, the journey thru life has shocking twists and turns. Pride had deceived Azalea into believing that she had it all; until the unexpected happens. Azalea suddenly found herself thrust into a situation, where she would be tried and tested beyond her limits. Azalea's path she'd chosen, had led her to achieve the pinnacle of success in life. Would success alone be enough to see her through her trials and tribulations? Would God's path ultimately lead to *"Her Divine Destiny?"*

Chapter

1

The Birth

The year was 1955; the 8th day, in the month of July. The morning was extremely hot, and humid. The heat was almost unbearable; as the rays from the scorching hot sun, penetrated the tin roof of the little white cottage. Somewhere in a small southern town, all attention in the little cottage; was focused upon the birth of a baby. The baby is being born to a young working class mother; who grew up in a very close knit community. The community was situated in a small southern town, known as Sapphire Blue; located in the beautiful State of Georgia. The town of Sapphire Blue; was located just four miles north of Cherry Blossom, Georgia; the largest city on the seat of Claret County. From beyond the walls of the cottage, the cries of a young woman's voice could be heard, as she had now labored for hours to deliver her baby.

"I'm so thirsty Papa," Azalea cried. Her lips had become parched from the heat outside that was causing the tin roof to make the inside of their tiny cottage feel like an oven.

"I'm going to fetch you a cool glass of water Zale," replied Papa.

Papa always called Azalea "gal," since she was a little girl. He always said that the name Azalea was a mouthful for him to say, so he either called her gal, or on occasion; Zale. If ever there was an occasion, this was definitely one.

"You just hang on gal;" Papa said nervously, trying to remain calm. "Giving birth is just a woman's lot in life." Papa did not want Azalea to sense the fear he still felt; from her mother dying immediately, after giving birth to his precious Azalea.

The midwife; Miss Ella was a devout Christian woman, who attended church regularly, and read the bible daily. She had delivered Azalea when she was born, and was now well into her sixties, but had not slowed down a bit.

Miss Ella always wore a bright smile; that could quickly turn to a frown, if anyone tried to cheat her at the market. She was a tall stout woman with arms that were strong enough to plow her fields for harvest. Her husband had died years earlier, but had paid off every dime he owed so that she would own the property out right. She had one son, named Charles, who had gotten married and moved to Apple Village, South Carolina. Charles worked as a smith in town, but would always come home during harvest-time, to help his mother harvest the crops, to sell at the farmer's market.

Miss Ella was known for saying to young mothers-to-be that; "The good Lord made women's bodies; to be able to stand the pain, despite how delicate they be."

Azalea was now about to give birth to her second child born out of wedlock, so this second pregnancy was completely unexpected. Although Papa tried in every way he knew how, to be strict on Azalea, his sister Aunt Mae would oftentimes say to Papa; "Hank, you can't watch a girl twenty-four hours a day. If they are going to sneak out and see some boy, then you can't stop them." This meant that in another year the baby would be one, and little Clay would be just three years old. Although, Azalea was a strong young independent woman, Papa still treated Azalea as though she was his little girl.

Azalea was giving birth to her second child, in the month of July; arguably one of the hottest months of the year. Just at that moment, the midwife; Miss Ella arrived.

Miss Ella asked, "Is that child bout ready to deliver Mr. Hank?" "I don't rightly know Ella; but I suppose she be close to her time now, replied Papa."

"I best be getting washed up quick then Mr. Hank," said Miss Ella "I already done got all the towels and hot water ready Ella," said Papa."

Miss Ella said, "You done good Mr. Hank getting everything ready for me." Papa replied, "I had lots of practice; with Lil Clay when he was born."

"Look like I got enough to help deliver the baby," said Miss Ella. Miss Ella then went into the bedroom where Azalea had been in labor for the past eighteen hours.

Don't worry child," said Miss Ella; "because I delivered you with these same two hands.

Papa had prayed Azalea and the baby would be alright, and that the tragic history of her own birth, would not repeat itself. The grace of God surely would not allow the same tragedy that happened to Azalea's beautiful Creole mother to happen again to Azalea. Papa thought surely history could not repeat itself in such a tragic way in the Stevens household.

Moments later, the sound of a slap could be heard, followed by an infant's cry coming from the bedroom. Papa could hardly control his emotions as he knocked on the door. "Ella," said Papa "is that gal, and that baby alright?"

Just at that moment, Miss Ella opened the door, "Mama and baby is both healthy and doing fine Mr. Hank. It's a beautiful baby girl," replied Miss Ella.

"Papa shouted with excitement; "I got me a girl grand baby now!"

"Come on in and see for yourself;" Miss Ella said with a beaming smile on her round face. Papa for one fleeting moment thought of the grim look Miss Ella had on her face when she'd opened the door, after having delivered Azalea. He thought of the sad news she'd given him of Mama Lucille not making it. Papa then thanked the Lord. "God be praised!" shouted Papa in excitement.

Azalea said, "Papa I have a little girl, isn't she a beautiful baby?" Papa replied repeating himself, "She sure is; she sure is."

"Papa I want to name her something so different from anyone else Papa." Papa asked, "What is her name going to be? Azalea replied, "I am going to give her a very unique name Papa. Her name will be Matisse. "

Suddenly, little Clay ran into the bedroom peering down at his brand new baby sister and shouted with excitement, in his baby voice and a big smile on his round chubby little face, "Mommy, Mommy; baby sister, baby sister!" Little Clay was so happy that he would have a sibling in the house now to play with. Although, little Clay had been hoping for a little brother, he was just as excited about having a baby sister to look out after.

"Matisse Stevens made her grand entrance into the world on July 10, 1955. Papa was as excited as Azalea to have a little baby girl in the home now. Papa had gone all out to make the cottage as comfortable as possible for the new baby. Papa had constructed a cradle with his own two hands; that rocked back and forth, just like a rocking chair. The cradle was made of oak scrap wood; that Papa had been given by Mr. Ralph; the kind-hearted gentleman who owned the local lumberyard.

Papa had decided to wait until the baby was born, before painting it. Once little Mattie was born, Papa went to the little woodshed located out back, behind the cottage, and removed the cradle to paint it. Papa used a can of oil paint, left over from when he trimmed the shutters of the cottage, and the little white picket fence that surrounded it. When he'd finished, the little cradle glowed under the rays of the sunlight. After sitting out back under the hot sun, the cradle was completely dry in one hour, but Azalea didn't want the smell of fresh paint around little Matisse, for fear of her coming down with asthma, like Papa. Papa decided to leave the cradle in the wood shed for about a week, before bringing it inside.

Azalea's childhood friend Shelia; was just as excited as Papa about the birth of the new baby. The next day, on Saturday morning; there was a knock on the front door of the cottage.

"Hello, Shelia shouted, "You in there Azalea?" "Come in Shelia;" Azalea replied, "Now where do you suppose I'd be only hours after giving birth Miss Nosy Rosy?"

"Well I don't rightly know Azalea, since you seem to have gotten the hang of giving birth down to a science." Shelia replied with a girlish giggle. "Besides girl, you sure aren't one to talk."

Azalea replied, Honey child, you are something else. Now what's inside of that wrapping paper, you're holding so tightly in your arms?"

Shelia replied, "My goodness Azalea, Now who's the nosy one?" "I'm not nosy, replied Azalea with a self-assured smile on her face, "I'm just curious?" "Besides," Azalea added, "I've told you a hundred times Shelia, to please use proper English.

"My English is just fine," Shelia replied in an icy tone of voice. "So you just have to excuse me Miss Azalea, with your bourgeois self."

"Azalea said, "Oh Shelia, "Please don't be angry with me. I apologize for my comment. I suppose it's my hormones, from giving birth."

Shelia quickly replied as her smile suddenly faded by Azalea's comment.

"Now don't you dare go blaming that precious little baby for anything you say outta your mouth honey child, because even when we was little girls, every weekend you got back from being around that little Constance, you talked that way. I try Azalea, but I'm just not you, with all that proper culture stuff."

"Azalea began to cry, as she said, "Please forgive me Shelia. You are as dear to me as any flesh and blood sister God would have given to me. I love you Shelia. You are my best friend in the whole wide world. I would never deliberately do or say anything to hurt you. Please say you forgive me Shelia?"

With tears in her eyes, Shelia sat on the bed next to Azalea, and said, "I forgive you, my dear friend; I forgive you." Shelia then embraced Azalea, as they made up once again, just like they always had, and always will, with a lasting friendship that would endure the test of time.

Shelia grabbed a couple of tissues, as

she wiped away her tears, and placed the large wrapped package on Azalea's bed, and said, "I hope you like it girl, because it took me forever to make it. When Azalea opened the package, it was a beautiful pastel pink, blue, and yellow crocheted blanket, with a matching sweater, and booties of the same soft colors.

Azalea said, "Oh my goodness Shelia, there're absolutely beautiful. I love the colors, as well as the crocheted design. I promise you I will cherish them always," Azalea added, "You are so gifted in your hands Shelia. You mark my words; you and I will someday establish a fashion design company, and you will be my right arm. We will work side by side, to turn it into one of the most successful design houses in the State of Georgia.

Shelia laughed as she answered and said, "You sure do dream big girl." Azalea replied, "It's much more than a dream I have a plan to turn it into a reality, and you'll see someday my friend."

Shelia replied, "You sound so convincing girl, that I almost believe you myself"

Azalea replied, "That's because it's true my friend. That's because it's true."

Azalea then yawned, and said, "I'm so sleepy Shelia, can you watch baby Matisse, until I take a nap; or until Papa return from the store. He went to buy more milk." Shelia replied, "I can do that, but I thought you were breast-feeding girl?" Azalea replied, "I am you silly girl, the milk is for little Clay's oatmeal." As Azalea dozed off to sleep, her mind began to drift back to the past; recalling the stories of her ancestry, as told to her by her late Aunt Mae, and her Papa.

Azalea was now eighteen years old and had already given birth to a little boy two years earlier on, June 17, 1953; whom she had named Clayton. Clayton was named after Papa's father; Clayton Henry Stevens, who was born in 1867. Clayton Henry Stevens; after he'd reached later became a respected farmer, and preacher in the community. Many in the little community of Sapphire Blue; purchased his vegetables at the farmer's market, because he was known for his honesty; as well as his integrity. He was a man of devout faith.

When Clayton was only a baby, his mother; Iris Callie-Stevens, and father; Kent-Hollis Stevens had both died in a fire, while asleep in their cabin. The neighbors were only able to rescue baby Clayton, when the door was kicked in, because his cradle sat nearest to the door, but the smoke was too thick, and the flames too hot to rescue his parents.

Clayton was raised by his late father's brother's wife; Sadie Mae Stevens. Aunt Sadie was a widow. Her late husband had been a sharecropper. Jess Stevens seemed to have a knack for handling money. He could tell if he was a penny short. This is why it came as no surprise, least of all to his wife Sadie when he worked out a deal to purchase the land he sharecropped. He made enough off of his share of the crops he sold at market to make payments on the land. After his death, Aunt Sadie found out that he not only had nearly finished buying the property, but had made arrangements for market to accept the sale of crops from his wife Sadie. Aunt Sadie thought of little baby Clayton, as a blessing sent to her. She nurtured and cared for him, since she had no children of her own. Aunt Sadie sent him to a broken down school held in an old cabin. One day, she said to young Clayton; "I can barely read myself child, but you going to learn, if I got anything to say about it.

His Aunt Sadie; had taught him about the Lord, by bringing him to church every Sunday. His Aunt Sadie would also bring Clayton along, whenever she went to prayer meeting. When Clayton reached fourteen years of age, he began to complain to his Aunt Sadie about going to prayer.

Aunt Sadie was a very stout built woman, with strong arms from plowing for many years. She grabbed him by his ear one day and said, "Boy you going to learn to prayer to the Lord who done made you, or I'll hit you with this here Holy Bible." Clayton replied nervously, "Yes, yes Ma'am Auntie Sadie."

Aunt Sadie could not read well herself, but believed in carrying the Bible every Sunday to church. She believed that it was Holy, and was the indisputable "Word of God." She would have Clayton read the scriptures, and explain them to her. By the time Clayton turned nineteen, he had not only learned to read the bible scriptures, but could quote them; as well.

Clayton worked on the farm every day, and was a blessing to Auntie Sadie, as she seemed to be getting older, and slowing down now. Clayton had just turned twenty, when he told Aunt Sadie one day, that he had decided he wanted to be a preacher someday.

"Glory," shouted Aunt Sadie, "Praise the Lord!" Auntie Sadie shouted. "I knew you would be something good on this earth child." Clayton said, "Auntie Sadie, I hear there's a Pastor in the town of Sapphire Blue, Georgia, that helps young men became preachers, who sat under his ministry a while."

Auntie Sadie asked, "What is you saying child?"

Clayton replied, "Aunt Sadie, I want to go to Sapphire Blue. It's my best chance to become a real preacher someday."

Aunt Sadie said, "Child, I suppose I done taught you all I knows about the Lord."

Clayton replied with tears in his eyes, "Auntie Sadie, no school could ever have taught me what all I have learned from you. I love you Auntie Sadie, and the town is only seventy miles away, so I'll be back every chance I get."

"I know you will my son," replied Auntie Sadie with tears in her eyes.

"I promise that I will help you harvest, and help you plow," said Clayton to Aunt Sadie. Aunt Sadie gave Clayton a hug, and said, "I am so proud of you son."

The next morning Clayton set out from the farm; driving the smaller of the two wagons Auntie Sadie owned. The large wagon; was used primarily during harvest time, to market crops. Auntie Sadie stood waving goodbye to Clayton, as he headed to the town of Sapphire Blue, Georgia, to begin a new life.

The Mt. Bless Baptist Church, was preparing for its' Annual Church Fair. Lily;

the pastor's young daughter; had volunteered to help her mother at the baked sale table. Lily loved to bake cakes and pies. Her peach lattice top pies; were said to be the most delicious sold each year. Lily never would share the secret spice that made her peach pies stand out from all the rest. Some said it was pure ground nutmeg, with brown sugar; while others speculated that it was a mix of ginger, and cinnamon. Whatever the secret was, it enabled her to win the coveted "Blue Ribbon" each year at the fair.

Lily was just beginning to set up her pies; as well as other cakes and pies for sale, when she heard an unfamiliar male voice say, "Hello pretty lady." Lily looked up, as her eyes trailed upward, to the handsome face of the tall young man standing before her, with the winning smile.

"How may I help you?" Lily asked. Clayton replied, "Which one of these delicious pies and cakes are yours pretty lady?" "I baked the deep dish apple you're looking at; as well as this here lattice crust peach pie," Lily Mae replied. Before Clayton could say another word, Lily Mae, who was flustered by this handsome young man who stood before her continued; "I also baked this red velvet cake. I've been told my peach pies are the best though," she said with a sweet shy smile. "Why it has won "Blue

Ribbons" the past three years.

"Well, replied Clayton, "I suppose I'll have to buy a peach pie then pretty lady."

When Lily handed Clayton the pie, their hands touched, and they both felt a sudden shock of static electricity. "My goodness," Lily said softly, "What on earth was that?" I believe that it's called love," replied Clayton. "You certainly do think very highly of yourself," said Lily.

"Well if I don't pretty lady, then who will?" Lily replied, "I suppose you're right. My name is Clayton Henry Stevens," he said. Lily replied, "Lily Mae Bell is my name; so pleased to meet you Clayton."

"That is a very pretty name, for a pretty lady," Clayton replied. "It is a pleasure meeting you Miss Lily," replied Clayton.

"Have you been staying here in town very long," said Lily, "because I don't recall seeing you before?"

"I just arrived in town, and I'm going to study to be a preacher someday," replied Clayton. "My father is a preacher who helps young men become preachers," she replied.

Clayton asked, "He must be the Pastor I am looking for." Lily replied, "Don't you even know his name?" Clayton replied, "I only know the name of his church."

Lily replied, my father is Pastor Jacob Bell; of Mt. Bless Baptist Church." "That's the name of the church I'm looking for," Clayton responded gleefully.

Just at that moment, Lily heard her name being called by her father, "Lily," shouted Pastor Bell, "who is the young man you been talking to for so long now? You know we have got to sell these bake goods before sunset."

"Yes sir Papa," replied Lily. "This here is Mr. Clayton Henry Stevens, and he is going to be a preacher like you Papa." "Well," said Pastor Bell, "Not if he doesn't keep his mind off you long enough to study with me, my daughter. Are you in town for my daughter or me son?" "No sir," stammered Clayton. "I mean, yes sir Pastor Bell; I really want to be a preacher, and learn from you sir."

"Then let's get a move on son, replied Pastor Bell. Times a wasting while you standing around, and staring at my Lily. I got rooms built behind the church for my student preachers. You will share a bath and kitchen the other ministry students."

"Yes sir," replied Clayton, as he waved goodbye to Lily. "I will see you at church Sunday Mr. Stevens, said Lily." "I will see you at church then," replied Clayton. Clayton proceeded to follow Pastor Bell behind the church to his living quarters.

Clayton was determined to become a preacher. He studied faithfully with Lily's father, and worked around the church, whenever he was needed. Pastor Bell almost immediately took a real liking to Clayton, and respected his strong work ethic.

Clayton Stevens; had eventually become a meticulous fine young man, of twenty years old, who was greatly admired and respected for his cleanliness. He was a man who prided himself on how neat he dressed. He would eventually fall in love with, and marry, the lovely young Lily Mae Bell. Mae was as short, as her husband was tall. She stood about five feet tall; whereas Clayton stood six feet, two inches tall. She had thick long hair; that she wore in beautiful braids, usually tied in back with satin bow ribbons. She had a beautiful smile that lit up any room that she walked into. Her skin was a beautiful chestnut brown; that was flawless. Her skin simply glowed in the sunlight. Her mother sewed all of her dresses by hand. Lily Mae had learned to sew by the time she was fifteen years old. This was a gift that would be passed on.

A year later, Clayton Stevens, now twenty-one; and who was now a young deacon, under Lily Mae's father, Pastor Jacob Bell, began to notice that Lily was blossoming into a beautiful fine young woman of seventeen. Lily's father; Pastor Bell was married to Lula Mae Bell for twenty years, and had only one child. Lily's father had always wanted a boy, but his wife never became pregnant again. Lily Mae became her father's pride and joy. Pastor Bell was impressed by Clayton Stevens, the very first time they met. He had told Clayton; that he was very proud of how far he had come in a year's time, sitting under his ministry. Pastor Bell; had even went so far as to say he wished he had a son like him. Clayton often referred to Pastor Bell, as his adopted father, since he never knew his father, since he died when Clayton was just a baby. Shortly after completing his bible studies with Pastor Bell, Clayton got word that Auntie Sadie had taken ill, and needed him to come home. Auntie Sadie was so glad to see Clayton.

Clayton sat by Aunt Sadie's bedside holding her once strong, but now fragile hand in his, as she spoke; "I know you going to make it son, she said. I done raised you to love the Lord." Clayton held Auntie Sadie's hand, and said, "I love you Auntie Sadie," as he wept. Auntie Sadie then closed her eyes, as she drew her last breath.

Auntie Sadie left everything she owned; including the farm to Clayton. She also had some money she kept inside of a box that she kept under her bed. It was enough for Clayton to pay off the farm, and some left over. Clayton now owned the farm outright; as well as the crops. Clayton became not just a farmer, but a well-respected businessman in the town of Sapphire Blue, when he returned. Clayton asked for Lily Mae's hand in marriage, and received her parents' blessings. Pastor Bell performed the wedding ceremony at Mt. Bless Baptist church in the springtime. Clayton and Lily Stevens later had two children. They had a son, whom they named Henry Stevens, and a daughter, whom they named, Cassie Mae Stevens, but was called Mae by all those who knew her.

Cassie Mae was a very attractive young lady in her day, and was one who dressed very well. Rev. Clayton Stevens her father, was now the Pastor of Mt. Bless Baptist Church, where his wife Lily's late father had once been the pastor. Cassie was known as one of the best dressed girls in the town of Sapphire Blue. This was because her mother had taught her to sew when she was just a little girl; just as her grandmother had taught her mother to sew. Mae had hoped to someday pass this skill on to her own daughter.

When Mae was only fifteen years old; she dropped out of school in the 10th grade; to go to work in a dress factory as a seamstress apprentice. Mae was by all accounts, a fine built woman. She would never be called skinny Mae loved baking pies and cakes whenever the church had bake sales.

Hank and his sister, Cassie Mae grew up in church, and would always help out at the church whenever their father needed them. One fine summer day, Mt. Bless Baptist church, was having their annual bake sale. Mae was wearing her thick soft hair pulled back in two braids with a red bow around the tip of each one. She had bangs that nearly covered her eyebrows. Mae was wearing a white peasant blouse that hung slightly off her shoulders, and a red flared skirt, that had a wide waistband that zipped up in the back. Mae also wore a red and white checkered apron with a wide bow tied in the back.

While Mae was selling her bake goods at the church fair, a cocky, handsome young man walked up to her table. The young man's name was Eric Larson. Hank never cared much for Eric Larson, from the minute he laid eyes on him. Mae was Hank Steven's baby sister, whom he loved dearly, and was very protective of since both of their parents had died. Hank was five years older than Mae, and had always taken care of her.

Mae was barely seventeen when she met Eric. Hank Stevens was just about to buy his baby sister's last sweet potato pie, when suddenly, he heard the young man say; "Hey there girl, I know you aren't going to sell my pie to this here cat?" Hank Stevens interrupted before Mae could respond, "I don't see a name on any of these here pies." "Eric asked, "I suppose you already know this fine lady?"

"First of all," Hank replied, "my name is Hank Stevens, not cat." "Secondly," Hank added, "I've been looking out for this here young lady since she was two years of age. "Eric asked, "Just how is that?" Hank replied, "Because, I'm her big brother." Suddenly Mae shouted, "Will you both stop talking about me like I'm not even here?" "I apologize for my forwardness Ma'am; but I was just driving by, and could not continue on, until I had met you," Eric said. Mae replied, "Well, my name is Cassie Mae Stevens. "Allow me to formally introduce myself; Eric Larson is my name," he said; "and I'm a trumpet player." Mae asked, "You are a real musician?" "Why sure," replied Eric. "I done played in all the juke joints all round, and in the city of Blue Ocean, Louisiana, where I'm from. Make a good living at it too," Eric said.

Mae would later fall in love, marry, and run off against Hank Stevens wishes, ran off with Eric, when she was barely eighteen years old. Mae looked forward to being a loving and supportive wife to Eric Larson, and a nurturing and loving mother, to their children. Mae's life with Eric; had not turned out at all, as she had hoped it would. In the beginning, it seemed like an exciting life to Mae; until she tired of Eric dragging her from small town to small town, barely earning enough money, to make ends meet. Eric told Mae, that he needed to return to his home, where jazz music was more popular. Mae gave in, and finally followed her husband Eric to the city of Blue Ocean, known for its' jazz; where he played in juke joints to small audiences.

Mae had yearned for her and Eric to conceive a child. When nothing had happened within a year, she sought medical advice at a local clinic, located across town where women who had the same type of medical problem, went for medical services in Blue Ocean, Louisiana. There was also a small building located at the back entrance adjacent to the local hospital in the city; in the event of an emergency. The prognosis was not what Mae wanted to hear. She was told that she was infertile, and would never bear a child. Mae was devastated by the news.

In order to survive, Mae decided to

get a job to help supplement Eric's small income. She started working part-time as a seamstress, and part-time as a waitress in a restaurant known for its soul food country cooking. Mae was known for being a very hard worker on job, and felt extremely tired one day, so she had decided to get off early from work one day.

Much to Mae's chagrin, she had arrived home unexpectedly to find Eric in bed with another woman. She immediately dropped her bags onto the floor, and ran into the kitchen. Mae was acting on shock and emotion, as she grabbed the container of lye out of the utility cabinet. She ran back into the bedroom yelling as tears flooded her eyes.

"Why, did you do it Eric?" "Get on outta here," Eric shouted. "I done been so good to you," Mae cried. I loved you with all my heart, and now you hurt me like this?" Eric said, "What are you rambling about?" "Well now I'm going to hurt you too," Mae shouted. Tears streamed down her cheeks; revealing the agony she felt from Eric's betrayal." "Eric shouted, "You crazy woman, get on outta here." Eric then reached into the nightstand grabbing his 22 automatic, shooting and wounding Mae in her left shoulder, but not before she was able to throw the lye upon Eric, and the "other woman," lying in bed with him.

A next door neighbor, who had heard the arguing, had called the police; as well as an ambulance. Mae was rushed to the local hospital emergency room for immediate medical attention to remove the bullet from her shoulder.

Fortunately for Mae, the bullet had traveled thru her shoulder, leaving an exit wound. Eric and the other woman were both rushed to the same hospital; as well for second and third degree burns; that they had sustained from the lye; that Mae had thrown on the both of them in the heat of passion. Mae was informed by the police, who waited for her, that she would be arrested for assault with a dangerous substance, and was told that she would be tried once she had recovered.

The judge in the case ruled that Mae had acted in "the heat of passion; and her actions were a result of the shock, of finding her husband in their bed with another woman. The case was dismissed. Several months later, Mae received word that, Eric had been killed in some type of bar brawl supposedly over another man's wife. Mae not having a child for Eric had been a blessing in disguise.

Chapter

2

Henry "Hank" Stevens, as he was affectionately called by those who knew him; later met and fell in love with the beautiful Lucille Wright, who was the daughter of Rev. Taylor Wright, and Marie Dupree-Wright, in the small town of Sapphire Blue, Georgia; on September 18, 1927. Lucille's mother Marie Dupree; was Creole, while her father Taylor Wright, family were from the Caribbean Islands. Marie Dupree; had a beautiful olive complexion that looked radiant in the sunlight. Taylor Wright was a handsome young man when he met Marie. Hank Stevens family came originally from the Island of Martinique, along the Caribbean coast. had decided that he didn't want to go into the ministry like his father, so Rev. Wright became the Pastor of Mt. Bless Baptist Church, when Hank's father; Pastor Clayton Henry Stevens died.

Hank Stevens, and his wife Mama Lucille, had prayed for a baby. Everyone called her Mama Lucille, because, in the winter, she would bake delicious chocolate chip cookies, and give them out to all of the children in the neighborhood. Mama Lucille was also known for making the best homemade banana ice-cream in the summertime. Whenever a child would go to the corner store for her ingredients, she would reward them with a large scoop of ice-cream on a cone.

The Stevens had tried for many years to have a child, and was blessed to conceive a child later on in years; Lucille was in her late thirties, and Hank was in his forties. When Lucille finally became pregnant, it was a happy time for her, and her husband; Hank Stevens. The Stevens, Hank neither Mama Lucille, were prepared for the tragedy that was to follow their months of joyous anticipation. Hank and Lucille were so excited about the upcoming birth of their first child. They had decided that if it was a boy, he would be named after Henry Stevens. They had decided that if it was a baby girl, they would name her after Lucille's favorite flower; which was Azaleas.

When Lucille's time came to deliver her baby, Hank Stevens had run nearly a mile to the small farmhouse, located in the country, just outside of town where the mid-wife, Miss Ella lived. Miss Ella had monitored and delivered most of the babies in their little community for a number of years.

"Come on Miss Ella;" yelled Hank Stevens. "Hurry woman," he cried; "because that baby is coming fast.

Miss Ella said to Hank, "Follow me," as she jumped into her wagon used to carry produce to market. When they arrived, they could both hear Lucille screaming. Hank and Miss Ella rushed into the room to find Lucille biting down into a sheet, that she had gathered tightly into her small delicate hands, to ease the pain. Sweat was pouring down heavily from her forehead onto her brows.

"Thank the Lord, we made it just in time;" Hank cried, as his voice trailed off.

"Hurry, go on." said Miss Ella. "Get on outta here" she shouted, as she ran Hank out of the bedroom.

Hank Stevens anxiously awaited the birth of his first baby, as he sat in a rocking chair just outside of the bedroom door. Suddenly, Hank could hear the screams of Mama Lucille cease, and the cries of a baby began. The door opened. The mid-wife, Miss Ella, exited from the room carrying a blanket that bundled a baby girl. Papa was so excited.

"It's a baby girl, Hank," she said. "I got me a baby girl," he shouted with excitement in his voice. Miss Ella did not reply, and Papa suddenly noticed the grim expression on her face, and asked; "How's my Lucille doing Miss Ella?"

"I am so sorry Hank," she cried. I did all I could to save Lucille, but couldn't."

"Oh no," shouted Hank. "You are lying to me Miss Ella," he cried.

Miss Ella replied, "I am so sorry Hank, but you got to know that I tried my best to save her."

"This isn't true," shouted Hank, as tears rolled down his cheeks. Stop that lying, he said."

Miss Ella then tried to explain to Hank Stevens, in her own simple words, how that his wife; had suddenly started experiencing complications during labor. She told him that Lucille had said if it came down to a choice, that she wanted her baby to live.

Miss Ella told Hank, that Mama Lucille told her, that she and her husband Hank; had waited many years on a child. Miss Ella then told Hank, that Mama Lucille; had made her promise; that if it came down to her life or the baby's; that she; Miss Ella, was to save the baby. Miss Ella then told Hank, that his wife; was willing to give up her own life; rather than lose the child she had nurtured, and carried for nine months in her womb.

Because there was not a hospital within fifty miles; to give adequate medical care, the midwife was the only medical care she had. Miss Ella explained to Hank, that the baby was born breech birth; which meant feet first. Miss Ella told Hank Stevens, that she just did not possess the medical knowledge, nor the medical equipment needed to save both mother and child in that situation.

Hank Stevens was not an educated man, and was not able to fully understand the complexities of what had just happened. All he knew; was that he had lost a fine wife; and didn't know how he would go on without her in his life. Hank Stevens named his baby girl after his wife's favorite flower, which was an   Azalea. Hank and his wife had grown up in the small country town of Sapphire Blue; just four miles north of Cherry Blossom, Georgia. Everyone knew everyone there.

The Butcher was Mr. Carson, who had known Azalea since birth. Mr. Carson was considered a blessing to the community, because if you were not able to pay in cash, he would barter. Sometimes Mr. Carson would receive payment such as a basket of eggs (2 dozen) for a pound of pork chops, or carved wooden pieces to sell in his store window in exchange for 2 quart bottles of milk, and a pound of churned butter.

Often times he didn't really need the items, but his acceptance made the people feel they were paying their way, which left their dignity intact. This was why he was so well liked by the community. His family, were Italian immigrants from the "old country."

He had grown up in the northeast, but had moved his wife and children down south after the economy was hit hard back east. He had made a new life for his family after settling in Sapphire Blue. Hank Stevens would sometimes walk up the street to Mr. Carson's store just to say hello, and talk about the boxing matches.

Hank Stevens, was so devoted to little Azalea, that he was called "Papa." He was given the nickname by the mailman, Mr. Richard right after Little Azalea had born. When little Azalea began to talk, she called Hank Stevens Papa; as well. Mr. Richard had known Papa for many years. One day when Hank Stevens was just a little boy, he and his father were at the corner store, when he was occupied playing with his ball. Suddenly, little Hanks ball rolled out the door of the store into the street. When little Hank ran to get his ball, he felt a hand jerk him back onto the sidewalk.

The next sound heard was screeching tires as a car rolled over his ball. When little

Hank got up he noticed a smiling face of a little boy who said, "You sure are lucky I was passing by here." Little Hank walked over to the little boy and said, "You just saved my life. You like a real hero." The little boy replied, "Why I'm no hero, I just go to Sunday school, and they teach me that Jesus gave his life for me is all." Little Hank said, "My name is Henry Stevens, what is your name?"

The little boy replied, "Richard O'Brian, but my friends call me Richie." Little Hank asked, "Can I call you Richie?" "Sure," he replied. "Besides my Dad says if you save someone's life, you are responsible for it, so I suppose I will have to look out after you now." From that day forward; the two little boys formed a unique bond.

Papa had decided to retire from the Southern Railroad Company; to try and care for his baby girl. Papa had worked twenty-five years, and would soon be turning fifty. The winter months were freezing in the little white cottage and summers months were scorching hot. Papa often times would have to chop wood for their wood burning potbelly stove to keep the family warm.

Papa had begun to experience asthma attacks since the loss of his wife, which hindered him in taking care of little girl. The next door neighbor, Mrs.

Thompson, often helped him out.

Folks used to say Papa Stevens, was never the same after Mama Lucille died. Papa knew he had to continue to live for his little Azalea. He had no idea how to care for a little girl and sent word to his sister, Cassie Mae, that he needed a woman's hand in helping him do so.

Mae was ready now ready to move back to Georgia; where she lived in a rooming house. She had found a job as a maid for a very old and very rich Southern family by the name of LeBlanc. The Leblanc's were one of the oldest aristocratic families from Cherry Blossom, Georgia. Mrs. LeBlanc was born of French heritage, and had insisted that Mae refer to her as Madame LeBlanc. Mae was then hired on as their maid. She had worked for them for a number of years following the incident with her husband Eric.

The only people during that time, for her to lean on, were the Leblanc's. The LeBlanc's; who become very fond of Mae, had treated her like a member of the family. Therefore, it came as no surprise; that Mae immediately told Mrs. LeBlanc of her good news. Mae had received word that she was needed to help her only sibling; Hank Stevens, her brother, raise her little niece.

It all began one morning, when Mae

arrived at her job, Mrs. LeBlanc handed her a letter. "Mae," said Mrs. LeBlanc; "This letter arrived for you late yesterday evening, after you had already left for home."

"What is it Madame LeBlanc, she asked? "I don't know Mae," replied Mrs. LeBlanc, "You know very well that I don't read other people's mail."

Mae was able to read pretty well for herself. Reading had always been her favorite subject; before she had dropped out of school. Although she often spoke broken English, she had prided herself on being able to read well.

When Aunt Mae opened the letter, and began reading, her eyes filled with tears. Aunt Mae did not see a name on the envelope, but recognized the return address. Papa; had asked his dear old friend Mr. Richard, to mail the letter for him, and had asked that Mr. Richard send it special delivery. Papa had decided not to put his name on the envelope; for fear that Mae might reject him after so many years.

When Mae opened the letter, she saw that it was indeed, from her brother, Hank Stevens. Papa had found out by word of mouth; that his long-lost sister Mae, had finally moved back to Georgia. Mr. Richard, Papa's best friend, and a mailman, was able to locate her whereabouts. Papa had no idea that Mae lived so close to him. She was roughly within a five mile radius southeast of him, in the city of Cherry Blossom, Georgia

"Madame Leblanc," said Aunt Mae, "I'm going home, my brother needs me!"

"Why Mae," replied Mrs. Leblanc; "What on earth are you rambling on about?"

"Looks like I'm going to live with my brother now Ma'am; since his wife died. He says he needs me to help him raise his little baby girl," Aunt Mae replied with excitement in her voice.

"What pray tell," cried Mrs. LeBlanc, "am I supposed to do if you're leaving me now?"

"I don't know Ma'am," replied Mae, with a sad tone in her voice.

Mrs. LeBlanc replied, "Haven't we been good to you Mae?" Mrs. LeBlanc now had tears welling up in her eyes.

"Yes ma'am," replied Mae.

"Well then pray tell, sobbed Mrs. LeBlanc, "Just what am I to do now without you Mae?"

Mae quickly replied, "I'm not leaving yawl Ma'am, I promise; but could I bring my little niece with me to work on the weekends?" My brother gets that asthma real bad and he about fifty years old now," said Aunt Mae. "He be getting on up in age. He be too old now to run behind a young'un, especially a little girl child," said Aunt Mae.

"Why of course Mae," replied Mrs. Leblanc. You most certainly may bring her on weekends, if you insist." "Your little niece could keep little Constance occupied, whenever I have the ladies from the Cherry Blossom Society Club over for tea on Saturdays. However Mae," said Mrs. Leblanc, "We need to be perfectly clear about one thing." Mae replied, "Yes ma'am?"

"You will need to keep her in the kitchen at all times with you, is that understood?" "Yes ma'am," Mrs. LeBlanc, Aunt Mae replied.

"Besides," replied Mrs. LeBlanc, "you know how active Little Constance can become, when she feels like she's being ignored," said Mrs. Leblanc.

"Yes ma'am "Mrs. Leblanc," replied Aunt Mae. Mae had been a faithful employer to Mrs. LeBlanc, and was happy Mrs. Leblanc was willing to accommodate her little niece, but was saddened inside by what seemed to be Mrs. LeBlanc's lack of compassion for her family's situation; following her years of loyalty to their family.

One day that Mr. Richard delivered a letter from Hank Stevens sister; Cassie Mae. Mr. Richard the letter to saying she was coming to live with him, and little Azalea.

The day that Mae arrived in the taxi, was one of the happiest days of Hank Stevens life. The only two other days he was so excited, was the day he married his late wife Lucille, and the birth of little Azalea, which was somehow overshadowed by the loss of his wife, Lucille during childbirth.

Hank Stevens now felt that he was long overdue for some happiness. His sister, Cassie Mae would bring that happiness to the little cottage of where her brother, Hank Stevens, and his little girl Azalea lived.

Little Azalea was waiting on the front porch, when her Aunt Cassie Mae arrived. Mrs. Thompson had dressed little Azalea in one of her Sunday best dresses. Azalea wore a little white flared cotton dress with a beautiful light petticoat underneath. The little dress had little puffed short sleeves, and a little rounded collar. The dress was covered with a light pink and white dotted-Swiss pinafore made of chiffon, with a big bow tied in the back. Azalea wore light pink socks; that were turned down, and were trimmed with white lace. Mrs. Thompson had styled little Azalea's hair pulling her thick, long curly hair back, with a pink ribbon tied around her ponytail, and soft curly bangs on her forehead.

The minute Azalea spotted the taxi; she immediately ran indoors shouting so as to use the full capacity of oxygen her little lungs. "Papa, Papa, she's here, she's here." "I'm coming child, Papa replied." "Hurry Papa," shouted Azalea.

When Papa stepped onto the porch, and saw his sister Cassie Mae paying the driver the fare, he took little Azalea by the hand, and hurried to meet her before she could even step out at the taxi. When Mae finally stepped out of the taxi, she hugged Papa so tightly, he could hardly breathe. "I missed you so much Hank," said Cassie Mae. "I missed you too, replied Papa."

Little Azalea stood smiling, seeing her Papa so happy for the first time.

"This here is your niece, Little Azalea Stevens," he said to Cassie Mae. Cassie Mae swooped little Azalea up off the sidewalk, and hugged and kissed her.

"Put me down," said little Azalea, "I am a big girl."

"You sure are," replied Cassie Mae, with a laugh." Cassie Mae then placed little Azalea back down, and told her just how pretty she looked in her little white dress and pinafore.

"Thank you," replied little Azalea. Cassie Mae replied,

"Now child," said Cassie Mae, "you just call me Aunt Mae from now on." Azalea replied, "Yes Ma'am Aunt Mae."

Aunt Mae said to Papa, "that child show is mighty proper talking for a little girl." Papa replied, "I know Mae." Mae asked, "Who she learning that from?"

Papa replied, "My next door neighbor is a retired school teacher, and she been helping me look after my little Azalea since she was born."

"Well that is my answer," Mae replied. "It makes a lot a sense to me now."

Aunt Mae looked at little Azalea, and said, "We going to get along just fine child." Little Azalea smiled, and said, "I love you Aunt Mae."

Azalea quickly bonded with Aunt Mae. In no time at all, Aunt Mae became like the mother Azalea had lost. Hank Stevens had so much joy now. Azalea loved weekends at the LeBlanc's.

As time passed, Constance and Azalea became very close. Constance loved poetry, and had taught Azalea how to read with expression the poetry and prose of some of the world's most famous writers. Azalea often times could hear the classical music of famous composers being played whenever Mrs. LeBlanc entertained her society club on Saturdays.

Through Constance, she had learned to distinguish between the artists, and composers of classical music. Azalea was receiving a formal education at Mrs. LeBlanc's, that she would never have received otherwise, had it not been for her friendship with little Constance, and the years of hard work, and loyalty of her Aunt Mae to the LeBlanc family.

Every Saturday morning Little Azalea arose out of bed with much anticipation for what new and exciting adventure the day would bring her. As the bright sunshine beamed through her bedroom window, Little Azalea pressed her forehead to the window eyeing the beautiful pink azaleas; that were her favorite flowers. Little Azalea loved them especially, since she had been named after them.

She had helped her Aunt Mae plant them in front of the little cottage that used to look so dreary, but had now been transformed by Aunt Mae's feminine touch. Aunt Mae had loved sewing, and had sewed beautiful curtains for little Azalea's bedroom window. They were pink cotton with ruffled lace trim.

Aunt Mae had also bought little Azalea's an antique bedroom suite. Little Azalea's bedroom was a Queen Anne style that was fit for a little Princess. Aunt Mae hand crocheted a gorgeous pink cotton quilt with eyelet design. She had also given little Azalea for a birthday gift, a beautiful writing desk. Little Azalea loved spending hours at her desk reading books Aunt Mae would bring home from work.

Mrs. Leblanc's daughter Constance was required to read books often by her teachers. She'd sometimes become bored with books she had read, or didn't find particularly interesting that she owned. Once she had read them, she would give them to Azalea; who had come to enjoy reading.

Azalea would literally become captivated by the books she read. It was a way for her to travel to faraway places, and see sights she could only dream about, in the world in which she lived every day. Over and over again she buried her head in books. She loved fiction, such as romance novels; as well as, non-fiction; such as books of historic significance.

Azalea grew to love reading so much, that she became known to her closest friends as a bookworm. One particular Saturday, as Aunt Mae was preparing for Mrs. Leblanc's tea party with her social ladies club; Mrs. LeBlanc walked into the kitchen, and asked Aunt Mae;

"Where's Azalea Mae?" Aunt Mae was so afraid to tell Mrs. LeBlanc, that Azalea was in the upstairs parlor, where little Constance was always teaching her friend, little Azalea about etiquette and southern culture. Constance was being taught at Miss Carol's School of Southern Charm and Etiquette, and loved having Azalea as a pupil.

"She is up in the upstairs parlor with Miss Constance," Aunt Mae replied in a hesitant tone, as though almost afraid of the consequences.

"Why Mae," Mrs. Leblanc replied, "Surely you didn't think I had no knowledge of the hours she spent with my little Constance, did you?"

"I didn't know Mrs. LeBlanc, replied Aunt Mae. "I am so sorry Ma'am."

"No Mae," replied Mrs. Leblanc, "It is I who am sorry."

Aunt Mae asked, "What do you mean you sorry Ma'am?"

Mrs. LeBlanc replied, "Yes Mae, I'm sorry about the way I behaved, when you told me about your brother and little niece; so will you please forgive me Mae?"

Tears appeared in each of their eyes, as Aunt Mae replied, "Oh Mrs. LeBlanc, there is nothing to forgive. You all have treated me just like family when I didn't have anybody to lean on."

Aunt Mae then placed her arm around Mrs. LeBlanc's shoulder as she wept, and said,

"We have all grown so fond of that child Mae. She has brought a special purpose to all our lives," replied Mrs. LeBlanc. "You mark my words this day Mae;" she continued, that child is going to make you proud one day."

Although she had little friends at school, with the exception of little Constance; whom she saw only on Saturdays and rarely on Sundays; little Azalea remained largely to herself when she was at home; until she met a little girl named Shelia. I suppose Azalea and Shelia became such good friends because they had both experienced the loss of their parents at a young age. They became like sisters. Shelia had been adopted by her grandparents, the Thompsons, since both of her parents had been killed in an automobile accident.

Shelia was only five years old at the time, and had only met her grandparents once, since her mother had left the south, and moved up north with little Shelia's father, before she was even born. Life for little Shelia; considering the sudden tragic loss of her parents, would have been almost unbearable for little Shelia; had she not been introduced to little Azalea, who lived next door.

Azalea didn't particularly like going with Aunt Mae to prayer meetings, but looked forward to the time that there were revivals held at the church. This was because on the last day of revival, there was always a grand fellowship held behind the church.

Azalea and Shelia both; enjoyed the good eats that were always served on the last day. The six picnic tables where everyone sat down to eat; were covered with red and white checkered table cloths. On two other large picnic tables covered with red and white checkered table cloths, was an abundance of was mouth-watering, delicious southern country cooking.

The buffet spread out on each table included, crispy fried chicken, collard greens, candied yams, corn bread, biscuits, fried fish, barbecue ribs, and fried okra. She also loved the desserts which included; coconut, and red velvet cakes; peach and apple pies. There always at least two large jugs of ice cold lemonade on each picnic table.

Because of Aunt Mae's job as a maid for the LeBlanc's, Azalea had acquired a deep passion, and love of reading books. This was her way of dealing with the fact that her mother had died in childbirth leaving her for her papa to raise alone. Since Papa had to work on the railroad to provide for little Azalea; she was alone and often times comforted by her friendship and talks with little Shelia, until Aunt Mae came to live with Papa and Azalea.

Aunt Mae had taught Azalea to sew

like a real seamstress, so by the time Azalea was fifteen years old, she was able to get a part-time job working at Parkinson's dress factory; while attending Lilac's School of Design.

Azalea had dreams of becoming a famous fashion designer for the rich high society set in Georgia. Azalea worked by day, and attended school at night. Parkinson's department store; was the location of the most sought after off the rack dresses in the city. Azalea loved Aunt Mae so much.

Azalea lived only a short distance from her job which was located right in town. Aunt Mae still worked for the LeBlanc's in Cherry Blossom; which caused her to always make it home after Azalea. Azalea didn't mind this little fact at all, because she loved waiting for her Aunt Mae to surprise her with something special.

After getting home from her own job at the dress factory; Azalea loved relaxing in her favorite scented bubble bath called. In the summer, she would put on one of her many blouses, and a pair of her comfortable shorts, and sat on the front porch anxiously awaiting Aunt Mae's arrival.

Although Azalea was a teenager, Aunt Mae still treated her as though, she was still little Azalea. Azalea had always been treated so well as an only child. Aunt Mae would always bring home delicacies like crab cakes or fried shrimp; that had been prepared with fresh seafood caught off the coast of Cherry Blossom. Sometimes she would bring home real French puff pastry like cream puffs or chocolate éclairs which was Azalea's favorites.

The Leblanc's, whom Aunt Mae worked for, were always having elaborate dinner parties. Mrs. Leblanc always insisted Aunt Mae take some of the leftovers home with her. Aunt Mae was a very proud woman; but she knew that Azalea would love these treats. Azalea had become accustomed to the ritual of Aunt Mae arriving home with delicate pastry treats.

One hot Friday evening didn't feel right to Azalea. She had always had such anticipation of Aunt Mae coming home, but Azalea could not shake this feeling of dread this particular day. Aunt Mae stepped out of the taxicab with two pink bakery boxes for Azalea who was waiting with opened arms.

"Aunt Mae," Azalea said, as she ran out of the front door to meet Aunt Mae; "What surprise treats do you have for me this time?"

"Azalea," replied Aunt Mae, "I sure spoiled you child. Give your Aunt Mae a big hug." Suddenly, Aunt Mae collapsed in Azalea's arms.

The white bakery boxes fall to the ground; the tiny fancy chocolate and white frosted cakes rolled to the ground.

"Aunt Mae," shouted Azalea, "Please get up Aunt Mae"? "Please, Aunt Mae won't you get up?" Azalea cried, "Oh Lord; please help me?" "Papa, Papa," cried Azalea."

"What on earth is going on gal?" Papa yelled.

"It's Aunt Mae Papa," replied Azalea, "she just collapsed in my arms Papa."

"Quick, you run next door gal and call for help." Papa held Aunt Mae while Azalea ran next door to use the phone and call an ambulance for Aunt Mae. When the ambulance arrived Aunt Mae was not breathing. The coroner was called and pronounced Aunt Mae dead.

"No, no, no, no, this can't be happening," Azalea screamed. "Not Aunt Mae," she cried, "Not my Aunt Mae.!"

Tears flowed from Azalea's eyes like a dam had broken, releasing every ounce of water it had held back for years. The results of the Coroner's autopsy determined that Aunt Mae had suffered a massive stroke.

"I don't care what some coroner's report reads, said Azalea. "It was hard work that killed my dear sweet Aunt Mae," cried Azalea. "I tell you Papa," she repeated, "It was nothing but hard work that killed her."

"I promise you Aunt Mae," Azalea had cried at Aunt Mae's funeral, "I will never have to work hard like you did, and I will make something of myself, that you will be proud of."

It was shortly following the passing of Aunt Mae, when Azalea gave birth to a baby boy. When Azalea became pregnant, and had her first child at sixteen, it was hard for her to finish her education, and so she dropped out of Lilac's School of Fashion Design, and decided to work fulltime and earn extra money to help support her son, little Clay, and help Papa who had raised her.

Papa was a blessing to Azalea, since he had now officially retired, and was able to babysit his grandson. Although Azalea had promised her Aunt Mae that she'd never work hard, factory work seemed very tiring at times, especially during the hot summer months. Azalea really missed the love and nurturing of her Aunt Mae. Papa tried his best to fill her shoes for Azalea.

"Where is that baby bottle? That child is crying too long."

"Why Papa, replied Azalea, she's alright, I'll be right there. I just have to test the warm temperature of the milk."

"How you do that?" said Papa. "I just hold the bottle upside down and let a drop fall on the back of my hand," replied Azalea. "You show do thinks of everything child," he said.

"I showed you what to do before Papa; don't you remember?"

"I reckon so gal, but I'm getting on in years now, and I can't remember like I used to." Azalea replied, "Why Papa, stop talking such nonsense, because you're just as spry as you ever were." "Azalea my child," Papa replied; "You is a blessing to me gal, and a good Momma to them babies."

Azalea worked very hard to support her children, whom she loved with all her heart. It goes without saying the love she also had for her Papa, who had stuck by her side through thick and thin. Hank Stevens had tried his best to shield his daughter and only child from heartache in life, but once Azalea had become with child, it shattered his expectation of her purity remaining with her until she'd one day meet the man God had chosen for her to marry.

Chapter

3

Shortly after Aunt Mae had died, Azalea met a young man who had a reputation. He was known in those days, for being a scalawag, by the name of Winston Sanders. Winston was said to be a notorious liar, who sought after the most vulnerable young ladies he could find.

Azalea had just turned sixteen, and was very naïve of the ways of the world. Winston knew that her Aunt Mae had died, and saw how Azalea had blossomed into a fine young woman. His motives for spending time with her were driven by nothing more than his own lust for her body. To him, Azalea was as ripe as a peach, and twice as ready for the picking by him. Winston cared nothing about her feelings.

Azalea had begun keeping company with Winston, without Papa's knowledge. Her best friend Shelia; had repeatedly warned Azalea about Winston's reputation, but to no avail. Azalea was convinced that Winston had genuine feelings for her. One day after work, Winston had given Azalea a ride home. Winston told Azalea, that he loved her and wanted to marry to her someday. He then proposed marriage to her, and Azalea accepted. Winston first drove Azalea to his tiny apartment, where he said he needed to pick up her engagement ring; that he had so conveniently forgotten to bring with him. He then poured her a glass of red Bordeaux wine, and told her to relax.

"I'm not accustomed to drinking alcoholic beverages," she said. "Don't worry baby," replied Winston in a deep voice, and with a lecherous grin on his face. "I just want to show you how much I love you."

"I'm so very afraid Winston," replied Azalea. "I've never done this before." "My Papa and Aunt Mae were so strict on me growing up."

"Aunt Mae brought me to church every Sunday and stressed the virtue of a girl saving herself for marriage."

"What do you think we're doing wrong baby?"

"It just doesn't feel right Winston." Azalea replied. "My Aunt always said I should save myself for marriage."

"We getting married," he quickly responded. Azalea asked, "When Winston?"

"You show do smell good," he replied; as he sniffed her blouse; evading her question. "Your skin looks so soft and beautiful. I love you," he said. Azalea was very naïve to the ways of the world, and slick men like Winston. She finally gave in, and surrendered to his persistent advances.

Afterwards, she was awakened to Winston's voice; "Come on girl, hurry and get on up outta here," Winston said, "because this isn't just my apartment." "What?" Azalea replied feeling a bit disoriented by this time.

"You hear me girl," replied Winston, "a friend of mine rents it with me, and he going to be home from work soon; so you got to go baby;" he said. "I need to freshen up first Winston, replied Azalea.

"Okay, okay," replied Winston, "But make it quick." Azalea hurried to the bathroom to freshen up, but wondered what had happened to the ring Winston had promised her. When she walked out of the bathroom, she asked;

"Where is my ring Winston?" "Don't worry girl," he replied, "I'll bring it the next time I pick you up from work. Now hurry so we can go. "

Azalea asked, "How did you know my ring size Winston?" Winston replied, "Because, your friend Shelia told me."

Azalea knew Shelia did not care for Winston at all, and wondered why she would keep such a secret from her best friend in the first place.

"Come on now girl, we have to go. I'll drop you off at that bus-stop on the corner, closest to your house, said Winston."

"Okay," replied Azalea, as she began to get a sick feeling deep down in the pit of her stomach; that Winston had deceived her. As the days passed without even so much as a word from Winston Saunders, Azalea began to regret that time spent with Winston, that cost her a precious gift of purity, that Aunt Mae had told her was priceless. Aunt Mae had always said "the Lord gave you that gift my child, meant to be for your husband, as his gift from you to him on you all wedding night." Azalea felt as though something was not right, but knew that what had happened, could not be undone.

Azalea's intuition proved to be correct, as it turned out to be a very long time before she would even lay her eyes on Winston again. Nine months later, she would give birth to her first born; a healthy baby boy, that she named Clayton Stevens. He was given the nickname of little Clay. Azalea loved little Clay dearly. She used to call him her "little man," because he was always trying to help her with the laundry, whenever she folded clothes she had washed.

One day while it was raining, Azalea

waited at the bus stop under her umbrella for her ride to work. Suddenly, a car stopped at the corner, and the driver blew his car horn. Because of the hard downpour of rain, Azalea was unable to see clearly just who the male driver was, until she peered closer to the window.

"Hey girl, need a ride?" It was Clay's long-lost father Winston Sanders. Azalea had not seen Winston in two years; not since he ran off from Sapphire Blue, Georgia to Blue Ocean, Louisiana; to marry the woman he left her for. Winston was a light-skinned man with an ego the size of a snow capped mountain. Azalea had found out a year ago that the beautiful young woman had later left Winston because of his cheating ways. Azalea often wondered when he would surface again. Winston was said to be like "a bad penny." He was always "turning up at the wrong time." Winston had never given Azalea a silver dime towards the support of little Clay.

"Hello Winston," Azalea replied coldly. "Is that all you got to say to me girl?" he asked.

"What else is there to say to you Winston?" replied Azalea. "Don't you even realize that when you left me, you just didn't just leave me, but you deserted your own son? He was just a sweet innocent little boy, who had never hurt anyone, including you;" replied Azalea. "Look here, I just wasn't ready to be no daddy at that time girl," shouted Winston defensively.

Azalea replied, "I don't believe you'll ever be ready to be a father to my son Winston." Winston replied, "So how is my boy doing anyway?" "

What do you care Winston?" replied Azalea. "Look here girl, he's mine too. I'm the one who made him, and I got every right to see that boy," he replied defiantly.

Azalea would not be bullied nor taken advantage of this time. "How dare you even attempt to claim any rights to my son Winston? You gave up any rights you had, when you walked out on him." Now go away, and leave me alone," replied Azalea.

"So, you still the snooty; and stuck-up Miss high and mighty. Girl you ain't never gonna change," Winston replied with sarcasm in his voice. Just then Azalea spotted her bus; "You just stay away from me and my son, or I'll call the law on you Winston, you hear me?" Azalea yelled to Winston as she boarded her bus.

"Sure thing, I don't need any more problems no ways girl," Winston shouted back at Azalea, as he drove off.

Azalea took her seat and began to read a novel, that she had wrapped in cellophane, and tucked in her raincoat pocket; as she often did while riding on the bus to work. She needed to get her mind off of the encounter she had earlier with little Clay's father; that had a left a bitter taste in her mouth. Azalea not only had little Clay to think about now, but also little Matisse.

An entire year had gone by and Azalea was still working at the dress factory as a seamstress. This was of course a blessing, since she would once a month secretly sew a new dress for her beautiful little Matisse, who was now a year old.

"Azalea," Jeanie yelled; over the noise of the machines sewing, "Are you still going to the party for Shelia; Friday after work?" Shelia was now working alongside her dear friend Azalea, as a seamstress in the Parkinson's dress factory, which manufactured women's and girl's dresses for Parkinson's Department stores. Azalea was lost in her far away thoughts again, and didn't hear Jeanie.

"Azalea Stevens," shouted another co-worker, named Linda; "Would you please stop day dreaming and tell us your answer?"

Jeanie said, "Azalea," "We really need to know whether or not you are coming, to make certain there's enough to eat for everyone."

"Of course, I'll be there Jeannie,"

replied Azalea. "You know very well I wouldn't miss it for the world."

"Just checking," replied Jeanie.

Azalea then declared, "You all know very well, that Shelia and I are best friends." Azalea had volunteered to help with the planning, but Jeanie; and the other girls knew Azalea's hands were filled with caring for two young children, and her Papa was getting on up in age, and not always feeling up to the task, they'd thought.

When Papa was younger, he loved going to the local juke joint every week-end, shoot a few games of pool, and have a few beers with his friends from the railroad. When Aunt Mae had come to live with Papa and little Azalea, he would sometimes take little Azalea with him after school on Mondays. The old juke joint, that had now become a quiet place, where all the old timers, gathered together to watch the baseball game on television.

Some years later, after Aunt Mae died, Azalea and his two grandchildren, little Clay and little Matisse; were now all Papa had left in the world. He absolutely adored his grandchildren. Papa was content now to just keep a watchful eye on little Matisse, while little Clay was in school and, Azalea worked hard each day. Little Clay and little Matisse were such a joy to Papa each day that he spent watching them for Azalea.

Matisse's' absentee father; Jacque Marquette, a handsome light skinned man of Creole decent had seemed to be in love with Azalea. Jacque's family lived in the upper-class part of Cherry Blossom, reserved for Creole society, or those of aristocratic mixed blood lines. Azalea had grown up learning all the finer points of the aristocratic life-style when Aunt Mae worked for the LeBlanc's.

It was Azalea's intellect and classy ways that intrigued Jacque; but he would only visit Azalea whenever Papa wasn't home. Azalea was delighted to spend quality time with Jacque. She'd prepare delicious meals for him. Jacque's taste buds acquired a taste for Azalea's country soul food.

Jacque's favorites were collard greens with salt pork, cornbread; crispy southern fried chicken. Jacque also loved whenever Azalea served as an appetizer; fried green tomatoes and onion rings made. Azalea would always prepare a large serving of this entrée joined by either key lime pie or red velvet cake for dessert. Jacque loved ice tea; but his drink of choice was a fine, and mellow Southern bourbon.

Azalea had often times been told by her best friend Shelia; that Jacque was not sincere and that he was just using her for his own self-gratification; but Azalea had been swept away by his charm and good looks. Azalea was riding on the Cherry Blossom ferry boat when she spotted Jacque for the very first time. Jacque was wearing his military uniform having just returned from fighting. Azalea had a beautifully shaped body which Jacque noticed immediately. Jacque began picking Azalea up from work every evening. He'd offer Shelia a ride as well. Shelia knew that it was just for appearances, so that there would be no gossip about he, and Azalea.

There seemed to be an instant chemistry between the two of them. Jacque would visit Azalea in the beginning, always bringing with him, flowers and a box of chocolates. Papa never seemed to trust Jacque's charming ways; but Azalea had fallen deeply in love with Jacque. Papa's concern; was because of the fact that Azalea who already was the mother of a little boy didn't have time to play games. Papa wanted a man who would love and cherish Azalea. Papa was getting on in years and wanted to know that Azalea and her little boy Clay would be provided for.

Jacque was so suave and debonair. He was a very dapper dresser. He was often referred to by those who knew him as the "The Best Dressed Man with the Plan." He sure had a plan alright. He planned to seduce

Azalea and leave her with a child to bring up
on her own. Jacque always seemed to want to
stay home with Azalea never taking her out
in public. Azalea was a beautiful woman, and
possessed a radiant light-skinned
complexion, with Azalea's close friends, who
knew Jacque, said he treated Azalea this way
because although she had a light-skinned
complexion, because she was of multi-
cultural heritage; Creole/part French,
Spanish, Cherokee Indian, and Caribbean);
her ancestors were of an African lineage
traced by to the 1850's, so she wasn't what
was known as, "Passé Blanc." Jacque
frequently sought Azalea's company behind
closed doors. Whenever he would go spend
time with Azalea, he always made it a point
to leave before Papa would come home from
his Wednesday and Friday night deacon
meetings at the church. Azalea became
increasingly tired of this treatment.

Azalea was beautiful on the outside,
but she possessed an inner beauty which
made her even more radiant. Azalea had such
pride and dignity. She loved the poets. She
cherished the classical music composers. She
loved the paintings of great artists. Azalea
also loved to read great novels; as well as
non-fiction and reference books. Azalea's
reading explorations had educated her as if
she had a graduate degree. Azalea was also a

connoisseur of fine art.

It was mid-November when Papa had gone to visit an old friend he knew from the railroad when he was younger. His friend Mr. Jackson had run into Papa at the corner hardware store. Although Papa had just turned seventy-five years old in October; he still liked to go on the corner and buy some type of small tool like a screwdriver or talk with the old timers he knew. It seemed to make him feel younger.

Papa also loved to fish now and then but, taking care of Lil Clay while Azalea worked, hadn't left much time for fishing. When Mr. Jackson told Papa that his youngest son was taking him on a fishing trip Papa was so excited. Mr. Jackson told Papa that he had a little grandson about the same age as Lil Clay who was seven years old, and that he would be going along with Mr. Jackson, and his son on the fishing trip. He told Papa that they would be staying in a cabin his son had rented, and that there was more than enough room to bring Lil Clay along. Azalea was excited for Papa. Not only was it a perfect opportunity for little Clay and Papa to spend time together; but it was also a golden opportunity, for Azalea and Jacque to share a romantic evening without fear of interruption.

Saturday evening arrived not a

minute too soon; as Azalea had worked all day to prepare the perfect intimate dinner for Jacque. The table was set with the fine china Aunt Mae had left Azalea. The china had been a gift to Aunt Mae one Christmas from the Leblanc's. It was made in France. The table was covered with a French lace tablecloth that had been a gift as well. The table was light with two long spiral candles held by two antique candelabras.

The dinner was a Chef's salad served with French dressing. Warm French bread with butter. The main entrée Azalea served Jacque was a thick succulent steak with a baked potato topped with butter sour cream and chives with yellow rice served on the side. She had also baked lobster served with butter on the side. Dessert was chocolate éclairs; Azalea's favorite ironically, was Jacques's favorite dessert as well. She had also prepared fresh squeezed lemonade to wash it all down. Azalea had even managed to purchase a bottle of Jacque's favorite southern bourbon.

The evening seemed to progress well, with the soft sounds of romantic music playing on the phonograph. Jacque whisked Azalea onto her feet and began dancing with her. Azalea had never felt this way before. The night was perfect. She just knew that Jacque would propose to her this beautiful autumn night. Jacque and Azalea walked outside to look at the stars. Jacque gently lifted Azalea's chin as he placed a very soft kiss upon her lips.

"I love you Azalea, you know I do, said Jacque.

"I know in my heart, that one day we will marry, and be so happy Jacque, "replied Azalea. "Jacque said,

"My dear sweet Azalea, I don't want to wait any longer, will you marry me?" "Yes Jacque," replied Azalea, "I will marry you!" This was the happiest night of Azalea's life. She was so in love with Jacque; that evening, Azalea melted in the passionate warmth of Jacques' loving and strong arms.

The night Azalea had spent with Jacque had ended on a very romantic note. Jacque hurried as he dressed. Even though it was Saturday, and Papa wasn't due back until Sunday evening, Jacque did not want to take any chances. He was hoping that he'd be gone by the time Papa returned from his fishing trip. Azalea spotted Jacque as he was leaving.

"Jacque," said Azalea, "you're not leaving so soon are you? I've fixed a nice breakfast for you," Azalea said. Azalea had the table set with an aluminum pitcher of fresh squeezed orange juice, buttermilk pancakes topped with hot buttery syrup, pork sausage links, thick country ham, grits, bacon and scrambled eggs.

"Well I just thought you needed some time to prepare for when Mr. Hank gets home Azalea," replied Jacque."

"Oh no Jacque, I'm just fine," replied Azalea." "You sure are baby;" Jacque replied, as he grabbed Azalea around her petite waist; in a flirty tone of voice referring to Azalea's beautiful shapely figure.

Azalea said with a little laugh, "Jacque, will you please stop flirting so I can fix your breakfast?"

"Sure baby, replied Jacque; "After all, you know I have to keep up my strength," Jacque replied with a smile.

Azalea asked, "Would you like to attend Shelia's party with me as my escort Jacque?"

"I'm not sure," replied Jacque, "I believe that I have something important I have to take care of on that evening Azalea," he added in a not so convincing tone of voice.

"But Jacque, everyone will be there and I don't have a date, and you've never taken me out before," said Azalea.

"I know, replied Jacque, but I have other plans."

"Are you ashamed to be seen in public with me," said Azalea.

"Of course not woman, that's not it at all," replied Jacque. "I just have some other business that requires my immediate attention on that evening," said Jacque."

Azalea replied, "Business so important, that it would keep you away from one evening out with me Jacque?"

Jacque responded in an agitated tone of voice, "Azalea will you please stop nagging me about a silly party?"

Azalea snapped back; "Was last night silly to you as well Jacque?" "Tears began welling up in her big beautiful brown eyes that were now filled with sadness."

"Of course not Azalea, you know that I love you, it's just that my family; Jacque paused; you do understand Azalea, don't you?" "I just can't afford to lose my inheritance.

"All I understand Jacque, is that you say you love me, yet your actions say something else." "You know very well, that my family has threatened to disinherit me if I continue seeing you;" Jacque replied." "We'll need that money to make it once we're married;" Jacque added.

"All I need is you Jacque," replied Azalea, "and besides that, both of us already have jobs, so why do we even need their money to live on Jacque?" "You just really refuse to understand Azalea; I love you but we're talking about a sizable chunk of money"; replied Jacque.

"We have love, and that should be enough," replied Azalea; as she poured Jacque's coffee. "Look, I'm sorry Azalea," replied Jacque.

Azalea replied, "Please tell me what it is that I don't understand Jacque? "Azalea replied. "Azalea," said Jacque, "You are such a romantic woman, but love won't pay bills."

Azalea replied, "Neither will words."

Jacque said, "Exactly what do you mean by that Azalea?"

"I simply mean that your constant need to keep me a secret from your wealthy family has practically bankrupted our relationship," she replied. Jacque retorted, "As far as I'm concerned, this discussion is closed." From that point on, you could literally hear the sound of a feather if it were to hit the floor. The kitchen atmosphere was thick with tension.

Azalea suddenly became silent, as though she had withdrawn into her world of books she loved to read when she was just a young girl. She thought that somehow she could perhaps tune out the crackling sounds of twigs burning out on a campfire; that had once burned with the love, desire, and passion of a forest fire. Time seemed to fly by; as Jacque hurriedly tried to finish his breakfast, and rush out the front door. "I'll see you on Monday," said Jacque as he made a hurried exit out the front door. Azalea was once again left alone to dream about marriage to her elusive fiancée.

Chapter
4

When Papa returned from his fishing trip with Clay, Azalea was excited to see them. Papa it's so good to have you and Clay back home again, I really missed you both so very much" she said.

"Well," replied Papa, "we are glad to be back gal." Papa sat his fishing tackle box down next to the kitchen door, and sat down at the table, as Azalea poured him a nice cold tall glass of iced tea, with a lemon slice. "You know Zale, them mosquitoes is so bad in the summer; especially round all that water," he added. "I certainly do Papa," Azalea replied. "Child," asked Papa, "what is the matter with you?" "Nothing Papa," Azalea replied. "I suppose I just feel under the weather." "I sure hope that boy hasn't been round you," replied Papa. "I told him to stay away from you" Papa said.

"Oh Papa," replied Azalea, "I love him, why can't you understand that," she responded? "Gal you don't know the meaning of that word," replied Papa. "You done already made one mistake, now don't you go and make two," he added.

"Winston was a mistake Papa," replied Azalea, but not little Clay," she replied.

"I love that boy with all my heart," Papa replied. "Its' them no good men that comes sniffing round you child;" said Papa. "I just don't trust any of them," he added.

Azalea began to cry. "Papa I know that you love me and little Clay, but you have got to let me grow up," she replied.

"I just can't help worrying about you gal. You my only child," said Papa.

Azalea replied, "That's my point Papa, I'm not a little child anymore, and I want you to see that I am a grown-up woman, and that I'm going to make mistakes in life."

Papa lowered his head, and a tear rolled down his cheek to his white beard; as he said to Azalea, "I knows all that already, but it still don't stop me from trying to protect you Zale.

Azalea began to cry, and said, "I don't mean to hurt you Papa. Lord knows that I don't; but I have got to be allowed to live my own life Papa;" she said.

"Zale," replied Papa, "I sure do hate seeing you so sad all the time."

"I'm fine Papa," replied Azalea. "I'm never sad when I have you and little Clay around," "I know assuredly that you both love me very much."

On Monday morning, Azalea and little Clay were up bright and early, to eat breakfast, before Azalea would be leaving for work. Papa had already prepared a nice breakfast for them. "Papa," said Azalea, as she and Clay walked into the kitchen, "You spoil us," she said. "My mouth is watering for your delicious light and flakey biscuits."

"I just try to do my best for you all," he replied. "I promised my sister Mae, God rest her soul; I would take good care of you all."

Once Azalea had left for work, Papa began to reminisce about the time when Azalea was just a little girl, and her mother; his wife became very ill, and died. Mae came to live with him and little Azalea after Mama Lucille died. Papa realized that even though he and Mae had not seen one another in years; he knew that she would be there to help him with his little girl. He and Mae had been raised to believe that "blood was thicker than water, with the exception of her best friend Shelia, who was like a sister to Azalea since childhood. Papa recalled the day that he told little Azalea about the fact that she had an Aunt named Mae, and that she was coming to live with him and little Azalea. Papa recalled in his mind the conversation.

"Come here child," Papa said to little Azalea. "Now you know I got to take care of you, and don't know much about caring for no little girl child."

Little Azalea interrupted her Papa, and cried, "Oh no Papa; I love you so, please don't send me away. I promise I'll be a good little girl."

Papa replied with tears in his eyes as he hugged little Azalea; "Child, I won't ever sends you away, cause I loves you too. My sister Cassie Mae is coming to live with us, and she is going to help me take good care of you."

Papa thought about how much of a blessing Aunt Mae had been to him and little Azalea. Papa thought how time had just seemed to fly by. Papa was left to now take care of Azalea and her little boy; Clay.

On Tuesday morning, Papa had gone to the Brass Band Club Hall, to play bingo and watch television with some of his brothers who belonged to the Club. Azalea heard a knock at the door; "Knock, knock!"

"Azalea," Shelia yelled, "are you in there girl?"

"My goodness gracious Shelia," replied Azalea. "Are you trying to wake up everyone in the neighborhood?"

"Not really; just you sleepyhead;" replied Shelia, with a giggle.

"Come on in," replied Azalea. Shelia was so very anxious so hear of Azalea's evening with Jacque, that she could hardly keep her voice down.

"Well Azalea," asked Shelia, with excitement in her voice. "So tell your very best friend what happened last night?"

"Simmer down Shelia," replied Azalea. "Can't you be quiet for one minute?" "Yes," replied Shelia.

"Then, you just hush your mouth and finish enjoying your breakfast Shelia," said Azalea. "I will Azalea," replied Shelia; "but only if you promise to fill me in on all the wonderful details." Azalea poured a cup of tea for Shelia, and served tea cakes that Aunt Mae had taught her to bake when she was a little girl.

Azalea had also prepared; fried bacon, eggs, and creamy buttered grits. Azalea and Shelia both loved this for breakfast since they were little girls.

"Would you like milk in your tea Shelia?" "Yes, and two sugar cubes," replied Shelia. "Azalea," said Shelia, "You already know how I like my tea. Boy oh boy, that Jacque must really have your head in the clouds this morning honey child."

"He most certainly does not,"

replied Azalea.

"Come on," said Shelia. "The suspense is killing me Azalea," she added. "Now tell me what happened before I just burst."

"Well, Miss Nosy;" replied Azalea, "We had a lovely dinner, and the evening was so very romantic. I tell you Shelia, it was just like right out of one of my romance novels I love reading, and I could not have written it better myself."

Shelia asked with anticipation, "You didn't let him make love to you, huh Azalea?"

"I'm not able to eat breakfast this morning Shelia," replied Azalea. "So what does that tell you?" "Oh my gracious," replied Shelia, "I hope you were careful Azalea."

"Shelia, Jacque promised me that he was very careful." said Azalea. "Well, if you say so;" Shelia replied, with skepticism in her voice.

Azalea waited with anticipation on Monday after work, for her ride with Jacque as usual. "Azalea, I really don't think he's coming to pick you up today," said Shelia.

"Please hush up Shelia," cried Azalea. "You have no idea what you are talking about, because, Jacque loves me. He said so when he proposed to me on Saturday night," said Azalea; "and what's more, he's taking me to Blue Ocean City, for our honeymoon."

"Azalea," replied Shelia; "You know that I love you like the sister I never had, so I must tell you how I truly feel."

Azalea asked, "Could I even make you shut-up right about now Shelia?" "I don't mean to get you all upset Azalea," replied Shelia; "Nor hurt your feelings in any way, but where's the ring?" "What?" Azalea replied; "What was that you asked me Shelia?"

Shelia replied, "I asked you, where is the engagement ring?"

"Why I don't know," replied Azalea, in an agitated tone of voice. Maybe Jacque will surprise me this evening when he picks me up from work today. Now stop talking Shelia," said Azalea.

After waiting an unusually long time on Jacque to pick her and Shelia up from work; Azalea walked back inside the department store to see if Jacque had called, and perhaps left a message for her.

Azalea asked the desk secretary Gail, "Has there been any phone calls for me today from my boyfriend?"

"There were no phone calls come in here today from your boyfriend," replied Gail. "Azalea," said Shelia, "We had better just go on; call a taxi, and split the fare; because it's starting to rain."

Since Shelia and Azalea were next door neighbors, it was the economical thing to do, especially since it was obvious, that Jacque would not be coming to give them a ride home today. As Azalea and Shelia rode in the taxi, Azalea began to think about her last romantic evening with Jacque.

Suddenly Azalea's thoughts were interrupted by the taxi driver who said, "Sure looks like an all-day rain huh?" Azalea nodded, and replied, "It certainly does."

Azalea's mind then immediately drifted back to her private thoughts, as soft raindrops fell upon the windows of the taxi. Azalea began to analyze her last evening she spent with Jacque systematically and methodically. It suddenly began to dawn upon Azalea, that she may have made a mistake in trusting Jacque. Jacque had stopped picking Azalea up from work. He had also stopped coming to the cottage to see Azalea, even when Papa was not home.

A couple of months later, the fairy tale really ended for Azalea when her monthly cycle was late, and she began to feel sick early in the morning. Her tea cakes, eggs, bacon and grits would not stay on her stomach. This was Azalea's favorite breakfast so she knew something was wrong. Azalea told her best friend Shelia how she had been feeling lately and about the romantic night she and Jacque had spent together when Papa was away on his weekend fishing trip.

"Oh Azalea," said Shelia. "You must see a doctor; you sound as though you might be pregnant again."

Azalea began to weep, and asked, "Oh Shelia, what am I going to do, I just can't be pregnant again?"

"Try not to worry Azalea," replied Shelia. We'll figure something out; I promise."

"But Shelia," replied Azalea, "Lil Clay will just barely be two years old; by the time this baby would be born. Don't you see Shelia? I just can't be pregnant again. It will just kill Papa."

Azalea just did not realize how strong Papa really was. He was in fact, stronger than she had thought he'd be after finding out.

When Papa found out Azalea was pregnant again, he knew it had to be Jacque's baby. Papa noticed that Jacque had suddenly stopped coming around to spend time with Azalea. Papa had also heard ugly rumors being spread about Azalea being with child again and not married yet. Papa was there for Azalea and her unborn child. Jacque had been warned by his aristocratic family to stay away from Azalea, whom they considered to be of a lower class. Jacque's family had threatened to disinherit him if he continued to see Azalea.

Two years had now come and gone; since Azalea had given birth to baby Matisse. Little Matisse was now two years old, going on three, and little Clay was about to turn five before very long. In all the time that had passed, Jacque's desire for Azalea had still left a burning desire for her; which is the reason why he showed up late one night at Azalea's door intoxicated.

Jacque became very angry; because Azalea refused to let him inside of the house. "Open this blasted door Azalea, right now or I'll kick it in."

Jacque then became very threatening toward Azalea. "Woman, you'd better open this door right now," he yelled.

"Go away Jacque, I mean it or I'll call the police."

Jacque's aggressive behavior made her fear for herself as well as her Papa's safety. Jacque yelled, "I'll kick in this blasted door if you don't open it right this minute."

Azalea didn't respond, instead she called the police. She was told by the police to lock herself, and any family members in a room, as a safety precaution. So Azalea, Papa, Clay and little Mattie were in a bedroom safely behind a locked door.

"I know you're in there Azalea," shouted Jacque. "I know that you can hear every word I'm saying to you woman."

Azalea refused to answer Jacque's slurred outbursts, as he continued alternating between knocking on both, the door; as well as the window.

When the police arrived on the scene, Jacque was arrested for drunk and disorderly conduct. Azalea was determined to keep Jacque out of her and Matisse's life this time. She filed formal charges with the hope that he would not be locked up, but rather that the courts would restrict his coming around her again. Although a court date was set, Jacque never showed up. The case was later dismissed.

Azalea always believed that the case was dismissed was because of Jacque's family influence. Although there was never any formal court ruling, Azalea was not to see, nor hear from Jacque for some time to come, following the incident that had left many of her so-called friends talking about for a long time. Many had thought Azalea should never have started a relationship with Jacque Marquette to begin with in the first place.

Chapter
5

Azalea had now moved on with her life and was actually enjoying her freedom. She had gotten dressed, and was about to leave home on this particular evening, to attend Shelia's party. It had been quite a while, since Azalea had any social life, what with work, Papa, and two children only two years apart. Azalea had really anxiously anticipated attending the party on tonight. Just as she was about to leave for the evening, she heard Papa's voice.

When Papa spotted Azalea leaving he asked, "Azalea, where on earth are you going this time of the evening; its 8:00 o'clock already, and getting dark outside?"

"Papa," replied Azalea, "Haven't we had this discussion before?" Papa replied, "We show have gal, and you just don't listen to me. You just put those babies to bed, and now you sneaking out the front door."

Azalea argued, "I just can't believe this, will you please stop treating me like I was still a little girl Papa?"

"You are acting like a child," Papa argued back. "Look Papa, I'm a grown-up woman with two children," replied Azalea."

"You show don't need to remind me of that Zale. That is why you need to listen to me," replied Papa. "This party is for Shelia's birthday Papa," replied Azalea. "You know that I wouldn't miss it for the world."

"You are too hard-headed child," replied Papa. Azalea just shrugged her shoulders. Papa continued fussing; "You forgets about them two babies daddy's that went and ran off on you," "Papa this is a surprise birthday party being given for my best friend Shelia, replied Azalea, "and I don't plan on missing it."

Azalea had adorned her best light green taffeta dress that was gathered at the waistline with an A-line skirt which accentuated her figure beautifully. Azalea had worked many late hours while Papa babysat little Clay and Baby Matisse. Working late nights presented Azalea the opportunity to sew her design that she had created. Azalea had saved her extra money to buy the right pair of shoes which were pale green satin. Azalea had made her mistakes, but she stood her ground. She didn't run away from her responsibility to her children.

"You not leaving here tonight gal," said Papa; "and I mean it!" Azalea shouted, "Papa you get from in front of that door and I mean that!"

Papa was so angry, that he slapped Azalea across the face with the palm of his open hand, on the side of her cheek. "Oh no Azalea my child," cried Papa, "Please forgive me?"

Papa sounded as though he was tortured by what had happened. Papa had never even so much as spanked his precious Azalea when she was a child growing up. Papa seemed to be in pain for what had just happened. Azalea stood still; her lips quivered, as tears ran down her cheeks. "Papa I love you," Azalea replied; "but you must let go."

Papa replied, "I loves you too child." Azalea replied, "Then you can trust me now, can't you see that I have learned my lesson?"

"I'm getting on up in years, and just can't help worrying bout you gal," replied Papa. Azalea replied,

"Papa, as much as I love Mattie and Clay, I will never bring another child into the world ever again without a ring, and a vow before God."

"I believe you gal," said Papa. Azalea embraced Papa, washed her face, and applied her make-up once again; which consisted of light face powder and lipstick.

"Papa," said Azalea, "I almost forgot Shelia's birthday present." "I didn't even kiss baby Mattie or little Clay goodnight," said

Azalea.

Azalea then walked into the beautifully decorated bedroom she shared with little Mattie, and brushed her curly soft hair from her brow, before kissing her chubby rosy cheeks goodnight. "Momma loves you so very much Matisse," said Azalea. Although little Clay liked calling her Mattie for a nickname, Azalea loved calling little Mattie by her full name. After Azalea tucked Mattie in, she turned on the lamp light with the soft pink rose light. Azalea then walked into the bedroom that Clay shared with Papa. Clay yelled, "Look Momma, I put my jammies on all by myself." Azalea replied, "You're Mommy's big boy."

Clay then asked, "Mommy, can I stay up with Papa? I want to watch some babe ball. Azalea chuckled and replied, "You mean *baseball* my little man Clay."

Clay asked, "What is it called Mommy?" Azalea replied, as she tickled little Clay's belly, "*B-a-s-e-b-a-l-l*; spells *baseball*."

"Can I stay up Mommy," Clay repeated, without any thought to what his Mommy had just told him. "Yes Clay," replied Azalea. "You may stay up for one more hour, and then it's time for bed Clay," said Azalea.

Clay immediately hopped out of

bed, and reached for Azalea to give her a hug. "Thank you Momma, said little Clay, but it's just Clay now, because I'm a big boy right Mommy?"

Azalea replied, "Yes you sure are Clay; you sure are. "Goodnight Momma's big boy Clay," replied Azalea.

Time seemed to just keep rolling along, as Clay had finally turned five years old, and wanted to be called Clay; since he was now called Clay by all his schoolmates and teacher at kindergarten.

"I'll be home soon Papa; don't worry." Papa stood in the doorway watching as Azalea walked up the street to the party being given for her friend Shelia; while three year old, wide-eyed little Mattie leaped out of bed; and stood with her plump little hands holding onto Papa's pajama pant leg as she watched her mother from the bottom portion of the screen door. The screen door had an indention where Mattie, would press her forehead against it to watch her mother until she was out of her sight; whenever she would leave for work.

Little Mattie had taken her completion partly from Azalea and partly from her father Jacque. Mattie had beautiful big brown almond-shaped eyes that sparkled when she looked at you. Mattie had been born with a light-skinned completion; that was a combination of her mother's beautiful dark brown mahogany skin tone, and her father's fair complexion. Although Matisse was a beautiful little girl, she still did not have fair skin, so she was not accepted by her father Jacque's snobbish family. She had high cheek bones like her paternal grandmother's Cherokee Indian ancestry, and her thick hair came from her mother's Creole- Caribbean ancestry. Mattie's hair was of a cross grain texture. Her hair was very long but thick and curly. The texture of her hair was thick yet, had very silky curls that were so soft to the touch. Her little lips were thin yet full and almost heart-shaped Papa loved Clay and little Mattie so very much. They were indeed, the joy of his life.

When Azalea was gone, Papa settled in for the evening. He left little Clay asleep in the bedroom, while he sat on the front porch a while. Papa loved sitting on the porch in his rocker; as he listened to the birds singing; and watching to see, who was passing by the house in the evening. He often times held conversations with those folks he knew from the neighborhood. This particular evening, he talked to someone else, that he usually didn't talk with on these evenings. Papa was getting older now, and was concerned about Azalea and the children.

He began to talk to the Lord in prayer "Lord," Papa prayed, "I don't know how much time I got left; but I need to know that Azalea and those babies will be taken good care of when you call me home." "I need to hear from you Lord," he prayed. "Lord my child done met the wrong men before." "Please send her the right man to take care of her and my grandbabies." "I show do, thanks you Lord. "Amen," said Papa. Papa then tilted his head upwards, looking toward heaven; as though he could see the Lord from where he had knelt and prayed. Papa had reason to be concerned about his Azalea, since she was not only his only daughter, but his only child; as well.

Azalea and Shelia had a very close friendship, which is why the last thing Azalea wanted to do, was not attend Shelia's party. The real turning point that sealed their friendship, began one morning, during the time that Azalea was first pregnant with little Matisse. Azalea was experiencing morning sickness so bad, that she was not able to go in to work that day. When Shelia went next door that morning to pick Azalea up for work, as she always did; Azalea told her what the problem was.

"I can't go in to work Shelia," said Azalea. "I'm having morning sickness so bad, and can't hold anything on my stomach."

"I'm so sorry Shelia; that I won't be there with you today." Then, without a moment of hesitation; Shelia immediately asked her friend, Azalea, "Since Papa Stevens has been picked up for his doctor already, would you like me to stay home with you?"

"Thank you so much for caring Shelia, replied Azalea; but I'll be alright on my own, until you or Papa get home." "Okay girl," replied Shelia; "but don't you hesitate to call me at work if you need me." "I won't," replied Azalea.

"Well," replied Shelia, "I'll see you later." "Okay," replied Azalea; and you take care not to work yourself too hard at the factory today." "I'll try to do just that," replied Shelia, as she hurried to the bus stop to wait for bus ride to work.

Shelia had no idea what was to transpire on her job that day. Shelia and Azalea's friendship was so very close, that they were always scheduled to work on the same days, and off on the same days. The manager over the seamstress at Parkinson's Department store dress factory; had no problem accommodating their request, since they were the best two seamstress he had working at the factory.

It was just around lunch time, that Shelia was passing the factory break room. She was on her way to the snack room, to buy her usual sandwich and a soda; when suddenly she could hear laughter and talking coming from the company break room.

"Child, I told you Azalea was no better than the rest of us," said a co-worker named Hilda. "I mean she walks around here like she's so high and mighty. I mean just look how she done gone and got herself pregnant again. She ain't no little princess, I'll tell you that much."

"You sure is right about that fact Hilda," replied another co-worker named Dorothy; "I done heard that she been sneaking around behind her Papa's back again, and seeing that Creole man, Jacque."

"He show is good looking though; I'll say that much for him," replied Hilda. Just then, Shelia pushed the door open, and began yelling at the two women who were talking about her best friend Azalea, behind her back.

"I'll thank you two gossiping evil witches to mind your filthy mouths," Shelia shouted. Hilda shouted back, "Just who you think you calling a witch?' Shelia replied, "Just who do you think you little evil witch?"

"How dare you," screamed Dorothy, "Why you can't talk to us like that!" Shelia screamed back pointing her index finger in Dorothy's face, "I'll do more than just talk, if I ever catch either one of you talking about my best friend like that ever again. Why Azalea has more class in her little finger, than two of you combined. As a matter of fact, now that I think about it; the two of you have no class!"

"You got a lot of nerve girl," Hilda retorted, just as she slapped Shelia across her face. Shelia saw stars from the slap, but she quickly recovered.

Then suddenly, without giving any thought to the consequences, Shelia grabbed a salt shaker off the table, quickly throwing salt into the other co-worker Dorothy's eyes, so she would be free to take care of Hilda. "Look what you've done," Hilda screamed, as she tried to run for help, but was blocked by Dorothy who was still rubbing her eyes, as she was trying to find the exit door herself.

Dorothy began screaming, "My eyes are burning, my eyes are burning;" Fearing Shelia's wrath, she tripped over a chair near the door, and then quickly fled the room scrambling to get out on her hands and knees, leaving Hilda to face Shelia alone. After fleeing the room, Dorothy screamed, "Help me somebody, Shelia threw salt in my eyes, and now she's beating poor Hilda." Shelia had quickly grabbed Hilda by her hair, and said, "Just where you think you're going? Shelia then literally threw Hilda onto a table,

where she began slapping, and choking
Hilda, as she shouted at her, "You take it
back!" "You take it back!" "I'd better not
hear you mention her name again, do you
hear me?" Knowing Dorothy and Hilda as
they did, none of the factory workers had
come to 'Dorothy's aid. Suddenly, the
supervisor on duty rushed out of his office,
and shouted; "What in the world is going on
out here?" "Why are you screaming
Dorothy?" Dorothy screamed, "My eyes are
burning, my eyes are burning. Help me,
Shelia; just threw a handful of salt in my eyes
for nothing, and now she's in the break room
beating Hilda. We didn't do her anything.
Hurry, you gotta help poor Hilda."

Dorothy neglected to tell the
supervisor that she and Hilda had been
gossiping about Shelia's friend Azalea,
causing Shelia's anger. The supervisor said,
"Come on over her to the sink;" as he led
Dorothy by her hand over to a sink water
basin in the corner of the factory. This was
where workers washed their hands before
lunch, and at the end of their work day.

The floor supervisor immediately
began flushing the salt from Dorothy's eyes
with cold water, and hollered for a worker to
run, and get the manager to help stop Shelia
from beating Dorothy's friend, Hilda. But by
the time the manager arrived on the scene,

the fight was over. Shelia was adjusting hair, and her blouse; that had been ripped as Hilda tried to get away from her, and Hilda was slumped on the table, clutching what little of her blouse was left, after Shelia had shredded it. Hilda's other hand was rubbing around her neck as she screamed; "Shelia choked and beat me for nothing."

Fortunately for Shelia, there were two other co-workers, who had just happened to hear the entire exchange between all three women; Shelia, Hilda, and Dorothy. The workers were witness to the entire incident. One of the witnesses was so very candid, that she described the incident as; Hilda and Dorothy both got what they were asking for, a well-deserved beat down.

Hilda and Dorothy were the biggest gossips working in the dress factory. They were even known for fabricating lies. Both eyewitnesses to the incident; told the manager the truth of how the fight had started. Both Hilda and Shelia were both suspended two days from work, without pay, for fighting on company time, and in the building itself. Dorothy was suspended for one day, without pay Dorothy's suspension was for taking part in the controversy; that culminated into a violent altercation, between two fellow co-workers. Shelia never regretted defending her best friend. When Azalea found out about the fight that Shelia had in which she was defending her, Azalea knew for certain, that whatever happens in their futures; her and Shelia would be friends for life.

Since their childhood, Azalea and Shelia had always been inseparable. They not only had they grown up together, but were also next door neighbors which made their friendship even closer. Azalea's Aunt Mae, and Shelia's Grandma, would very often allow the girls to have little pajama parties. They would have to continue making good grades in school in order to have a pajama party twice a month; on alternate weekends. Both Azalea and Shelia studied very hard to enjoy this privilege.

Azalea and Shelia also loved to go on church hay rides during the summer time. Azalea and Shelia both loved putting on their short sets, and jumping onto the back of a wagon filled with fresh hay. They would each share a picnic basket full of delicious food, like fried chicken, potato chips, pickles, and chunks of Aunt Mae's chocolate cake. The church always supplied the ice and choice of fresh lemonade or iced tea.

Probably their most exciting times were whenever they would go shopping together. It was during this time spent together when they talked about their hopes and dreams for the future; and usually culminated into a fun day of hot dogs, sodas, banana splits for dessert, laughter and giggles.

Unbeknownst to anyone, including Shelia and Azalea, destiny was about to step in, and change the course of Azalea Stevens' life for the better.

Chapter 6

When Azalea arrived, the birthday party for her best friend Shelia was already in full swing. "Why Azalea, you look absolutely beautiful in that dress," Shelia shouted, so her voice could be heard over the selection that was playing on the phonograph.

"Thanks Shelia," replied Azalea. "You are always so kind to me." "I suppose it comes from you and I being like sisters," replied Shelia. "Yes, that is so true," said Azalea."

"After all, girl we have been best friends since you were seven years old and I was five," Shelia said, unable to control her laughter. "Now there you go again Shelia," replied Azalea, "Once again exaggerating the difference in our ages." Shelia replied in a defiant tone of voice, "I most certainly am not Azalea!"

Azalea said with more defiance, "Oh yes you are Shelia, because you know very well that I'm only one year older than you are." "Come on girl, you know I'm just kidding," said Shelia.

Azalea shrugged her shoulders, and said, "I don't know any such thing Shelia." "Azalea, you know girl; you really do look very pretty, as well as chic tonight," said Shelia. "Will you please forgive my earlier comment?"

Azalea replied, "Why of course I forgive you Shelia, you are after all, my oldest and dearest friend; and besides I never could stay upset with you for very long."

Shelia replied, "Same here girl." After a warm embrace of friendship, Shelia said; "You know it's been a long time since that Jacques has been out of your life girl."

Azalea said, "I don't miss him one single bit either."

Shelia said, "Azalea, I couldn't help but notice, that you have not dated anyone since." Azalea said, "What exactly are you trying to say Shelia?"

"I mean it's just not normal for a lovely young woman like you, not to date every now and then Azalea. I mean you don't have to marry, or be intimate with a man just to go on a date to the movies; or out to dinner with him."

Azalea replied, "What has whether or not I date, have to do with anything, and just how is that any of your business Shelia?"

Shelia replied, "Because you are my best friend Azalea, and I want you to be as happy as I am."

Shelia added; "Don't you realize, that there isn't a woman at the dress factory, that wouldn't give her best dress, for a figure like yours honey child?"

"There *isn't*," said Azalea.

Shelia replied, "What?" Azalea responded, "Don't you mean there *isn't* a woman at the factory, Shelia?"

"Azalea you are awful girl, just awful," replied Shelia. All that reading done went to your head honey child," said Shelia. "Oh excuse me Miss Azalea, I mean, all of that reading *has* gone to your head," laughed Shelia. "Azalea, now you even have me correcting my own English," said Shelia.

"That's the idea Shelia," replied Azalea. "We may not be rich in money; but we can be rich in words. Believe me my friend; once you are rich in words, you never have to worry about losing it, or any one stealing or taking it from you."

Shelia replied, "I believe I know what you mean Azalea."

Azalea said, "It's true Shelia, once you are rich in words, you have been empowered to reach any heights.
"Remember, Shelia, that one of the keys to success, is having knowledge" said Azalea,

"My goodness Azalea," replied Shelia. "Azalea, it's no wonder you haven't met anyone else," said Shelia. "It is because your head stays up in the clouds." "Come on girl, and try and relax for just one evening," said Shelia. "I mean lets' focus on fun, and forget all that serious stuff."

"Okay," replied Azalea, "I promise not to take life so seriously for one evening;" Azalea said with a smile.

"Let's remember it's a party Azalea," replied Shelia laughingly. "So let's just try to have some have fun".

"You got it Shelia," replied Azalea. "Let's throw caution to the winds." Azalea had no idea that her life was about to change that evening. The party was just under way, when suddenly Shelia said, "Azalea, there's a gentleman who just arrived here, that I want you to meet."

"But Shelia," replied Azalea, "I really don't want to meet anyone." "Papa has had enough worries brought on by me," said Azalea. "But Azalea," said Shelia, "He's a really nice man and a hard worker too, and besides," said Shelia; "He's not a playboy type like Jacque."

"Okay Shelia," replied Azalea." Does this so-called gentleman have a name?" Shelia replied, "He most certainly does. "His name is Lane Jenson," Shelia replied; "and he is definitely a gentleman. Just wait until you meet him Azalea. You'll see what I'm talking about."

Azalea asked, "Does this gentleman Mr. Jenson, even have a job Shelia?" Shelia replied, "He sure does. He works with my boyfriend David, building and painting homes for the wealthy."

"I'm sure he's probably a really nice man Shelia," replied Azalea; "but I'm just not interested at this point in my life. "

"Why Azalea," replied Shelia, "David assures me that Lane is one of the most skilled carpenters that he's ever laid eyes on." Azalea replied; "Really Shelia?" "Yes, and that's not all," replied Shelia. "What more is there to this gentleman of whom you speak Shelia?" "Well for starters, David also told me that he's studying to be an architect at Dawson University in Cherry Blossom City, located right here in Georgia. He is also a member of a real union; that ADL union for carpenters." "That all sounds very impressive Shelia, but I'm still not sure that I want to get involved with another man at this point in my life," replied Azalea.

Shelia asked, "Girl what are you waiting on Azalea?" Azalea replied, "I'm just not ready to venture out right now Shelia."

"You must be waiting on one of those movie stars, that you always staring at on the big screen," said Shelia. "Girl, you just got too much pride in you," said Shelia.

"That is not it Shelia," replied Azalea; "and you very well know it."

"Don't get me wrong, pride is alright in its place, but you can't eat pride Azalea," said Shelia. "You got those two young children to feed and keep a roof over their heads, and besides, your Papa is getting on in years."

Azalea replied, "Don't you know that I am well aware of that fact?" Shelia asked, "How old is he now any ways Azalea?"

"He's nearly eighty years old now Shelia," replied Azalea. "Now can we please change the subject?" Shelia replied, "That's what I've been trying to do for the past twenty minutes Azalea." "Thank you," said Azalea.

"My goodness Azalea," Shelia said. "Just who do you suppose is staring at you this very minute?" "I don't know Shelia, but I'm sure you're going to tell me," replied Azalea.

"Why, it's that handsome Lane Jenson," replied Shelia. "He and David just walked in." "My goodness." said Shelia. "Honey child, he's walking right in this direction with David, and not taking his eyes off of you girl,"

Azalea was just about to turn her head to look, when suddenly, Shelia leaned closer to Azalea, and whispered, "Don't look Azalea!" No sooner had Shelia sounded her warning, Azalea heard a male's voice say,

"Well hello there. Good evening ladies." The voice belonged to Shelia's boyfriend, David Roy.

"Hello David," replied Azalea, as her eyes suddenly glanced towards the handsome gentleman standing next to David.

"Ladies, this is a friend and co-worker of mine, Mr. Lane Jenson," said David.

"Nice meeting you Miss Shelia," said Lane Jenson, as he shook Shelia's hand gently. "I have seen you from a distance before Ma'am, but have never been formally introduced to you. I must say, that I have heard very flattering things about you from your boyfriend David."

"I am very pleased to meet you too, Mr. Jenson," replied Shelia. Lane Jenson replied, "Please, just call me Lane."

Shelia replied, "The same goes for me. I'm just known as Shelia by my friends." Shelia then gently nudged Azalea.

Lane Jenson said, "I don't believe I know this lovely young lady." Shelia saw her chance to play matchmaker, and quickly introduced Azalea to Lane.

"Mr. Jenson, please allow me to introduce my best friend, who is like a sister to me, Miss Azalea Stevens," said Shelia.

"Azalea Stevens," said Shelia, "I'd like you to meet Mr. Lane Jenson." Azalea said, "It is a pleasure to meet you Mr. Jenson."

"I can assure you Miss Stevens, the pleasure is all mine," Lane responded in a deep strong voice. "Let's just dispense with the formalities, and call me Lane, Miss Stevens."

"The feeling is mutual Lane, you may call me Leah," replied Azalea.

Azalea had never allowed anyone, with the exception of Papa; not even her best friend Shelia to call her anything but Azalea. Shelia's eyes widened in astonishment, at the mere suggestion from Azalea, that Lane could call her Leah. From that moment on, Shelia believed this was truly, a match made in heaven between her best friend, Azalea Stevens, and the handsome Mr. Lane Jenson.

The evening was beautiful. The sky was lit up by a luminous moon, and bright stars that were the essence of romance. Azalea could not remember when she'd had such a wonderful time. Between working, and caring for Lil Clay, Papa, and little Matisse; Azalea had no social life to speak of; so she decided to relax for one evening, and really enjoy the company of the handsome Mr. Lane Jenson. The evening seemed to progress so quickly, Azalea lost track of time.

"Azalea, it's getting late," said Shelia, we should be getting on home." Azalea replied, "Shelia I know you're right, but I haven't had such fun since, I don't know when."

Shelia said, 'I could not be happier for you my dear friend, than I am right now." Azalea replied, "Let's just relax Shelia, and enjoy what's left of this evening." Shelia remembering her earlier words to Azalea said, "You're right Azalea, after all; it is Friday, and neither one of us have to work on tomorrow."

Shelia then turned and walked away with a mischievous smile on her face. Azalea and Lane danced the night away as they talked about their hopes and dreams for the future. Lane Jenson said that he did not plan on working as a skilled laborer the rest of his life, but that it was simply a pathway leading to his dreams. Lane dreamed of one day owning his own construction company. Lane did not think of building as work, because he possessed a passion for it. Lane also revealed to Azalea that he'd been taking college classes at night. Lane told Azalea that he was majoring in architectural designing.

She had longed for and dreamed of meeting a man with Lane's ambitions and integrity. Since Aunt Mae began teaching

Azalea how to sew, Azalea had dreamed of becoming a fashion designer. Azalea shared her dreams of designing for rich high society patrons one day with Lane. Azalea also shared her most intimate details of how those dreams had been derailed by getting involved with the wrong men. Azalea hoped Lane would not be frightened off by the fact that she had two children that were born out of wedlock. Some other man might have been scared off, by Azalea's willingness to share such intimate facts of her life with them, upon a first meeting, but not Lane Jenson. Lane seemed to hang on Azalea's every word, as she spoke.

Azalea found herself really beginning to open up to Lane about her life. Lane Jenson listened to Azalea as she revealed her dreams, desires, and passions to him with his undivided attention, which really impressed Azalea. Azalea knew that she was taking a risk sharing so much with this fine man that she had just met, but thought to herself, that it was, either, "now or never." Azalea thought that she may never get this chance again, so she became a very bold woman.

Azalea also shared with Lane, some of her unfortunate choices she had made in life along the way.

Lane after listening to what Azalea had shared with him said, "You shouldn't blame yourself for being deceived Azalea. No one is perfect. You must know that everyone at some point in life; is persuaded by someone who is not sincere, and whose own selfish agenda is what drives them."

"Lane," said Azalea, "I've never met a man with your compassion before."

"Azalea," said Lane, "don't you realize that you are a beautiful and intelligent woman?" Azalea just smiled rather shyly. Lane added, "You were a trusting woman, who was just naive to the likes of men, who did not have your best interest at heart," said Lane. Azalea replied, "Do you really think so?"

Lane replied, "I know so. There was never anything wrong with you Azalea. The problem was that both of those men were self-indulgent, egotistical jerks."

Lane seeing Azalea's expression said, "I'm sorry Azalea. I don't mean to sound so judgmental about your choices, and I do apologize if I sounded a bit harsh; but I just find it so very hard to even imagine the very thought of someone treating you in this manner."

Lane went on to say, "You are such a wonderful woman Azalea, and you deserve the best that life has to offer."

"I accept your apology Lane," said Azalea. "Lane Jenson, you are such a fine gentleman," said Azalea.

"The feeling is mutual," said Lane. I see you as a very fine lady Azalea, with the promise of a very bright future ahead of you."

"It has truly been an enlightening experience meeting you Lane," said Azalea. I've really enjoyed meeting you too Azalea," replied Lane.

Azalea just smiled and lowered her head as though she were some shy young girl on her first date.

Lane then asked; "Azalea, may I have the honor of calling on you sometimes?"

"Why I'd be delighted to accept your company Lane," replied Azalea. "Then it's settled Azalea," said Lane.

"Come by my home next Saturday evening for seven o'clock pm," said Azalea. "Seven o'clock pm would be perfect Azalea," replied Lane.

Azalea said, "Here are my address Lane; as well as my phone number."

"I'll expect you at that time," said Azalea. "I will definitely be on time. No question about it," Lane replied. "I'll prepare a delicious dinner for you, if you don't mind making it a family affair," said Azalea. "I don't mind at all," replied Lane. "A home-cooked meal is a rare opportunity for me, and besides, I look forward to meeting the man who raised such a fine young lady."

Azalea was speaking of the fact that Papa, Lil Clay, and Matisse would be joining the two of them for dinner. Azalea knew that although she was a grown-up woman; that any man that she met, would have to first meet with Papa's approval; as well as her children.

Azalea adored and respected her Papa's opinion, and knew in her heart that if there was any chance of a relationship blossoming between the two of them, her children would have to accept Lane; as well. Azalea felt that Papa would have to be impressed with Lane Jenson's hard work ethic, not to mention his character and ambition in life.

Lane Jenson was born on April 9, 1932; to Lana and Wyatt Jenson in a small country town named Sanderson, located 26 miles south of Miller, Tennessee. Lane Jenson was known as a man of integrity by all those who knew him. Lane had decided to settle in Louisiana, after traveling the northeast and southern region of the country. Lane had been orphaned in 1939, when he was only 7 years old, along with his 3 brothers; Jarrett, who was the eldest, who was 10 years old, and his two younger brothers, one of which was named Justice, who was 4 years old, and the baby brother named, Darnell William who was only 2 years of age. He was born on January 5, 1934. Lane's dear sweet mother Lara; had died at 38 years of age from breast cancer. No one in medical science at that time; knew very much about how to fight the disease. Lane's father Wyatt; had been a farmer who was ten years older than his beautiful young wife. Lara was beautiful and was the daughter of a well-respected farmer and a Cherokee Indian princess. Wyatt Jenson promised her family that he, Wyatt, would take very good care of Lara.

He felt so blessed to be getting such a jewel for a wife. Wyatt Jenson had always provided for his family, but when he lost Lara, he could not bear living without her, even though he had the boys. Wyatt began drinking heavily and eventually succumbed to pneumonia. Wyatt's sons became wards of the state, and were sent to an orphanage. When Lane was 13 years of age, he and his older brother Jarrett, who was 3 years older, determined that no one was ever going to adopt older children. They especially knew that no one would be willing to keep 4 brothers together by adopting all of them. So with this in mind, Lane and Jarrett, decided to run away from the orphanage leaving their two younger brothers behind, with the hope and promise of returning for them one day.

As life has its twists and turns, their plans would not turn out the way they had hoped for.

The year was 1949, and four years had quickly gone by. Lane was now 17 years old, and had finished high school because of his big brother Jarrett was now 20 years of age, and had worked very hard to make certain that Lane got an education. They worked odd jobs that almost always had to do with construction. Lane had acquired a yearning to someday own his own architectural and construction company. Lane had dreams of building tall buildings known as skyscrapers.

One scorching hot day in August, Lane and Jarrett, who had just gotten off from work, stumbled upon a robbery of a well attired gentleman taking place in an alley behind a fancy restaurant. The two robbers, both of whom looked like they were homeless, had assaulted the man as he struggled for his life. They had probably come from the near-by soup kitchen. The city council had heard complaints from local patrons, who frequented the restaurants in the area, about having it moved to another location; but the county commissioner's office had said that it was outside of the city ordinance.

Lane and Jarrett immediately came

to the aid of this gentleman by chasing off the two robbers; who ran off with the man's wallet they had stolen. "My wallet," shouted the man, they stole my wallet."

Jarrett ran behind the robbers in an attempt to retrieve the man's wallet, but was shot in his upper thigh by one of the robbers, before he jumped in the boxcar of a slow moving train. Jarrett was rushed to the hospital, but his gunshot inflicted wound to his thigh, proved to be fatal. Jarrett later died that evening from his wounds. Lane was devastated by the loss of his older brother. The gentleman they had rescued; told Lane that he appreciated their sacrifice, and insisted on paying the cost of Jarrett's funeral; as well as his burial.

The gentleman turned out to in fact be one of the most prominent citizens in all of Cherry Blossom, Georgia. His name was Mr. Benjamin Carlton III. He had built a construction empire from his inheritance. He was educated at Saxon University, receiving a Bachelor's Degree in Drafting; and later graduated from Lexington University, receiving a Masters of Arts Degree in Architecture and a PH.D in Literature.

Benjamin Carlton had written two books that were best sellers. Both of his books were non-fiction. One book was on architecture designing, and the other was written about literary giants of our times.

Mr. Carlton was very sorry by Lane's loss of his older brother. Mr. Carlton met with Lane following Jarrett's burial, and found out that Lane had carpenter skills, and had dreamed of becoming an architect someday. Lane had wanted to go into business with his brother Jarrett, should the opportunity was to ever present itself. Mr. Carlton decided that he could assistant Lane in some way that would inspire him to pursue his dream of building great structures someday.

Mr. Carlton asked Lane, "How can I be of help to you?" Lane thought about how much of an honor it would be to his brother Jarrett, if he were to pursue his dreams, and become the architect Jarrett had always known, and encouraged him to become. Lane replied, "Well Mr. Carlton sir, I would love to be able to go to college someday. My brother worked and made sure that I finished high school, but I never went to college." Mr. Carlton replied, "I will help with your education." Lane replied, Thank you sir, I promise I will not let you down. I'll study really hard." Mr. Carlton replied, "There is something else that you need to know, and that is this arrangement will require something more of you Lane." Lane replied, "What is it sir?" I will only cover one half of your college tuition, but if you are the industrial, determined young man I believe you are, you will work hard to pay for the other half." Lane replied, Mr. Carlton sir, all I've known my whole life is hard work. I will accomplish all of my goals in life sir." "I see," Mr. Carlton responded, "I'll have my attorney make the necessary arrangements to pay your tuition costs each month to the college of your choosing." Mr. Carlton asked, "Where are you staying?" Lane replied; "I'm staying at Capp's Boarding house across town. Mr. Carlton gave Lane his business card, and told him if he needed anything to call his office.

Lane called only once, to say thank you for all Mr. Carlton had done. Lane found out that Mr. Carlton, who knew someone on the Board, had actually arranged for Lane to work part-time on the school grounds while at Dawson University in Cherry Blossom, Georgia, to help pay for his tuition. Lane wanted to show Mr. Carlton his appreciation for believing he could accomplish is dream of becoming an architect. During the day, Lane either worked in the cafeteria, or in maintenance. During the night he attended classes, and on weekends he worked in construction.

The year was now 1958. Seven years had passed, since Lane Jenson had begun pursuing his dream of becoming an architect. Lane was now 26 years old, working hard as a skilled laborer in construction.

One day while working on weekends at his construction job, Lane walked to get lunch at the sandwich truck that he frequented, while working on weekends. The sandwich truck would come around at lunchtime each day. A young lady named Cassandra helped her mother and father prepare meals, during the summer months, whenever she wasn't in school. She had always wanted to be a secretary, and was taking classes in stenography at a nearby secretarial school. Lane first met Cassandra when her father had initially prepared Lane's sandwich, and had put mustard on it, which Lane did not eat. Lane went to return the sandwich with a complaint,

"I thought I told you not to put any mustard on my sandwich," he shouted. .

Suddenly he was greeted by a beautiful young lady who said, "Has anyone ever told you that it's impolite to stare," she asked?

"Why no, I mean yes," Lane stammered. "Where is the man that fixed my sandwich?"

"You mean my father," she replied. "He had an errand to run, but I would be more than happy to prepare that sandwich the way you like it," Lane replied, "I'd be much obliged."

In no time, Cassandra and Lane were wed in a very small ceremony at her home. Lane loved her very much, but had very little time to spend with her because of his endeavors. One day Cassandra became very ill after spending all day working in her ailing father's place on the sandwich truck. She came down with pneumonia. When Cassandra died, Lane thought his life was over, but little did he realize, that it was just beginning.

Lane really struggled to get back on an even footing following the tragic untimely loss of his beautiful wife Cassandra. This wasn't easy for Lane, who was a loner, since the loss of his older brother, Jarrett, and the separation from his two younger brothers, after he and Jarrett ran away the orphanage to find a better life, and return for them. Lane had just started working for Jones Construction, who built homes for rich; as well as small office structures, when he met David Roy. David was a carpenter who learned his craft from his father. David Roy and Shelia; had begun dating in high school. It was "love at first sight".

Shelia and David would sat on the front porch just holding hands, while her grandmother was either baking in the kitchen, or sewing in the parlor, as she sat near the window, with a view of the young couple. Eventually, David was allowed to come to see Shelia every Saturday evening, and twice a month, he was allowed to pick her up for a date, and bring her to see a movie at the local theatre. Shelia loved the smell of hot buttered popcorn at the theatre. Shelia and Azalea had spent a lot of time together, since Azalea hadn't dated in a very long time.

Azalea had no idea, that her life was about to take another turn, but this time, it would bring her something she had long hoped for in her life.

Chapter
7

The evening had finally arrived for Lane to meet Azalea's family.

Azalea awaited Lane's knock at the door with much anticipation. Azalea was wearing a beautiful white cotton dress with a floral design of pastel pink roses with light green leaves. The neckline was about four inches from the neck and fell slightly just off the shoulder with two inch sleeves that were puffed and gathered. Azalea wore her favorite white sandals with light green crisscross straps;

"Papa," said Azalea, would you please hurry and finish getting dressed. Lane should be arriving any minute now;" said Azalea, in an anxious tone of voice.

"Good Lord girl," replied Papa. "You need to calm down, because you just too excited about that boy.

"Papa," replied Azalea, "If I've told you once, I've told you twice, Lane is a man, and quite a gentleman at that; so please do not refer to him as a boy when he arrive. Have I made myself perfectly clear?"

"Okay child," replied Papa. "I promise to do what you said," Papa replied in a disheartened tone of voice. "The way you carrying on, I know that I have to meet him now," said Papa.

"Believe me Papa," replied Azalea; "When he arrives, you will see what I mean."

Suddenly, at that moment, Azalea hears a knock at the door. Azalea could feel the excitement in her voice when she opened the door and said, "Good evening Lane, won't you please come in?"

When Lane walked inside the house, he appeared even taller and more handsome than when Azalea's had last seen him. He was dressed in dark blue jeans, a white long-sleeve, cotton ivy-league shirt, with the top button open and button down collar. Lane's outfit was accessorized with a stylish pair of alligator dress shoes. "Good evening to you too Azalea," replied Lane, as he presented her with a beautiful bouquet of pink azaleas in a decorative planter.

"Oh Lane there're so very beautiful," said Azalea. Lane replied, I thought you might like flowers that represent the origin of your lovely name."

"Why Lane;" replied Azalea, "Not only do you have a way with words, but are very creative; as well as thoughtful; to bring me flowers for which I was named. I'm so very impressed by your originality and sensitivity," said Azalea.

"Well," replied Lane, I'm so glad you invited me Miss Azalea. It's my way of showing my appreciation to a fine lady, such as you Ma'am."

Just at that moment Papa entered the living room. "Lane," said Azalea, "I'd like you to meet my father, Henry Stevens, whom I call Papa, but is known by everyone else as Hank," said Azalea." "Papa may I present Lane Jenson, said Azalea." "It's an honor to meet you sir, said Lane."

"Likewise son, said Papa." "I have been waiting a long time son, for a man like you to come into my Azalea's life," replied Papa. "Azalea is a fine young woman, and should have the best life have to offer;" said Papa. Lane replied, "I definitely agree sir."

Azalea was overwhelmed; as well as impressed by Papa's eloquent speaking. She thought to herself silently; "Did Papa just call me Azalea, and refer to me as a woman, instead of child, or gal?" Little did she realize until now, that Papa had picked up here and there, bits and pieces of Azalea's correct way of speaking English.

Papa knew that he was growing older with each passing day. He did not know how much longer he would be around to help Azalea with the children, Clay and little Matisse. Although Azalea worked at the dress factory for Parkinson's Department store, her income alone, was not enough to provide for her, the children, and pay household utilities and rent.

Papa's pension check he received each month from the Railroad Retirement Pension Fund; as well as his monthly social security check was a tremendous blessing to Azalea, and the children. Papa also received disability compensation from the railroad; because of an injury that he sustained working there.

This accident caused one of Papa's legs to be slightly shorter than the other; which is where he got his other nickname "Peg" Stevens, that only his dearest friends on the railroad, or the mailman, Mr. Richard, referred to him as at times. "Papa was now given the task of doing the very best he knew how not to embarrass his sweet daughter Azalea. In Papa's mind, he believed destiny had sent Lane Jenson into Azalea's life. Papa thought to himself, "Could this be the good Lord done answered my prayers?" Papa thought; "Time is growing short, because the Lord done sent the man to take care of my family, when I'm gone to be with the Lord in heaven." Papa believed Azalea's knight in shining armor had arrived, by the name of Mr. Lane Jenson.

Clay and Matisse both came running into the sitting room. "Stop that running children;" said Azalea. "Don't the two of you see that we have a guest present in the house?"

"We're sorry Mother," said Clay. Matisse was only three years old and simply smiled at Lane.

"What a handsome little fellow you are;" said Lane as he shook Clay's hand. "Thank you sir," replied Clay."

"I also see that beauty runs in the family, because little Matisse is a very beautiful little girl Azalea; just like her Mother." Azalea replied with a smile, "Why Lane you are such a flatterer."

"I like this young man already Zale," said Papa. "Lane will stay right here in the sitting room with me; while you get dinner ready for us men to eat."

"Alright Papa," said Azalea." Before Azalea walked into the kitchen, Papa said, "Excuse me son, I have to go in the bathroom for a minute."

While Papa was gone into the restroom, Lane took advantage of the time that Azalea and he were alone together. Lane walked quietly into the kitchen, so as not to be heard by Papa. "You and your Papa seem to have a very close relationship Azalea."

Azalea replied, "Papa is all I have in

my life, besides my two children, and my best friend Shelia. I sometime wonder, if he really knows, just how very much he means to me. I sure hope he does." Lane replied, "Well based upon what I've seen, and heard so far Azalea, I believe that he definitely does. Both you and your children; appear to be your Papa's pride and joy Leah."

Azalea looked into Lane's eyes, as he called her Leah, and said, "Thank you for your astute observations Lane." "It was my pleasure," replied Lane with a warm smile. Suddenly there was a type of intensity in the room between Azalea, and Lane. Just as Lane touched Azalea's hand to hold it, they heard Papa's voice.

We needs to talk right now," said Papa. "Yes sir Mr. Henry," replied Lane; as he rushed back into the sitting room with Papa.

"Just call me Mr. Hank son; because nobody else is proper round here, but my Zale. Go on, and close that door son," said Papa, "and have a seat right here next to me." Lane again replied nervously this time, "Yes sir, Mr. Hank."

Papa said, "I won't hit you son." I just needs you to feel comfortable, is all," said Papa, as Lane took a seat in a big comfortable sofa chair.

"So son, let's just get down to brass

tacks," said Papa. "What kind of intentions you got for my girl Azalea?" Papa did not hesitate to find this out, as he was getting older, approaching eighty-two years old now.

"Sir, I can assure you that I have the best of intentions for Azalea." "She is a wonderful woman sir." "I know you must be so very proud of the fine young lady you have raised."

"I sure am;" said Papa. "Do you smoke boy?" "Well sir, I may have a cigar or two on occasion;" replied Lane. "Just what I had in mind son; replied Papa.

"This is one of them occasion's son. The Champion Series baseball game is on today. All my favorite players are playing today. I got me some beer too. Would you like one?"

Lane was very relieved to see that he and Papa really seem to hit it off very well. "Sure Mr. Stevens," Lane replied.

"Now look here son," said Papa, "I told you to call me Mr. Hank, and I mean it."

Lane looked uneasy, and hoped he hadn't made Papa upset with him when suddenly, Papa burst out into laughter, and said, "I sure did get you with that one, huh boy?"

Lane realizing that the joke was on him, and that Papa had a great sense of humor, burst into laughter himself, and replied, "You sure did Mr. Hank, you sure did."

"Azalea," Papa yelled, brings me and Lane a beer." Azalea replied, "Yes Papa."

Papa then reached for his special hand carved wooden cigar box with his name engraved inside. This was a box that he only touched on Sundays or for his baseball games. Papa had been given this beautiful cigar box by his sister Aunt Mae, as a birthday gift, before she died. It was one of the few items that Papa cherished, besides his sword, passed to him by his father from his grandfather, who had once fought for freedom.

In the meantime, Azalea began sitting the table. Azalea used the embroidered cream- table cloth once owned by Mrs. LeBlanc. Mrs. LeBlanc had given it to Aunt Mae, which was passed down to Azalea. Azalea's china had been a family heirloom also passed on to her by Aunt Mae. The china was made in Cherry Blossom, Georgia, with artistry of some of Georgia's most beautiful plantations.

Azalea prepared for dinner as an appetizer, jumbo shrimp cocktail served on crushed ice with cocktail sauce in the center of a deep glass dish. The main entrée included, wild rice, stuffed flounder, stuffed with lump crabmeat and breadcrumbs, topped with hollandaise sauce. There was also asparagus spears served on the side. Azalea also prepared onion soap prepared with delicious onions grown in Georgia. Finally for dessert, Azalea was serving a delicious bread pudding topped with butter cream cinnamon sauce.

Azalea announced in her sweet tone of voice, "Lane, Papa, and children; dinner is now served." "Azalea, if your food is as delicious as the aroma," said Lane, then we're all in for a real treat this evening." "Thank you Lane, replied Azalea.

Lil Clay rushed to sit in a chair at the head of the table, as he had so often become accustomed to doing. "No, no Lil Clay." said Azalea. "Don't sit there, that chair is reserved for Mr. Lane." Lil Clay looked at his mother with a frown that showed his disapproval. It was the first time that Lil Clay had to share his mother's love with anyone besides Papa or Matisse. Lil Clay suddenly felt tinges of jealously towards Lane.

After dinner, it was now quiet time. The children had fully enjoyed their evening. It had been a while since they'd had so much fun in one evening. Azalea recognized that Lane Jenson had been a big factor in the scheme of things. Lane began to reflect on the wonderful dinner he had eaten.

"Azalea," said Lane, "you have really outdone yourself," Azalea replied with a smile, "Thank you Lane."

Dinner was scrumptious," said Lane. "I can't remember ever having eaten such a fine meal in my entire life." "Why Lane, what a wonderful compliment," Azalea replied.

Matisse ran up to her mother and hugged her legs ever so tightly. "Mommy I love you, said Matisse" "I love you too my dear sweet baby girl," replied Azalea.

"Give Momma a hug;" said Azalea as she picked Matisse up, and gave her a hug and a goodnight kiss.

Without saying a word, Lil Clay quickly ran into the bedroom; that he and Papa shared, closing the door behind him. Lil Clay slept in a folding bed that was placed in the closet during the day. The bed was made very comfortable with the feather mattress, which Azalea had purchased a year ago. Papa's bed was made of oak with four thick ball shaped posts. Papa's mattress was stuffed with feathers to alleviate some of his back pains. Papa now needed a thick pillow to support his back.

Azalea excused herself from Lane's company to put Matisse to bed. Matisse shared her mother Azalea's bedroom which she enjoyed playing in with her dolls. Azalea still had the Queen-Anne style bedroom suite that Aunt Mae had bought for her when she was a little girl. Fortunately the bed was a full size which she shared with little Matisse. Azalea was saving up money to purchase a child size bed for Matisse.

"Give Momma a kiss goodnight Matisse," said Azalea. "Goodnight Mommy," said Matisse." "Goodnight my baby Mattie, replied Azalea. Azalea turned the bright light off, and turned on the soft lamp light so Matisse could sleep without being in darkness which she feared. When Azalea turned doorknob of Lil Clay's room, it was locked.

Azalea walked into the sitting room, where Lane was waiting to say goodnight.

"Well Lane;" said Azalea. "The children are tucked in bed and Papa says it's past his bedtime, so he's going to sleep also."

"It's getting rather late," said Lane. "So I suppose I'd better be going; but I just want to say, that I cannot remember when I've had such a great time Leah."

Azalea replied, "Would you like a glass of a glass of lemonade before you leave Lane?" "Yes, Thank you Leah, replied Lane."

Azalea and Lane sat on the front porch watching the moonlight and the stars in the sky. It was a beautiful crisp cool fall night. The leaves were falling from the breeze blowing

. "Lane, fall is such a beautiful season, isn't it?" said Azalea

"It certainly is Leah, but not a beautiful as you," replied Lane. Azalea had always been taught that inner beauty is what really mattered, but appreciated the compliment that Lane Jenson had given her. Azalea had often received compliments on her beautiful figure. Azalea knew that there was no question of how curvaceous her beautiful body was. Azalea couldn't walk to the corner bus-stop without hearing the sound of wolf whistles coming from men as she passed by. Azalea was a very demure woman; especially after the hurt that she had endured with Lil Clay and Matisse's fathers.

Meeting Lane was truly a blessing for Azalea. She could hardly believe that this thoughtful, sincere, and loving man had such an interest in her.

"Lane, you are such a flatterer," replied Azalea.

"I mean every word I say Azalea," said Lane. "Although you possess an outer beauty; it is your inner beauty that has attracted me more. It is your inner beauty that shines, and illuminates from the inside out. That is what has fascinated me more than anything about you, my love."

Lane began to draw Azalea closer in his arms to kiss her lips. "Leah," said Lane, I believe I'm falling in love with you."

Just as their eyes met, Azalea cried; "No, No, this can't be happening again to me. No Lane! You must leave now, cried Azalea, as she began to dab her eyes with her dainty white handkerchief. Go away Lane, I mean it!"

"Azalea," said Lane, what on earth are you talking about? What have I done wrong?" "Please just go away," replied Azalea. "Azalea I'll go, but I'll see you again, Lane replied. I won't stay away," said Lane.

Azalea had been so hurt by the men in her past, that it was hard for her to comprehend the depths of true love.

Azalea said, "Don't you see Lane, that it will never work?" Lane replied, "I believe I know what is happening here, but I will never hurt you Azalea, because I've fallen in love with you."

Azalea said, "I just need some time and space Lane." Lane replied, "I'll say goodnight, but never goodbye my sweet Leah."

Lane then walked down the steps, alone the walkway that led to the driveway where his red truck was parked. Lane placed the key in the ignition of his truck, and looked up to see Azalea peering from behind the white ruffled organza curtains of her bedroom. Lane could also see Azalea's silhouette against the soft lighting of the lamp. As he drove off, Lane thought to himself; "Azalea Stevens is a fine woman in both body and mind. I would be a fool to allow such a jewel of a woman to slip thru my hands; and I'm certainly no fool. I'll be back my sweet Leah," Lane spoke verbally to himself. You can be rest assured Leah; I will definitely be back," Lane repeated.

In the meantime, Lane worked so very hard towards completing his studies, and achieving his dream of being a successful architect. He was the type of man that knew what he wanted in life and was determined to make whatever sacrifice it took to accomplish his goals. He had decided that the timing was wrong to pursue Azalea right now. She had already been thru enough hurt in disappointment in her young life to accept the genuine love he wanted to share with her.

Lane thought that it was too soon for Azalea to open up and share her true emotions with him. He sensed that she had built up a wall to prevent herself from ever being hurt again by love. Lane felt that Azalea did not deserve the hurt and pain she had endured from the other two men that had been in her life, and only wanted to take advantage of her kind heart. Lane felt that in time, thru his absence; that Azalea would come to realize that she truly love him.

Monday morning was a very windy day to work outside in construction. All types of materials were flying around. Tarps were blowing in the wind, felt paper and shingles were sliding off the roofs. Lane was very fortunate to have been promoted to assistant foreman and apprentice draftsman. Lane was right in the middle of going over plans for a new small library that Jones construction had contracted to build for the county. Suddenly there was a knock on the door of his small cramped module office. "Knock, knock. Come in," shouted Lane; over the noisy sounds of jackhammers, bulldozers, and other heavy equipment. The door opened, and in walked a very well dressed gentleman.

"Hello Mr. Jenson," said the gentleman. "You don't know me, but a longtime friend and business acquaintance by the name of Mr. Benjamin Carlton referred you to our firm."

Lane replied, "Mr. Carlton did speak to me concerning a visit I would be receiving from a representative of any firm. Who exactly are you, and what firm are we talking about?"

"Allow me to introduce myself; my

name is William Brighton II, of Brighton and Brighton Architectural Design Group. My father is William Brighton, Jr.; although he hates being called Jr. You see; Mr. Jenson, he finds it so condescending."

Lane Jenson's jaw dropped in amazement, because Brighton was the most prominent -owned architectural firm in the country. Lane Jenson knew he possessed exceptional architectural skills and intellect; but wondered why the heir of Brighton and Brighton would come in person to recruit him. Before Lane could respond, Mr. Brighton said; "The firm was originally founded by my great-grandfather, William Brighton Sr. You may have heard of him."

"Of course; Mr. Brighton," replied Lane Jenson. "Everyone knows that it happens to be one of the oldest architectural firms in the country; but how exactly, may I be of service?"

"We're looking for an architectural apprentice for our firm, and you came highly recommended by Mr. Carlton. Would you be interested in our offer?" "Of course, Mr. Brighton," replied Lane.

"Please just call me William; Mr. Brighton is my father." "Sure William," replied Lane. "The starting pay is not that much, but in one year, if you show great promise, we'll double your salary," said Mr.

Brighton. "I'll take it," replied Lane with enthusiasm in his voice. Lane started his new position almost immediately, and began to learn all he could while giving new and fresh ideas. Lane and William Brighton; had almost immediately formed a bond of friendship, that seemed even closer than the one that Lane had with David. They began spending a great deal of time together, even when they were not working together. William Brighton had suggested that in order for Lane to really move up in his field of architectural designing, that he needed to join the country club, and began playing golf. Bill Brighton had referred a golf instructor. Once Lane felt his confidence build, he began playing golf with Bill Brighton on weekends. Lane now began to realize that it was all about business, and it was all about moving up the ladder of success.

Azalea had not seen Lane Jenson for quite some time now, which was as she had requested. During the times that Lane was busy building up a reputation in his field, Azalea spent working extra hours at the factory, so that she would be able to buy her loved ones really nice Christmas presents this year. Azalea wanted to make this Christmas the best one yet for little Matisse and Clay. Azalea especially wanted to decorate the cottage nice with the hope that Lane Jenson would be paying her a visit for the holidays. Azalea also remembered the times when she was a little girl, and how beautifully Aunt Mae made sure that she was dressed each Easter; as well as Christmas. Azalea had wanted to make certain that both, little Matisse; and Clay were very well dressed on Christmas Day.

Although Azalea could not afford to buy Matisse's dresses there all the time, she loved to window shop, and one day, she had decided to sacrifice herself, and putting a collection of five beautiful dresses in the layaway on hold for little Matisse. Azalea could only afford to put so much down on the layaway, because she had shirts and pants on layaway at Parkinson's department store for Clay; as well. Azalea told the sales lady at Little Miss Cotton Candy Boutique for little girls, she'd try to pay more than the minimum payment; but could not promise, because she had a layaway for her son at another store; as well. One day the saleslady, whose name was Carol said, "You certainly are a very fine mother to your children Miss Stevens."

Azalea replied, "They are my little treasures in life." "Well," replied Carol, "I certainly hope when they grow up, that they are able to appreciate everything that you have done, and the sacrifices you've made."\

Azalea loved and adored both Clayton, and Matisse, but sometimes wondered to herself, if she may have perhaps doted on them a little too much. She felt as though she had to compensate for the fact that their fathers were never around, to show them the love and guidance; that every child deserved in life from their father, particularly a little boy. Azalea loved and appreciated her Papa for being there for her and her children.

Chapter
8
The Engagement

The fall had ended; and as winter drew nearer, the leaves that had fallen when Lane Jenson had last visited Azalea, had begun to lose their vibrant bold colors. The rustic orange leaves were now brown; the yellow leaves of the oak tree nestled in the front yard of the cottage were now rustic with dark brown hues, and the leaves that had once been bright red, were now dark maroon. Lane Jenson had decided to respect Azalea's wishes, by giving her some space. The remainder of the fall months leading up to winter, Lane had really thrown himself into his studies. His plan was to graduate by January, the beginning of the winter semester.

Lane Jenson was a very industrious young man. He had always dreamed of owning his own company; which made him decide years ago, on the advice of Mr. Benjamin Carlton, to begin investing his money. One-third of the money he earned from construction had gone towards his tuition, another one-third towards his living expenses, and one-third he had wisely invested in bonds and gold stocks. Gold stocks that Lane purchased provided a diversified portfolio. By that time Lane graduated, he would have enough money from his investments to purchase the ten acres of land he had eyed for some time now. After meeting Azalea Stevens, Lane knew that he wanted Azalea to be a major part of his future.

Winter had finally arrived and the bitter cold had set in. Christmas was just two weeks away. Lane decided that enough time had gone by since he had last seen Azalea. Lane went on a holiday shopping spree with the goal in mind of surprising Azalea, Papa, Matisse, and Clay on Christmas Day. Lane thoughts were of the warm reception he would receive from Azalea; upon his arrival.

It was now two days before Christmas, and Lane had not seen Azalea since October. Lane had been shopping all day for Christmas gifts. Lane's investments had really paid off. He was able to finish paying his tuition; which meant graduation in January. Lane had also purchased himself a brand new 1959 vehicle. The starting price was within his budget, but Lane wanted to add, fuel injection, power glide transmission, and power brakes; which made the total cost exceed his budget. Lane had become a man who knew what he wanted when he saw it, and Azalea was who he wanted. As Lane drove around shopping in his new car, he began to remember the great time he had meeting Azalea's family. Lane thought about Azalea's two children he had met for the first time.

He thought of the closeness he felt towards little Matisse and Clay. He knew that he would be sharing responsibility with Azalea to raise them as his own. He reminisced about him and Papa drinking a beer, and smoking a cigar; as they both watched the baseball game on television. He thought about the delicious aroma of Azalea's dinner she had worked so hard to prepare. Lane could almost smell the seasonings and herbs Azalea had added to her Cajun cuisine. Lane thought about the sensuous scent of Azalea's favorite perfume, as they stood on the front porch watching the beautiful silvery moon, and bright stars, as they illuminated the sky.

Lane thoughts and senses allowed him to feel and smell the cool crisp night air, as he held Azalea lovingly in his arms. Lane thought of the passion that he felt as he kissed Azalea's lips. Lane thought of how his evening was cut short by Azalea's emotions that had surfaced. Lane thought of the view of Azalea's shapely silhouette thru the window, captured by the soft light, as he drove off that evening. Finally, Lane thought of his last words to Azalea that evening; "I'll be coming back Azalea, you can be rest assured, I will."

In the two months leading up to Christmas, Azalea had worked extra hours at the dress factory, to buy gifts for little Matisse, Clay, Papa, and her best friend Shelia. Papa wanted Azalea to spend the money the extra money on Matisse and Clay, but Azalea would have none of that; because her love for her Papa was as great as her love for her children. Azalea also had purchased a gift for Lane.

Christmas morning had finally arrived, and the time had come for Lane to honor his last spoken words to Azalea. Although he would be arriving unannounced, Lane Jenson was "a man of his word." Lane firmly believed that "a man's word was his bond. Azalea had prepared a delicious dinner for Christmas that was enough to feed an army. The dinner included; baked turkey with cornbread stuffing, baked ham, baked macaroni and cheese, potato salad, collard greens with salt pork seasoning meat, squash and zucchini casserole, fried okra, and warm dinner rolls; as well as a delicious cornbread.

Azalea had prepared for dessert, three sweet potato pies, a red velvet cake; as well as a three layer coconut cake, with homemade cream cheese icing, topped with fresh shredded coconut. Azalea had also baked ginger bread cookies, with icing trim for little Matisse and Clay. The aroma in the kitchen was hypnotic to the senses of any man. Aunt Mae had always taught Azalea that the "way to a man's heart, was thru his stomach." Azalea quickly hoped that she'd see Lane for Christmas. Although her pride would not allow her to speak it out loud. Azalea had come to realize that "absence does indeed make the heart grow fonder." She'd hoped Lane felt the same about her.

Azalea was wearing her red poodle skirt, with a white cotton blouse. The blouse had a peter pan collar with a tiny green bow ribbon tied at the neck. Azalea wore her comfortable red velvet slippers. She also had on her white apron, trimmed with ruffles, and a large bow tied in the back. Azalea had made a special trip to her favorite beauty parlor in the town of Sapphire Blue, Georgia; to have her hair styled beautifully. Her hair was parted on the side with one side flipped behind her ear and the other side falling almost covering her right eye. She wore beautiful costume jewelry earrings that were hand painted tiny green and red Christmas trees. Last, but not least, Azalea wore the same perfume she had worn when she'd last seen Lane. The scented fragrance was mesmerizing to his senses. Azalea was taking the ginger bread cookies out of the oven, when suddenly; there was a knock at the front door of the cottage.

"Knock, knock!" Azalea shouted over the Christmas music playing on the phonograph, "Who's there?" "Lane Jenson," replied Lane. "I'll be there shortly," said Azalea. Azalea's heart raced; as she placed the cookies on the cooling rack high atop the counter, telling Clay and Matisse, "Don't touch." She then quickly removed her apron.

When Azalea opened the door, she was met by an even more handsome than before; Lane Jenson. This time, Lane stood tall in his boots and dark blue jeans with a turtleneck sweater and Navy blue blazer. Lane also wore a wide-brimmed cowboy hat. Lane removed his hat, before he stepped inside the cottage.

"Come in Lane," said Azalea. "My goodness Azalea," replied Lane. "You look beautiful Azalea." "Why, thank you Lane," replied Azalea. "You look very handsome yourself."

When Lane stepped inside, Azalea peered past him and spotted the new car. Azalea asked, "Is that yours Lane?" "Sure is," replied Lane. I have some presents I need to get out of the trunk; but I just wanted to be certain you were home, before getting them out the car. "Oh boy presents!" shouted little Clay. I sure do love Christmas Mommy?" "Yes little Clay," said Azalea, you most certainly do."

"Oh boy Mommy," little Clay asked; "may I please help Mr. Lane fetch the presents?" "Of course Clay, as long as it's alright with Mr. Lane," replied Azalea. "It most certainly is," replied Lane.

Azalea had decided that she would instill the importance of being polite, having fine manners, reading, and speaking proper English; in her children at a very young age. "Put that there coat on first boy," yelled Papa to little Clay. "Alright Papa," replied little Clay; who now wanted to be called Clay.

Lane and Clay walked back inside with the presents, and laid them down underneath the still brightly lii Christmas tree. "Please be seated in the parlor with Papa," said Azalea. "I have prepared a delicious Christmas dinner for everyone." "Azalea, your kitchen smells scrumptious, replied Lane. Azalea asked; "Would you mind very much if we opened the gifts before dinner Lane?" "Not at all Azalea," replied Lane.

Little Clay and Little Matisse immediately ran over to open their presents. "Wait children," shouted Azalea. "Mr. Lane will give each of us our presents himself."

"Okay Mommy," replied Little Clay, as he sat down on the rug next to Papa's feet.

Lane reached Matisse her gift first; which she quickly ripped the wrapping paper off with much anticipation. "I love my dolly mommy," shouted Matisse, as she held in her hands, a beautiful little baby doll with a dark curly coiffure; and medium brown eyes, wearing a pink frilly dress, with a tiny pink bow in her hair.

Matisse then ran to Lane, and as he leaned forward, she threw her chubby little arms around his neck and shouted, "Thank you, thank you.

Little Clay was a little more subdued, so as not to seem too anxious. When Little Clay began to unwrap his present, he spotted a green soldier and a brown soldier on the box. It was a box full of soldiers. It was what he had wanted. He loved playing soldier with his little friend Chuck's set, who lived next door to him. Thanks to Lane, he now had his own set.

"Thank you Mr. Lane, I really love it my present" said Clay, as he began to open the box with his eyes peering at the little soldiers inside.

Next was Papa's turn to receive his gift. "Here you are Papa," said Lane.

Realizing that he had just called Mr.

Hank, Papa; Lane said, "I sure hope you don't mind me calling you Papa, Mr. Hank. It just came out of my mouth so naturally."

Papa replied, "I don't mind at all sons." Lane said, "I hope you like your gift sir."

When Papa skillfully removed the wrapping paper, he saw vintage hand carved, wooden English pipe. There was also a pack of English tobacco inside. Papa was overjoyed with Lane's gift to him.

"Thank you so much son," said Papa to Lane, as he shook his hand. "Why you're welcome Mr. Hank, I mean Papa," replied Lane.

Azalea and Papa both laughed at Lane's efforts to become a part of the Stevens family. "I sure do see now, what my Azalea sees in you son," said Papa.

"Well," said Azalea, I suppose it's my turn now to see what my gift is from Lane. "I sure do hope you like it Azalea, said Lane. "I'm sure I will, replied Azalea as she began to un-wrap her gift.

There was an oblong black velvet box beneath the wrapping paper. When Azalea opened the box, she saw a stunning sterling silver and diamond necklace shaped like a string of leaves. "Oh my Lord;" said Azalea in a soft tone of voice. "It's absolutely breathtaking Lane," said Azalea.

Lane replied, "The leaves reminded me our first evening we spent here on the front porch, watching the leaves as they fell from the trees. The diamonds sparkle like the stars that illuminated the sky, and the sterling silver, reminded me of the bright silvery moon that shone that night."

"Oh Lane," replied Azalea; "I love it, It's so very beautiful." Lane replied, "I'm glad you love it Azalea. "Well Lane," said Azalea, "I may as well give you your gift before dinner also."

Azalea reached under the tree and handed Lane a soft package wrapped with a green bow around it. "This one is from Papa, Clay and little Mattie," "Thanks everyone," said Lane; as he held in his hands a wool scarf, with little white snowmen, wearing red scarves. "Just what I always wanted," he chuckled.

Azalea then reached under the tree and handed Lane a 14x16 white gift box with a big red bow tied around it.

"I wonder what on earth it could possibly be," said Lane. "I wasn't expecting anything at all, since you had no idea that I would be here today, said Lane. "I sure hope you like it Lane," said Azalea. When Lane opened the box, he revealed a 12x14 beautiful mahogany wood diploma frame.

"Congratulations Lane," said Azalea.

"It's for your Degree in Architecture," said Azalea. Lane replied, "Azalea it's the most beautiful frame I have ever laid eyes on. I will definitely make very good use of it," Lane replied.

"I actually have in my possession an invitation for you and your family Azalea. I sure hope you all will be there," said Lane. "Of course we will Lane," replied Azalea. "It's hard to believe that nearly an entire year has passed, and that you are about to graduate from college, Lane," said Azalea.

"Count me out," said Papa. "I'll watch these babies so you can go by yourself Azalea." Little shouted, "I'm not a baby." "You certainly are not," replied Azalea. "You are a big boy now Clay," said Azalea. "Well Lane," said Azalea, "you have your answer; I'll be there." Lane replied, "I'm really looking forward to it."

There was suddenly a knock at the front door. "Knock, knock. When Azalea opened the door, Shelia and David both stood smiling, their arms were full of Christmas presents. "What a wonderful surprise."

"Merry Christmas, and Happy New Year," they shouted. "Merry Christmas to you both; as well," replied Azalea. After hugs and kisses amongst everyone, Shelia said, "You didn't think David and I would miss celebrating Christmas with you all, did you? Azalea replied, "Certainly not, I knew you would show up eventually."

"I'll say one thing for you two, "said Lane; "you have perfect timing, because we were just in the middle of unwrapping gifts, when you two knocked at the door."

"Not only that," said Papa, we fixing to eat some of my Azalea's good home cooking too. "Well," said Azalea; "let me take your coats, while the two of you make yourselves comfortable."

David asked, "Hey Lane how's your new job at that fancy architectural firm going these days?" "Just fine," replied Lane.

"You sure are missed at the old construction site. The fellows are always asking me to say hello next time I see you." "I miss you fellows too," replied Lane. "I know I don't keep in touch like I used to David, but what with learning as an apprentice at Brighton & Brighton, and my studies, I have very little time."

"That's okay big fellow," replied David, as he grabbed Lane affectionately around the neck with a wrestling hold. After the gift unwrapping, Azalea said, "Shelia, could you please give me a hand in the kitchen?" "I sure will," replied Shelia.

Azalea said, "Shelia, you know I must talk to you about Lane." "Azalea," replied Shelia; "I sure hope you don't mind my saying it, but he sure is one fine man." Azalea replied, "Of course not Shelia. A woman would literally have to be blind not to notice it."

Shelia said, "Girl I just know he's the one for you. I can just feel it Azalea." I can feel it too," Azalea giggled "Shelia he's great with the children, and what's more, Papa took to him right away." "There's your biggest clue," replied Shelia. "The fact that your Papa likes him says it all girl."

"I know Shelia," replied Azalea. "It's like a dream come true." "Well Lord knows," replied Shelia, "those other two; Jacque and Winston didn't deserve a wonderful young woman like you in their lives; especially that Winston." "I agree," replied Azalea. "I just wish that it hadn't taken me so long to realize it. Shelia asked, "I wonder whatever happened to that Winston character?"

Azalea replied, "I'd really like to forget." Shelia replied, "Not that I miss him at all mind you, but I just haven't seen him in a long time hanging around these parts."

"You know I heard that the woman he left me for divorced him," replied Azalea. "Once a snake, always a snake," replied Shelia. Azalea said, "Shelia girl; can we please change the subject, and focus on a more pleasant topic of conversation?"

"You mean like your fine new beau; Mr. Lane Jenson?" "What else is there to discuss right now," Azalea replied smiling.

Both Shelia and Azalea both started giggling. David shouted, "Hey what's so funny ladies?" Lane then added, "Yes, what's so funny in there?" "Just girl talk," replied Azalea, as she and Shelia began giggling.

Azalea and Shelia then both began serving the Christmas dinner. "Sure smells good, said Lane." "Taste even better son,' replied Papa. "I can hardly wait to eat," said David.

After dinner, Lane, David, and Papa went into the parlor and lit up cigars, drank a beer, while they watched a football game on television. In the meantime Matisse and Clay enjoyed playing with their toys, while Azalea and Shelia cleared the table and exited to the kitchen to do dishes. Azalea was a meticulous housekeeper, and so was Shelia, They had both been raised to never leave dirty dishes in the sink.

"Azalea," said Shelia, "I've had a wonderful evening with your family. Mr. Hank has always made me feel as though I was a member of the family." "He thinks of you like you were a daughter Shelia," replied Azalea.

As the evening began to wind down,

David said, "It's getting late, and Shelia and I have a couple of more stops to make. I suppose we'd better leave now."

"We really have enjoyed your company," replied Azalea. "That goes double for me," Lane added. "Good night," said Papa; "You all welcome to come by anytime."

After a day of Christmas celebration with Azalea and her family, Lane Jenson was even more convinced that he wanted her in his life and in his future. Papa decided to turn in early that evening. After putting Clay and Matisse to bed, Azalea and Lane decided to recapture their first evening they had spent together, by walking outside and sitting on the front porch. Although it was cold, the sky was beautiful, as it displayed the moon in it fullness, and the stars sparkled like diamonds.

Azalea and Lane sat on the porch swing with Lane's arms holding Azalea wrapped in a festive red and green knitted shawl that Aunt Mae had knitted by hand for as a gift for her one Christmas. Azalea had always cherished the shawl, and always found a reason to wear it every year during the Christmas holiday season, each year since Aunt Mae died.

The perfect opportunity presented itself for Lane to reveal his romantic side to

Azalea. On tonight, Lane would make certain that there would be no doubt in Azalea's mind as to his intentions towards her.

"You look so very beautiful in the moonlight my dear, sweet, Leah" said Lane. "You are always so flattering to me Lane," replied Azalea. "It's not flattery," replied Lane; but the truth as I see it, and feel it."

For once in her life, Azalea could not find the words to speak; as she stood silently, and just listened, while Lane expressed his feelings to her. "Leah," said Lane. "The last time we were in this setting, you pulled away from me, but I know that the feelings that are in your heart for me, won't allow you to do so this time."

"I now know what I want Lane, and that is you; replied "Azalea. Lane replied, "Leah, I've waited so long to hear you express your feelings to me, because you must know just how much I love you." Azalea replied in a low whisper; "Oh Lane my darling," I love you too, and I promise I won't pull away this time."

Lane placed his strong masculine arms around Azalea's delicate feminine shoulders, and pulled her close to his chest. Lane and Azalea lips met in a passionate kiss.

"Azalea," Lane said, "You know how I feel about you; as well as those two very precious children you have; don't you?"

Azalea replied, "Yes Lane, I suppose I do." Lane Jenson then fell to his knee, as he pulled a small velvet box, out of his blazer jacket pocket.

"You won't have to suppose after tonight Leah, because I really love you, and hope that this proves to you, just how much." When Lane opened the box, there inside, was the most beautiful diamond ring, Azalea had ever seen. Azalea said, "Darling, it's absolutely breathtaking."

Oh Lane," said Azalea, as she placed one of her hands in Lane's hands. Lane held Azalea's delicate feminine hand in his, as he asked, "Will you marry me Leah?"

Azalea smiled, as Lane slid the beautiful two carat diamond engagement ring on her finger. "Oh yes Lane my darling," "replied Azalea. "Of course, I'll marry you."

Lane replied, "Someday, I will give you a larger one, and a diamond bracelet to match it." Azalea replied, "No matter what other diamonds you may give me darling, this is the one that I will always cherish the most."

"My dear sweet Azalea," said Lane; "You've made me the happiest man in the world, and I know that I'll have the finest, classiest wife there is, that any man could ever hope for."

Suddenly, the tall six foot two Lane

Jenson; swept the petite five foot two Azalea Stevens off her feet.

"My goodness Lane," said Azalea with excitement in her voice. "Put me down, put me down," she repeated as she giggled.

Lane ignored Azalea's requests by swinging her around as he held her lovingly in his arms. "I feel as though I never want this night to end Azalea," shouted Lane.

At that moment, there was a light tapping sound like a knock on the window pane. It was little Matisse. "Mommy," said Matisse, "You woke me up." Lane and Azalea looked at each other and laughed out loud. "I'd better let you go in Azalea," said Lane. "Darling," said Azalea, "I had the most wonderful day."

"Mommy," said Matisse, "I want Mr. Lane to come inside too, and read me a bedtime story." she said wearing a big smile.

"Why of course he will little Matisse;" Azalea replied. "I don't mind as long as Mr. Lane doesn't mind."

"I sure don't," replied Lane. "I would consider it an honor to say read you a story before saying goodnight, replied Lane Jenson.

Lane walked inside with Azalea, and they both sat down to read to little Matisse. Lane sat in the rocker next to Matisse's bed, while Azalea sat on the bed next to little

Matisse, as she held her hand, while Lane began reading Matisse a fairy tale bedtime story.

"Now just close your eyes," said Azalea to Matisse, while the "sand man" sprinkles sand in them. Azalea always used this expression with Matisse to get her to go to sleep faster. As usual, it worked like a charm, because; before Lane had finished the story, Matisse was fast asleep.

"I suppose it's time for me to be going Azalea, my love," said Lane as they stood on the front porch. "I'll miss you sweetheart," replied Azalea. "I'll miss you too, my love,' replied Lane, as he kissed Azalea goodnight.

While Azalea was preparing to take a bubble bath, she began to think about the wonderful life she saw ahead of her. She had so much anticipation about the new life she would have with Lane Jenson. After everything she had gone thru in her young life, such as the loss of her mother Mama Lucille, whom she doesn't even remember; because she had died giving birth to Azalea. Then there was the loss of her Aunt Mae, who raised her, and loved her dearly, and died when Azalea was only seventeen years of age.

On the other hand, there were those experiences in romance; that Azalea would rather forget. Her brief encounter with Winston Sanders and her one-sided relationship with Jacque Marquette; had left indelible marks upon her life. Although Azalea wanted to forget these two men, she could never forget the fact that she loved the two precious children that were a result of them.

Azalea felt as though Clay and little Matisse would both grow up to be a product of the love that she would show them, instead of like their fathers, who had deserted her, and them. Although at times, she had felt bitter towards Winston, for how he had deliberately deceived her, she never felt bitter about the baby that she had carried nine months in her stomach, as result of his deception. When Azalea met Jacque Marquette, she really believed that she had met the man that would share her life, her love, and her dreams.

Azalea woke up the next morning with the feeling of excitement she had never before experienced. She felt as though it was a beautiful dream, that she had the night before. If it was indeed a dream, Azalea never wanted it to end. Reality set in as she heard,

"Mommy, wake up," shouted little Matisse. "I'm hungry." "Mommy's up Matisse," replied Azalea; as she yawned. Azalea hurried to the bathroom to freshen up before preparing, and serving breakfast. When Azalea walked into the kitchen, she smelled the aroma of bacon, eggs, and buttered biscuits. Morning gal, said Papa. "I hope you slept good last night." "Oh, Papa," replied Azalea. "I sure did.

"Look Papa," said Azalea, as he showed Papa the engagement ring. "Papa shouted, "I never did see a diamond that big in my whole life." "Oh Papa." said Azalea. "Lane asked me to marry him on last night. Isn't it wonderful?" Papa replied, "Yes it is child, and he done backed up his words with his actions; when he gave you that big diamond ring. Azalea smiled and replied, "He sure has Papa.

Chapter

9

The year was now 1959, the month of January, and Lane was now twenty-six years old, and had finally completed his studies. Lane Jenson graduated from Dawson University of Cherry Blossom, Georgia; Magna Cum Laude, receiving a Master's degree in Architecture. Although Lane still worked part-time as a contractor, he was still an apprentice at an architectural firm in the city. Brighton & Brighton Architectural Design group; which was among the most prominent firms in the country, let alone the city of Cherry Blossom. Lane Jenson felt blessed to have received the letter of recommendation from his mentor and benefactor, Mr. Benjamin Carlton III.

Lane Jenson was yet to receive another surprise in his future from Mr. Carlton that he never dreamed possible after so many years. In the months that followed, Lane had encouraged Azalea to enroll in François School of Fashion Design. Shelia had volunteered to help out with Matisse and Clay on the night's that Azalea attended classes. Classes were only two nights a week over the next two years. During that time, Azalea and Lane saw very little of each other, except for occasional dinners at restaurants on weekends.

Lane felt that Azalea deserved the opportunity to explore her creative artistry in fashion designing. Over the next two years, Azalea studied very hard; learning all of the facets of dress design that she never knew existed. She had always thought that possessing skills to sew a dress; was sufficient enough to become a fashion designer; but soon came to realize how acquiring an education, would cultivate her gifts of drawing and sewing.

The spring of 1960, Azalea graduated from design school with honors, but was still working at Parkinson's as a seamstress. Nevertheless, things were looking up for her. Lane, Shelia, David, little Matisse, who was now five; approaching six years in the month of July; and Clay now seven, who would soon be turning eight; along with Papa, were all present for the momentous occasion. Papa who was now eighty-five, needed a walking cane to get around.

"I am so proud of you Zale," said Papa. "So am I," Lane added. Azalea was so very happy, but could not help but notice that behind the joy in Papa's eyes, there seemed to be a sense of resolve that she had never seen before. Azalea thought to herself, "What did it all mean?"

The fall of 1960, brought about "new beginnings" for Azalea Stevens; as well as for Lane Jenson. Little Matisse had turned five years old in July, and attending the elementary school's kinder garden. Clay, who had just turned seven years of age, was really excited about being a protective big brother to his little sister. Clay believed that he was finally his mother's big boy.

"Clay," shouted Azalea please hurry and finish your breakfast. You don't want to miss the school bus." "Okay Mom," Clay replied; "but Matisse had better be ready too then." "Don't concern yourself about that Clay," replied Azalea. "You just make sure that you're ready." I'm all ready to go Mom," Clay replied.

Azalea had insisted at a very young age that she wanted to be called; "Mother, Mom," or "Mommy," by her children. This is why, she was so glad that Clay had finally stopped calling her Momma, and had begun calling her Mom.

"I'll walk you and Matisse to the bus stop Clay," said Azalea. "Oh Mom," said Clay; "Do you really have to?" "I certainly do Clay," replied Azalea. "No matter how big you get, you both will always be my babies."

"Mother, please don't repeat that at the bus stop in front of my friends, "replied Clay. Azalea chuckled. "Don't worry Clay; I promise I won't," replied Azalea.

While Azalea was standing at the bus stop with Matisse, and Clay, she suddenly heard a horn blowing. When she looked, an unrecognized car pulled up alongside the curb.

"Well good morning Miss Azalea," said Winston; how might you be this fine morning?" "Winston," said Azalea. "What on earth are you doing, and what do you want?"

"Why so sensitive Miss Azalea?" "I'm just admiring those two fine children of yours," Winston replied.

Azalea replied, "I don't have time for this, so go away." Winston replied in a cocky tone of voice, "That sure is a good-looking boy you got there." "I'll bet he looks just like his daddy.

"I said go away Winston," Azalea snapped back. Winston replied, "Hey girl, what's that on your left hand ring finger?" "I'm engaged; not that it's any of your business," replied Azalea. "Well girl, I'll see you later," Winston said as he drove off.

Azalea was soon to discover in the worst way possible, that Winston really was like a "bad penny," turning up at the worst possible times.

Once Winston had driven away, Clay asked, "Mommy, who was that man and why was he talking to you?" "Just someone I knew once from my past Clay," Azalea replied with a somber expression on her face.

Just at that moment little Matisse spotted the school bus. "Mommy, here comes the school bus," shouted little Matisse with excitement in her voice.

"Give mommy a kiss Mattie," said Azalea. "Not me Mommy," said Clay. "Besides, I'm too big for that stuff now." "I'll see you later," said Azalea waving, as Matisse and Clay were driven away on the bus.

Clay and Matisse had just boarded the school bus, when suddenly Azalea heard a loud screeching sound. She turned to see a delivery truck try to avoid hitting Papa, but by the time the driver realized that Papa had stepped off the curb, it was too late. Papa, who would always stand in front of the gate to see little Clay off to school, had been told by Azalea to stay inside this morning, since his bronchitis had been acting up. Besides Papa's good leg was not as strong as it used to be, and his other leg had gotten even shorter over the years with age.

"No, no, no," screamed Azalea; "Oh no," she shouted, as she rushed to Papa's aid. Azalea began weeping heavily as she held Papa's head in her lap. "Please Lord, not my dear sweet Papa, Azalea cried." "Help me somebody. Please help me, somebody, please help me," Azalea screamed,

"The sirens of the ambulance seemed to be drowned out by the wailing of Azalea, she held Papa's head in her lap.

"Oh no, not my Papa," screamed Azalea. "Not my Papa." Papa died on the way to the hospital, with Azalea by his side. Before he passed away, Azalea sensed Papa need to say something to her, and leaned closer to his mouth.

"Tell them babies I love them," whispered Papa. "I will see you and those babies one day up yonder in heaven Zale," said Papa, as he drew his last breath.

Papa's funeral was conducted in a manner of the life he had led. Azalea read a scripture.

Azalea was so proud of the fact that Papa had worked so many years on the railroad. He was a member of the union. Papa was also a member of the Captains Brass band. After Aunt Mae died, Papa returned to his roots, and became a member of Mt. Bless Baptist Church. He had served faithfully in his later years, until his asthma conditions worsened, and he was not physically able to get around like he used to. It was therefore very befitting that all of these organizations were represented at his "going home celebration."

Azalea wore a stunning black three piece outfit that included a sheath fitted dress with a wide black patent leather belt, and matching short jacket. Azalea a black wide brim floppy hat, with a white rose in honor and memory of her Papa... Azalea accessorized with a string of white freshwater single strand pearls and pearl stud earrings. Seated behind Azalea on the second pew, was Lane Jenson.

Lane had not wanted to intrude on the family's grief publicly, but was there to show his support in Azalea and the children's time of mourning. Lane had developed a great deal of respect for Hank Stevens. Lane considered Papa a friend. While Lane sat somber on the church pew, his mind began to drift back to the memorable times he had spent with Papa. Hank Stevens had become like a father to Lane.

He thought of how Papa spoke to him in the parlor concerning his only child and daughter Azalea. Lane remembered when Papa said that he had been waiting a long time on him to arrive. Lane remembered that Papa wanted to know his intentions towards

Azalea right off the bat. It was now; while sitting in church, that Lane Jenson finally understood everything Papa said to him that evening. Once the service was ended, and everyone headed to the cemetery, Lane began to feel a sense of urgency towards loving and caring for the family Papa was leaving behind.

One week following Papa's funeral, Azalea was sitting outside on the front porch relaxing and reading her bible, as the children played in the yard. Since Papa's passing, Azalea had found herself relying more and more on scriptures to see her through each day. Azalea's trials she had been thru, only which seemed to increase her faith in the Lord. Azalea had come to believe, that it was perhaps indeed divine providence; that had brought Lane Jenson into her life at this particular time.

Considering the two men she had previously been involved with, Lane seemed to truly be a blessing. With each passing day, Azalea began to realize that so much of what Papa had tried to teach her about life was true. She realized that even though Papa seemed over protective often times, it was just because he loved her so very much, and did not want her be hurt, as she ended up being. Azalea felt blessed to have a friend like Shelia in her life.

Often times Shelia made life bearable for Azalea, when times seemed rough. Azalea had not seen Lane since the funeral, because he just wanted to give her some space. He knew that Shelia was right next door, and would check on Azalea. Shelia also relayed to her boyfriend David just how Azalea was doing. David in turn, would pass it on to Lane Jenson. Since Lane had graduated, he was trying to get established with the new firm he was working with. He remembered his talks with Papa, and therefore knew that it was imperative, that he had something to offer Azalea, before asking her to become his wife.

Azalea had not seen or heard from Jacque Marquette, Matisse's father since she'd had him arrested for disturbing the peace.

"Well, hello there pretty little girl." Azalea looked up from her reading to see Jacque standing at the front gate of the white picket fence smiling down at little Matisse.

"Azalea jumped up from the porch swing, and ran down the steps; up the walkway lined with flowers, and swept Matisse up in her arms.

"How dare you; even come near her after the way you have behaved towards both of us, said Azalea.

"Look here Zale," replied Jacque.

Zale was his pet name for Azalea when they were seeing each other, although sometimes, Papa had called her Zale also.

"I hear about old man's passing, and I just stopped to pay my respects. I meant no harm to her; but she is still my daughter. She is still my own flesh and blood."

"You should have thought of that a long time ago Jacque," replied Azalea. "Besides you never respected my Papa when he was alive, so why should I believe you now?" Azalea stood firm as she held little Matisse tightly in her arms. "Neither she nor I need you I our lives now." Jacque leaned forward as if to get closer to Matisse, and then responded, "How can you say that Zale, you and I once loved each other very much?"

"What we once had is dead and gone Jacque, and I've moved on since my dependence on you," Azalea said. She then tosses her head upward, as she proudly turned and walked away. Azalea felt powerful, as she left Jacque standing with mud on his face, and licking his wounds.

An entire year had now gone, by since the tragic accident that had taken Papa from Azalea, and her children; Matisse and Clay. Hank (Peg) Stevens. Azalea knew that life must go on for the sake of her children, Matisse and Clay. Papa would have expected no less from her.

The love that existed between Lane Jenson and Azalea Stevens; had blossomed into what many defined as a partnership. Each seemed to thrive off the other's ambitions and zeal for success. Their love was genuine, yet not invasive of each other's goals in life. They were each determined not to invade each other's space when it came to reaching the success they both sought after. Lane and Azalea both seemed to relish climbing the ladder of success. They each had a profound respect for one another as individuals. This was a rare quality found in most romances of their time.

Lane Jenson had now become an Associate of Brighton & Brighton Architectural firm. Lane had worked very hard to learn the intricacies of designing fine homes, and had begun learning about architectural structures of tall buildings. Lane had dreams of not just designing tall buildings, but owning them. Although this vision seemed a far off dream; Lane had begun to think of becoming a real estate tycoon.

Azalea was no longer employed by Parkinson's Department store; but was now a seamstress for Veronique's Fashion Design House, that catered to the most elite class of Southern high society, primarily in and around Cherry Blossom, Georgia.

The design house was located in the center of the fashion shopping district. Azalea worked very hard to prove at Veronique's. Her ambition; propelled her to climb the ladder quickly in the fashion industry. By sharing her design ideas with Veronique, Azalea was eventually given a contract, and became the first member of Veronique's design team, that was multi-cultural. Azalea was now meeting the Crème de la Crème of Cherry Blossom's bourgeoisie high society.

Azalea thought about how she was now benefitting from the avid reading of books as a child, novels; as well as reference books from her teen years into her twenties. She thought of the first time her Aunt Mae had brought her to her job as a child. Azalea thought of how Aunt Mae had told her to be sure that she curtseyed upon meeting Mrs. LeBlanc for the first time.

She reminisced about the times when she was just a little girl, and Mrs. Leblanc would have her recite poetry to her guests on different occasions. Azalea thought of how Aunt Mae and Papa had sacrificed so much to send her to charm school on Saturdays when she turned fifteen years old. Although she missed seeing Shelia on the job, she spent quality time with her. Azalea realized how blessed she had been that those old folks had prepared her for her life's journey into high society.

Azalea had decided a long time ago, that whatever happens between she and Lane; she would not let any obstacles stand in the way of her achieving the pinnacle of success that she had worked so hard for, and dreamed of having. When Azalea was at Veronique's, she was in her natural element. She fit in like a sheath dress that she had custom designed fit her very own sensuous body; that she had been blessed with. It was not very long, before Azalea's designs garnered more orders than any other. Her exquisite designs were second only to Veronique's Premier collection.

Although Azalea and Lane were both busy with their perspective careers, they still found time to spend with each other; as well the children. They would take Matisse and Clay to the corner pharmacy on weekends, where they would order banana splits, or ice-cream sundaes. Even though it wasn't fancy, but Azalea and Lane both felt as though it was very important to spend quality time with the children and each other, if they were going to one day be a real family. Lane knew that it was also very important that he form a bond with little Clay, if he was going to marry Azalea.

Clay had from the beginning, seemed

to feel as though he was in a competition for his mother's love with Lane. Azalea had always adored little Clay. He was after all, her firstborn child. Azalea had always referred to little Clay, as her "little man." When she saw some of the hostility that Clay seemed to show towards Lane, it troubled her deeply. She often wondered if perhaps her dependence on little Clay as the "little man" had somehow caused him to act in this manner towards Lane at times. Matisse was two years younger than Clay, and took to Lane immediately. It took no time for her to start calling him Dada. He was, after all, the only daddy she had ever known.

Lane had decided that it was time for him and Azalea to make their relationship official. He had been a very patient man, but wanted to begin sharing his life with the woman he love and cherished. Lane said to Azalea on day while they sat on the front porch.

"Leah, you know just how I feel about you my love." "Of course I know how you feel about me darling, she replied.

"I love and respect you very much," he said, but a man still has needs; that has to be met." "I appreciate your patience darling;" Azalea replied.

"Then let's begin planning a

wedding," he replied with a smile and a kiss. "I love you darling," said Azalea. "I love you too," Lane replied.

As time went by, Azalea threw herself into her work. She missed Papa so very much, and tried to become the strong woman that he had raised her to become. Azalea felt so blessed that she had met Lane the time she would need him most in her life. Lane truly became a rock to Azalea following Papa's passing. He was always there for her to lean on whenever she thought she couldn't go on. Azalea had once told Shelia, that although she loved her children; Matisse and Clay deeply, that she could never love them as much as she loved her Papa. Now she was faced with once again dividing her love between her children and the man who would replace Papa in her life.

Lane Jenson was the only man in Azalea's life; that Papa had accepted. Papa had given his blessings to Lane and Azalea. His dream for his only child was; that she would someday meet a man who would love and cherish his precious daughter; Azalea as he had. Papa's dream came true, the day that Lane Jenson walked into her life.

Lane Jenson began courting Azalea, as though he had just made her acquaintance for the very first time. Lane's time was now limited, because of his commitment to becoming an associate at Brighton and Brighton; but he always found time to spend with Azalea. Although, Azalea was busy learning all she could about the world of fashion, as a new designer at Veronique's; she also found time to be available for Lane.

Lane Jenson picked Azalea up every Saturday evening at 7:30 pm for a romantic dinner, at an exquisite fine dining restaurant of her choice in Cherry Blossom. Every time Lane arrived at the cottage to pick Azalea up for their evening out, he would have a dozen long stem red roses in one hand, and a box of fancy delicious chocolates in his other. Lane would then whisk Azalea away for an evening of dinner and dancing in the beautifully lit city of Cherry Blossom.

Azalea loved the lobster and steak dinners served at Aunt Bessie's Fine Southern Dining which was located along the coast of Cherry Blossom. Whenever Azalea chose Aunt Bessie's for their evening out; following dinner and dancing, Lane would take Azalea for a walk along the Cherry Blossom coast and look at ocean and the star lit sky, which were illuminated by the bright moon that shone.

Since Shelia and David were dating on Saturday nights; as well, Azalea would have Miss Ida, who was her next door neighbor, come and babysit little Clay and little Matisse, while she and Lane were out. Miss Ida was a spinster in the neighborhood whom all the children loved. Miss Ida had never married, and had no children or grandchildren. She was known for baking the best apple; as well as peach pies at the church fairs. Miss Ida was also known for her red velvet cakes and chocolate fudge walnut brownies; not to mention her chewy oatmeal raisin cookies. She had several "Blue Ribbons," to prove it.

She would sometimes send little Clay to the corner store whenever she would find herself needing one of her ingredients for baking. She would always give little Clay a nickel for going to the store for her. Azalea would tell Little Clay, to save two pennies out of his nickel, so that he would learn at a young age to budget his money. Sometimes that was easier said than done; especially when Miss Nora, the store owner, always had large clear plastic containers full of little Clay's favorite delicious hard candies sitting on counter.

Lane Jenson would also come over on Sundays, after Azalea had returned from church with little Matisse and little Clay. After Aunt Mae had died, and Azalea became pregnant, she had stayed away from church, fearing ridicule, and shame she felt that she had brought upon Pap's name. Since becoming engaged to Lane, and becoming successful in her own right; Azalea had felt a renewed sense of pride.

Azalea occasionally, would invite Lane to attend church services with her and the children, but he would always have a perfect excuse not to attend. Azalea persisted one evening in asking Lane to tell her the real reason he wasn't accompanying her to church, instead of making up what seemed to be convenient excuses.

Azalea said, "Lane why on earth won't you come with me and the children sometimes to church?"

Lane replied, "Azalea you know how much I love you; but once my mother died, my father needed me and my brothers to help work the farm every Sunday, so he never took us to church like our mother did while she was living."

"Oh darling," replied Azalea, "I'm so very sorry for what your life was like back then."

"Well that all in the past now," replied Lane. "Besides," he said, "I hardly expect anyone's sympathy now, least of yours."

"I know sweetheart," replied Azalea; "I suppose it's just the compassionate and nurturing side of me talking right now."

"Well my love, replied Lane; "It's

getting a little late, and I have a very busy
early morning waiting on me at the firm;
which means I'd better be leaving."

"By all means," replied Azalea. "I
have to get up very pretty early myself, to see
the children off for school before rushing
into the Design House."

"I'll call you on tomorrow my love,"
replied Lane. "I'll look forward to your call,"
replied Azalea. Lane then placed his strong
arms around Azalea's body; and drew her
close to him. Lane then gave Azalea a
passionate kiss to remember him by.

Once Lane had driven off, Azalea
began to think Lane's about "Not needing
anyone's sympathy, least of all hers." It was
as though he had no concept of having
someone who loved him showing empathy
where he was concerned. She thought that
this was not the Lane that had shown her so
much understanding when they had first met.
She realized that although Lane was capable
of showing compassion where she was
concerned, he did not want anyone to feel
sorry for the hard life that he had as a boy
growing up into a young man. Azalea
thought that this was a side to Lane Jenson;
that she had not seen before.

She could not shake the feeling, that
there was more to her fiancée than she had
originally thought. Azalea began to wonder if

Lane's private personality; was perhaps very different from the public persona that he projected. Nevertheless, Azalea knew one thing for certain; Lane Jenson loved her with all his heart, and held a deep fondness for her children, Matisse and Clay.

Azalea was so excited about her upcoming nuptials to Lane Jenson. She could barely sleep sometimes thinking about how her life was about to change for the better. Since Azalea had no sisters, Shelia was the obvious choice to be her Maid of Honor. After all who was closer to Azalea than her dearest friend Shelia? Since Lane had never been able to reconnect with his two brothers, after they were separated, David would stand in for him as his Best Man.

Although Azalea was a designer for Veronique's, it did not design bridal gowns; so she had decided to select her bridal gown, from one of the most exclusives bridal designs at House of Claudette Bridals, which catered to the multi-cultural high society, not only in Georgia, but around the country; as well. When Azalea and Shelia, arrived at House of Claudette's to select her bridal gown, they were both enamored with the atmosphere.

"Shelia," said Azalea, "Can you imagine working in a fabulous place like this?" "I know girl," Shelia replied. "It's like a wonderland of beautiful wedding gowns."

Azalea asked Shelia, "How'd you like to work in a place like this as a seamstress?"

Shelia replied, "Are you kidding me girl, they would never hire me to work in a place like this?" "Well," replied Azalea with her head raised; up in the air proudly, "Then I'll just have to own a Fashion Design House one day, so that I can hire you myself."

Chapter
10
The Wedding

Lane was now twenty- nine, and Azalea was now twenty-three; and celebrating her 24th birthday in September. The spring of 1961, would bring about the social event of the season; the nuptials of Lane Jenson, and his soon to be bride, Azalea Stevens.

Miss Azalea Stevens
&
Mr. Lane Jenson
Request the honor of your presence
At their Wedding Ceremony
On
May 28th of 1961; 5:00 pm
At
Mt. Bless Baptist Church, located
1120 St. Charles Ave.
Cherry Blossom, Georgia
Reception to follow at the Le Fleur
Columns

Shelia was selected by Azalea to be her maid of honor. This was expected, since Shelia was like the sister Azalea never had. They had known each other since they were little girls. Lane had decided that he couldn't find a better man to stand shoulder to shoulder, at his wedding as best man, than David Roy. David had become like a brother to Lane Jenson. Azalea was very excited as the day of the wedding had finally arrived. Lane and David were already at church, as Lane anxiously awaited the arrival of his bride.

The bridal party was running a few minutes behind schedule, which was not at all unusual. Lane Jenson stood tall at the front of the church wearing a white tux with tails, white wing-tip collar shirt with a light silver gray bow tie and light silver gray cummerbund. His tuxedo was accented with a tiny spray of white roses, with a hint of pale pink trimmed boutonnière. The boutonniere had silver gray ribbon attached. David; the Best Man, wore a steel gray tuxedo, with white wing-tip collar shirt, a pale pink bow tie, and pale pink cummerbund.

"I wonder what's keeping my bride," whispered Lane to his best man David Roy.

"Lane," replied David, "I've been told that it is quite customary for the bride to be late to her wedding." Lane replied, "Well, I suppose it does build the suspense," he said with a sly mischievous smile.

Just at that moment, the organist and pianist, both began playing romantic soft music; as little Matisse and Clay entered thru the double doors to the sanctuary; that had now opened.

Matisse; who served as flower girl, was wearing a chiffon silver gray tea length gown with a light pink satin sash with a big bow tied in back. She wore a tiara of light pink and white roses atop her head; with gray ribbons hanging in back. Matisse carried a white basket with light pink and white rose petals; that she tossed as she walked along the carpet. Clay; who served as the ring-bearer, was dressed handsomely in a white tuxedo, white wing-tip collar shirt pastel pink tie, with pastel pink cummerbund.

The music continued playing as Shelia; who served as the Maid of Honor to Azalea, began walking up the aisle. The white double doors were closed behind Shelia by two ushers dressed in white suits. Shelia wore a pale pink chiffon gown, with satin lining with a high bodice in front and cascading downward in the back, with tiny satin buttons streaming down the back. Shelia carried a small bouquet made of pale-pink and white roses, with silver gray ribbon wrapped the stems.

The church center aisle was decorated with a light silver gray carpet with tiny stars that sparkled like diamonds. Each pew in the church was decorated with mixed white and pastel pink rose bouquets; that had silver gray ribbons attached; which hung downward, six inches from the floor. The wedding planner had ordered two white and pastel pink rose floral arrangements for the front of the church.

The arrangements included light pink, white and light lime-green hydrangeas that accentuated the white roses beautifully. David smiled and winked at Shelia as she took her place behind Matisse in front of the church. Shelia smiled back. Suddenly the music stopped, and the white double doors opened; as the organist began playing the traditional "wedding march." Lane turned to see Azalea being escorted up the aisle by Mr. Richard; the now retired postman, who had been a close friend of Papa's since they were little boys, and Mr. Richard had saved his life.

Azalea's dress was an original, designed by a couturier from Veronique's

Fashion Design House as a wedding gift from her groom. Azalea wore a cream tea-length French lace wedding dress. The dress had a fitted bodice with a full skirt that accentuated Azalea's beautiful figure. The dress was strapless and gathered just below the bust line, giving a more sensual appearance. Beneath the French lace was soft glimmered satin.

The romantic look of the dress was emphasized by the delicate feminine short sleeve French lace shrug that covered Azalea's shoulders. Azalea wore a short cream veil, gathered at the top by three beige roses. The net of the veil fell just below her chin. Azalea wore cream satin shoes. Her hands were covered with soft lace fingerless cream gloves; that needed not to be removed during the ring ceremony. Azalea held a beautiful bouquet of cream roses with a hint of pink trim. Accenting the roses were light green hydrangeas. The stems of the bridal bouquet were gathered with pastel pink satin ribbons.

Lane Jenson was mesmerized by his bride's beauty. Azalea smiled at Lane with love in her eyes as Mr. Richard placed her hand in Lane Jenson's hand. The wedding vows were repeated and the rings were exchanged. Azalea's wedding set included her white gold two carat diamond solitaire engagement ring that Lane had originally placed on her hand when he proposed to her. Azalea's wedding ring was a simple white band that curved to enhance her solitaire engagement ring.

After the ceremony concluded, Azalea and Lane walked briskly up the aisle and out of the church to enter a white chauffer driven limousine that awaited them. Matisse and Clay rode in the only other limousine with Shelia and David to the reception held at the Le Fleur Columns.

The reception hall being at the Le Fleur Columns; was decorated beautifully with a rotating ball light that hung from the ceiling. The floors were marble with white columns at entrance of the reception ballroom. Each table was decorated with cream lace tablecloths and a tall three foot vase that held pink and cream roses with light lime green hydrangea accents and cascading light pink ribbons. The china was made in France. The crystal used to toast the Bride and Groom were a set of Waterford champagne glasses given as a gift by William Brighton III. They were arguably among the finest crystal made.

The toast by the "Best Man" to the bride and groom; Azalea and Lane, was about to commence, as David Roy raised his glass and said, "Ladies and gentlemen May I present to you, Mr. and Mrs. Lane Jenson, and may their marriage be blessed of the Lord."

Lane Jenson had indeed spared no expense to please his bride Azalea. Lane Jenson slid his arm around Azalea's petite waist as he drew her nearer to begin their dance. The ballroom lights included lanterns on the walls which were turn up as the main lights were turned down for a romantic ambience.

The menu was quite fancy. Being served was an appetizer was Oysters Rockefeller, miniature crab cakes served with a delicious Creole sauce, shrimp cocktail, and water crest finger sandwiches

For a main entrée, there was Baked Lobster served with butter, and grilled asparagus topped with a creamy hollandaise sauce, Filet mignon wrapped with a strip of bacon, served with garlic potatoes and baby spinach. For dessert, there was baked Alaska, miniature cheese cakes topped with a lemon sauce, and raspberry sherbet topped with a rich rum sauce, and fresh raspberries, with a mint leaf for garnish. The entire wedding was an unforgettable social event of the season. It was quite the bourgeois affair.

Shelia had volunteered to take care of Matisse and Clay, until Azalea and Lane returned from their week long honeymoon in Hawaii. School had just closed for the summer, so Azalea had enrolled Matisse and Clay in summer camp. Shelia picked them up each evening after work. "I am so very happy and excited for Azalea," said Shelia. "I am too," replied David. "They both deserve the best in life," said Shelia. David replied, "There's no doubt in my mind; that they will definitely succeed in business; as well as in their marriage." Shelia dabbed her tear-filled eyes as she replied, "I pray that they will David, because Azalea really deserves all that life has to offer her." David replied, "Don't worry sweetheart I'm certain that with Lane's ambition, and Azalea's love, that they're sure to have a marriage filled with joy and happiness.

Lane and Azalea had waited patiently for their nuptials to take place. They both had known from the moment they'd met that evening at Shelia's party; that they were meant to spend their lives together. They were finally man and wife. They were about to begin the next phase of their lives together. There was so much to look forward to.

The guests threw rice at the bride and groom, as they drove off in their car with cans attached to the back, and a "Just Married" sign to announce their newlywed status. Lane and Azalea both smiled, as they were off to their honeymoon.

Chapter
11
The Honeymoon

Upon arrival in Tropical Isle, Hawaii, Azalea and Lane were greeted by dancers who draped each of their necks with leas made of pink and white azaleas. Lane and Azalea rode in the Waikiki trolley to the hotel, and Lane rented a jeep for the duration of the remainder of their honeymoon.

Lane drove Azalea to the beautiful Hotel Aloha; that he had booked for their week-long honeymoon in Hawaii; located on the beautiful island of Tropical Isle. When the bellman opened the door to the bridal suite, Azalea was fascinated by the exotic beauty of her surroundings.

The entire room resembled a tropical paradise. There was a palm tree in each corner of the room. The ceiling fan was made of bronze with each individual blade designed to look like a large hand-held tropical fan. The bed was made on the order of a tropical style king size, white four poster maple wood bed. The posts included a canopy; that was covered with a white sheer mesh mosquito net. The bedspread was a white satin duvet, covered with sheer white organza.

On each side of the bed sat a white night stand with wicker veneer carvings on the drawers. The dresser was white maple with wicker veneer carvings on the top drawers, and a triple mirror that beautifully accented the dresser. In the corner next to the bed, underneath the palm tree sat a soft plush comfortable white chair with soft cushions.

The drapes were sheer panels of organza; that swayed in the breeze that was blowing thru the patio doors of the balcony. In the living room area of the suite; sit a white four piece wicker seating arrangement which included a settee, two chairs, and a coffee table with a beautiful bouquet of pastel pink and white calla lilies.

The wicker set also included thick soft cushions that were light pastel pink in color. In the far left corner sat a bar made of white wicker; which included two barstools. Atop the bar itself, sat two crystal champagne flutes, and a stainless steel champagne bucket of ice; which held a bottle of very expensive chilled champagne. In the far right corner of the room; sit a two-piece dining set. The center of the small dining table held a large bowl of tropical fruit which included; pineapples, melons, mangos, kiwi fruit, papayas, guavas, and coconuts. Azalea knew this would be a night to remember, and honeymoon she'd never forget.

"Oh Lane, this place is truly a paradise," Azalea said. "I feel as though I never want to leave here almost, were it not for Clay and little Matisse whom I love dearly." Lane replied, "I know exactly just how you feel, my love. In the meantime, we'll just enjoy this fantasy while it lasts," he added.

Azalea and Lane walked over to the patio doors. Lane slid open the patio glass doors, as he placed Azalea's hand in his and walked outside onto the balcony. The balcony overlooked the ocean.

Oh Lane, said Azalea, "This view is absolutely breathtaking out here." "I agree," replied Lane. "It's even more beautiful when you're walking on the shore," he added. Lane and Azalea had decided to order something from room service. Lane asked, "Are you hungry my love?" "I'm famished darling after that long flight."

"I figured you would be hungry after that long flight, and the fact there was a little too much turbulence to really enjoy your food," replied Lane; "So I'll order room service before we take our walk on the shore." That sounds like a very good idea darling," replied Azalea. Lane proceeded to order a light meal for the two of them. Azalea could not resist the fruit, and began to indulge herself with a taste of kiwi fruit, while Lane cut open the pineapple; and began skillfully peeling and slicing it.

"This is absolutely the freshest fruit that I have ever eaten," said Lane. "I must try a taste of papaya too," replied Azalea. "I think we'd better quit eating before we're too full to eat our delicious dinner."

"Let's shower, change clothes, and toast the beginning of our new life together before we take a walk on the beach," Lane said. "That sounds wonderful to me sweetheart," replied Azalea, as she rushed to beat Lane into the bathroom. "No peeking," she giggled. "Not until tonight," she added with a mischievous laugh.

Lane could not have imagined in his wildest dreams, that he would ever meet a delightful, engaging, intelligent, classy and alluring woman like Azalea. She was he thought; "the total package" of a woman. Azalea felt the same way about Lane. After two failed relationships of her past, she never thought that she would meet a man who not only loved her, but respected her as well. Lane actually encouraged Azalea to reach for her dreams. This was a man that she would love always.

Lane could hear Azalea singing sweetly as she lay in a bathtub of foaming bubbles, taking her beauty bath, before their walk on the beach. Lane anxiously awaited his bride to come out of the bathroom. While he waited for his turn to shower, Lane decided to taste some of the delicious tropical fruit that was on the table when they arrived.

Lane anticipated the intimacy he would finally share with his beautiful bride on this special moonlight night. On this night Lane and Azalea became one, as they consummated the holy vows of matrimony they had made in the presence of God.

The night was full of all the true love and passion that Azalea had long dreamed of; as she peacefully fell asleep afterwards; nestled in Lane's strong arms.

Azalea and Lane finished their breakfast the next morning, and began their whirlwind honeymoon in Hawaii. The time seemed to go by so fast. Lane and Azalea spent most of their honeymoon sailing, walking along the white sandy beaches, eating shaved ice and tropical fruit for snacks, enjoying some of the world's most scrumptious seafood buffet lunches and tropical drinks at the casinos by day; and some of the finest cuts of steaks, pork, delicious appetizers; and fine selections of wines for dinner in the evenings.

Sometimes they chose to eat dinner on their balcony by candlelight in the evenings under the moon and stars. The water was deep blue in the daytime, and the moon cast an iridescent light that illuminated the water

While lying on the beach shore one day, Azalea said "Oh Lane my darling, I know that I've said it before, but were it not for the fact that I have little Clay and little Matisse to return home to, I'd never want to go back home. This place is so beautiful."

"Well, my love," replied Lane; "I wish we could stay out here; as well. I mean it would be nice to never return to work, but is that what we would really want to do with the rest of our lives Leah?" Before Azalea could respond to his question, Lane said, "Remember my love, you and I have both worked very hard to be successful in life. I just can't even imagine giving up pursuing our dreams."

"Of course you are absolutely correct my darling, "replied Azalea, "but I can still dream."

As Azalea packed her bags to return home from her honeymoon with her new husband, she had no idea of the wonderful surprise that Lane had planned for her. The flight seemed much shorter returning home than when they had left for their honeymoon.

"Oh Lane," said Azalea, as she stared out of the window at Hawaii during take-off. I am so very excited to finally be Mrs. Lane Jenson. I believe I shall go by Mrs. Azalea Stevens-Jenson;" she said with a glow in her eyes much like a star-struck teenager.

Azalea then nudged Lane, who appeared to have fallen asleep. Azalea asked Lane, "What do think darling?"

Lane replied, "Whatever makes you happy my love; naturally makes me happy." Azalea was about to find out exactly what Lane meant by his comment. He literally felt as though he knew, and could anticipate her desire.

When the flight landed, there was a chauffeured driven limo waiting to drive Lane and Azalea to their destination.

Azalea asked Lane, "Why on earth do we need a limo darling to simply drive back to the cottage?" "You'll see Leah, my love, as soon as we arrive," replied Lane.

Azalea had no idea what Lane had in mind for their return trip home, but would soon find out. When the limo by passed the town of Sapphire Blue, where Azalea had lived her entire life, she became even more inquisitive. "Lane," shouted Azalea, "What's going on?"

Lane replied, "Just relax my love, and you will soon see for yourself." "My babies," she said. "I haven't seen Matisse and Clay in an entire week. I long to hold my babies," she said. "Sweetheart," replied Lane. "I promise you'll see both of them in soon. Just trust me."

In that moment, Azalea came to the realization, that she was no longer single living with Papa, but was married to the man she loved, and must now began to trust him with not just her life, but the lives and care of her children; as well.

Azalea had no idea of the sheer magnitude of surprises, that her new husband, Lane Jenson had awaiting her return from her wonderful honeymoon with him in Hawaii. It would not be long before she would discover that Lane was in fact a man who took charge of every situation. Lane was a man who waited for nothing to just "work itself out." Lane was a "take charge man."

Lane had learned when he was a young man on the streets, struggling to survive, that life didn't owe him anything, but rather he owed himself the right to make something of himself, and leave a legacy that his children would be proud of. Lane was determined to not only be successful himself, but to encourage, and motivate Azalea; as well as their children to be successful.

He felt that the best way he could do this was to "lead by example." Lane thought what greater way to inspire Azalea to pursue her dreams, than by starting fresh. Azalea would soon find out that after her marriage to Lane Jenson, her life would never be the same.

"Darling," said Azalea, I really enjoyed our honeymoon, but I'm ready to see my precious babies now. "I'm sure you are my love," replied Lane. "I'm even more certain that they can hardly wait to see their wonderful and loving mother." Azalea replied, "I hope they were good children for Auntie Shelia."

"Azalea you really worry too much. I believe you have nothing to worry about my love," Lane said. To tell you the truth Leah, from what I can see, both Clay and little Matisse couldn't love Shelia any more, if she were their real flesh and blood Aunt Shelia."

"I love you my darling," said Azalea, as she smiled sweetly, and snuggled closer to Lane. Azalea then laid her head upon Lane's chest, so as to find the security, and reassurance from a man who truly loved her. She felt deep within her heart, that Lane had been a gift to her sent by God. She thought of how they'd met, and how right the timing was. Just when she'd given up any hope of ever meeting the man who would someday marry, and cherish her, Lane had come into her life.

Finally, Azalea now saw the true beauty of shared intimacy of the marriage bed with her husband whom she loved; instead of mere lust with a man without the blessings of marriage that God had ordained from the beginning.

Chapter
12
The Bridal Gift

Lane had worked and planned every detail of his special surprise gift for his new bride. He wanted to overwhelm Azalea for her return home from their honeymoon. Shelia and David also play an important part in arranging Lane's surprise to Azalea.

Everything that Lane did for his new bride; Azalea, was done to make her happy. He wanted her to have the kind of life that she had dreamed of having. He was determined to give her the life that he felt she deserved.

From the moment that he met Azalea, he knew that she was a very special lady. He knew almost immediately that he wanted to share his life with her. What qualities that Lane felt most impressed him about her was her honesty and integrity.

Lane admired the fact that although she had made her share of mistakes in life, she was willing to strive to turn her life around. He was also impressed with the fact that she was willing to share intimate details of her life with him; which meant that she trusted him. The limo made a turn into one of the most beautiful neighborhoods in Cherry Blossom, Georgia; known as the Garden District. The homes were all so very picturesque, with beautiful floral gardens, green shrubs, rain trees; cherry blossom; as well as beautiful oak trees.

Suddenly, the limo pulled into the drive-way of a magnificent two story white French antique style home with a porch upstairs and downstairs. Each porch had a fenced in balcony and French windows and doors. Two beautiful dogwood trees sat in the front yard and three cherry blossom trees were located in the back yard area of the house, near the patio. The front yard had a cobblestone walkway leading up to the front porch flanked by beautiful, bright, light and dark pink azaleas. The landscape of the home was a magnificent work of art. The entire home, with four white columns, and azaleas gardens planted in front of the porch looked like a famous painting. There was a white swing on the front porch, and a white wicker settee, two wicker chairs and a coffee table; identical to the one on Azalea and Lane's honeymoon in Hawaii.

"Lane," Azalea asked. "Why are we stopping, and who lives here?"

Suddenly, the front door swung

open; as Clay and little Matisse, followed by Shelia, David ran out to meet Lane and Azalea.

"Welcome to your new home my love," said Lane. "This is my surprise gift to you, my love. "Darling," replied Azalea, "I'm absolutely overwhelmed by your generosity."

"Welcome home Mommy," said Clay. "I missed you Mommy," shouted little Matisse. "Children," replied Azalea, "I love and missed you both so very much too. Now come and give Mommy a great big hug," said Azalea. Azalea stretched her arms wide open to hug both of them.

"Azalea," said Shelia, "Congratulations and welcome home. David and I missed you both tremendously while you were on your honeymoon."

"Hey Mom," shouted Clay, "How did you and Mr. Lane take a trip over the moon?" "Why no Clay," Azalea laughed, as she explained; "We went on a trip called a honeymoon; that is a vacation a bride and groom go on right after their wedding." Everyone started laughing, as the limo driver finished unloading the luggage.

Azalea asked Lane, "How on earth did you manage to do all of this, with my knowledge Lane?"

"With the help and support of very good friends of course," Lane replied.

Azalea then asked, "What about all of our personal belongings back at the cottage?" "Don't worry Leah," replied Lane.

"I assure you darling," said Lane, "that everything has been handled, with the utmost attention given to even the minutest detail."

This home was already built when I purchased it, but the next one will be designed and built by me one day.

"Shelia supervised the packing of your personal belongs, and I hired a specialist team of professional movers for your furniture, which most has been placed in storage, and what I figured you'd like to keep; I had moved here."

"But Lane," replied Azalea, "How could you possibly know what I wanted to keep?"

"Because I believe I know your taste by now my love," Lane replied.

"Let's go inside Leah," said Lane. "Come see what your new home looks like. I had the inside designed by Upton's Interiors of Cherry Blossom, Georgia. Upton's Interiors also furnished the entire home to your liking as per my instructions.

"Darling," replied Azalea, "I am truly overwhelmed by what you have accomplished here."

"If there is anything you don't see

here already that you'd like to see in your new home," said Lane, "you can have delivered from storage, my sweet bride."

"You've really thought of everything darling," replied Azalea.

The home was everything that Lane described and then some. Lane had made sure to have central heat and air conditioning installed. There were 16 foot ceilings in the living and dining room areas. The living room and dining room each had beautiful crystal chandeliers in the ceilings. There was also a fireplace in the living room made of cream marble with light brown streaks. The living room floor had plush new thick cream carpet with a scotch guard covering to protect it from stains. There were also fancy soft vinyl carpet liners leading from the front door through the large wide corridor of the home. The dining room floors were made of glossy hardwood.

"Oh Lane," said Azalea, "it's absolutely breathtaking." "I am so glad you approve, my love," replied Lane.

"It reminds me of the home where my Aunt Mae used to work many years ago near here," said Azalea. "That's where I got the idea from Leah;" replied Lane. I just knew you'd love it."

Azalea finally began to live out her dreams with her knight in shining armor; but how long would the fairy tale last?

Nearly three months had passed since the wedding of Azalea and Lane on May 28th; of 1961. Azalea had returned to her fabulous career as a fashion designer. At Veronique's Fashion Design House of Cherry Blossom. Her marriage to a man of Lane Jenson's prominence; had only served to build her reputation in the fashion industry. Azalea was now seen as a fashion designer for the most elite woman in Cherry Blossom; as well as around the country. Azalea had become known as a very competitive, unapologetic and high powered woman among all those who came in contact with her. Nevertheless, she had one combined weakness; which was the maternal love she had for her children, and the passionate love that she felt for her husband.

It was now August, and little Matisse had just turned six years old in July. Azalea was so enthralled with her beautiful new home, and its lavish surroundings; that she initially found it very difficult to return to her career, but still felt a deep desire to capture the fashion world with her designs. Azalea also wanted to be the mother to her children that she did not have growing up. Azalea also realized that she wanted to be the loving and supportive wife that Lane deserved.

Azalea was planning a tea party with her best friend Shelia for some of her high society friends one day, when she suddenly became sick to her stomach.

"Azalea," said Shelia, "What on earth is the matter with you?" "I don't know," replied Azalea. "It must have been the fried sausages I had for breakfast." "But Azalea, replied Shelia. "I ate them too, and I'm not sick."

"Oh no," Azalea shouted, as she grabbed her stomach with one hand, and her mouth with the other. Azalea rushed into the bathroom just in time to throw up her breakfast.

After washing her face, and freshening up, she came out of the bathroom looking exhausted. Azalea then walked over to the refrigerator, and poured herself a cool glass of water. "Azalea," said Shelia, "Could it be that you're expecting again?" "Oh Shelia," replied Azalea; I spotted a couple of days in June; which is very unusual for me, and I haven't seen anything so far this month."

"Honey child," said Shelia; "You mean to tell me, that you didn't use any protection on your honeymoon?" "I wasn't thinking about such things at that time Shelia," replied Azalea. "Well that was the perfect time to think about such things if you ask me," Shelia replied. "Well no one is asking you Shelia, "replied Azalea.

"Look girl," said Shelia. "We've been best friends since we were little girls, and will be best friends until the Lord calls one of us home," replied Shelia. "You listen here girl," said Shelia; you know very well, that I only have your best interest at heart."

"Oh my dear sweet friend Shelia," replied Azalea as tears welled up in her eyes; "Will you please forgive me for being so abrupt with you?" "All is forgiven," replied Shelia; as she and Azalea embraced each other, like they so often did following a disagreement.

"Besides," said Shelia, "You know how that old saying goes girl, "time will tell." Shelia and Azalea both giggled the possibility

On February 18th 1962; nearly a year to the date of their honeymoon in Hawaii, a baby boy was born to Azalea and Lane Jenson. This would be the first born son and heir to Lane Jenson. Lane and Azalea had agreed upon him taking the surname of Lane's benefactor and mentor, Mr. Benjamin Carlton. The child's first name would be after Lane's youngest brother; Darnell William Jenson. Lane's first born son would be named, Darnell Carlton Jenson. Lane had already set very high standards for his son. He had his attorney set up a trust fund for Darnell that far exceeded the one that he had previously set up for Clay and Matisse.

Lane had made it perfectly clear to Azalea, that he wanted Darnell, to acquire an education from one of the most notable three ivy-league universities in the country. Darnell seemed to garner more and more of his father's favor with each passing day. Lane's eyes were not big enough to see Darnell. Because of her demanding career, Azalea had hired a nanny for her three children. When Lane's contracts began to expand, he began to insist that Azalea spend more time with the children. Azalea knew in her heart, that his interest was not just in the children, but rather in Darnell.

Although Azalea loved her sweet baby boy, she had the same love equally for all of her children. Azalea was very proud of the fine boy Clay was turning out to be. Another year had passed, and Clay was now ten years old. Clay studied very hard to please not just his mother, but also to make Lane proud of his achievements in school. It seemed that no matter how hard he tried to impress Lane, he was always overshadowed by the presence of Darnell. Matisse had begun growing more beautiful each year. Her smile was bright as the sun. Her eyes were a beautiful light brown color with long very dark eyelashes. Matisse's hair had grown very long, and her soft curly locks flowed down her back.

Although Azalea now lived in the Garden District of Cherry Blossom, and was now known among the high society set as a fashion icon, her friendship with Shelia never ceased to exist. Azalea loved giving tea parties occasionally, and Shelia was always on her guest list of invitees. Azalea had even encouraged Shelia to take classes in fashion designing. Shelia had a natural skill for being a seamstress, but just did not possess the ability and creativity Azalea had for fashion designing. Shelia decided to take typing; as well as study business courses. She graduated from Hawkins School of Business, and was later hired by Azalea as her personal administrative assistant. Shelia would later become a valuable business associate to Azalea; not to mention Azalea's most trusted confidant. Although Azalea had hired Shelia as her assistant, she still had not fulfilled her dream of owning her very own Fashion House and hiring her best friend to work by her side.

Azalea and Shelia worked very well together. Azalea felt so at ease having Shelia as her "right arm." She knew that she could trust her best friend Shelia with her life. Azalea and Shelia's friendship had endured since they were both little girls. Over the years, Shelia and Azalea's friendship had only grown even stronger. Upon Azalea's suggestion, Shelia had decided to study fashion consulting at Eileen's School of Fashion Consulting.

Shelia was already familiar with fashions from her years that she an Azalea both started out working as seamstress at Parkinson's Department store many years ago a young women. They had always worked well together, and believed that same connection would work well for them even all these years later. They became the sister that each never had in real life. Shelia had been Azalea's trusted friend and confidant. Azalea could share things with Shelia that she could not even share with Lane sometimes.

Azalea and Shelia sat one day at lunch, recalling the fun times that they shared working as seamstress at Parkinson's Department store dress factory.

Shelia said to Azalea, "Girl do you remember the time that you were too sick to come in to work, and I beat that mean old witch for spreading lies about you?" "I most certainly do Shelia," replied Azalea.

"I couldn't believe you defended me in such a way. "I felt like nobody was going to talk about my best friend like that and get away with it," replied Shelia.

Azalea replied, "I remember thinking when I found out what had happened; that I'll never need a bodyguard with a friend like you around Shelia." They both laughed.

"On a more serious note my friend," said Azalea, "I was so very fortunate to have met you when we were little girls." Shelia replied; I really believe that it was destiny that we would meet and be there for each other at that "particular time of our lives"? "Yes my dear friend," replied Azalea.

Azalea and Shelia then began to recall the times that they would go looking for jobs as seamstress whenever they were not working at Parkinson's Department store dress factory. Azalea and Shelia had nicknamed the dress factory; "The Hot Box," and "The Ice Box;" for two reasons: The first reason was because, it felt like an oven during the summer months; and like a freezer during the winter months.

Azalea recalled the day that she and Shelia decided to try and find seamstress positions at fancy fashion design houses down in the city of Cherry Blossom. On a whim, Azalea had thought, "why not?" Shelia was a little more apprehensive, but thought that even if they didn't get a seamstress job, it would be a great experience; not to mention fun, and exciting, just seeing the fabulous fashions creations that were in the exclusive design shops.

In the meantime, Azalea's love for Lane and her children; consumed the desires and dreams she once had for herself. Her dream of designing clothes had taken place; though not for an extended period of time. Her desire to meet the right man, had taken place when she met, and married Lane Jenson. Azalea decided in that fleeting moment, that she must fight hard to regain control of her strong concept of self-worth that she had once had. Azalea's self-confidence and sense of self-worth had lead Lane Jenson to fall deeply and passionately in love with her when they first met.

Azalea suddenly felt that she had become passive; and seemed contented to live her life in the shadow of her husband. She realized after hearing Lane's condescending remark to her, that she lacked the passion necessary, to rise to the top of the fashion industry. Azalea now realized that she had become nothing more than an ivory tower princess, in her husband's eyes. Azalea believed that Lane viewed her as a prized possession. A valuable trophy won, that he cherished, only to display on a mantle, and be adored. Azalea wondered; how long would she be able to remain on that mantle?

Azalea made up her mind on that

particular day; that she would now focus on her goals, she'd had her entire life. She was on a secret quest to recapture the zeal she once had; and regain the high self-esteem she'd always had inside of her. Even thru adversity in her life, she had never lost sight of her dreams and aspirations. Azalea had voluntarily relinquished her goals she had set for herself; redirecting them rather on Lane's ambitions in life. Azalea had lost the drive to achieve her search for true fulfillment and purpose in life, after her marriage to Lane Jenson. She was bound and determined to do whatever it took to recapture the spunk that had once made her a driving force to be reckoned with in the fashion industry.

"If we have enough money for Lane to purchase a new car after a business trip, she thought to herself; then surely, we have enough money to provide child care for the children. I am now more determined than ever to achieve my dreams and aspirations in life."

No longer would Azalea be the passive woman she had become. Azalea finally began to realize thru her increasing dependence upon Lane; and that because of it, she had slowly begun losing her inner self. She suddenly realized that her life had merged with Lane Jenson's in a way that she had not anticipated. She found herself catering more to Lane and the children needs, and less about herself. This was not what she had envisioned for her life.

Every time she attended church with the children, people spoke of how well behaved the children were, and well-dressed they were. Every Easter Sunday, the church would have a fashion show after service to select the "Best Dressed," in different age categories. Azalea's children would always take first place award in each category. Although she was proud of her children, and the success that Lane had become, she felt unfulfilled. Finally, Azalea was pushed over the edge, when Lane yelled downstairs one Saturday morning;

"Leah," he shouted, "where's my navy blue and silver gray striped tie?" "I suppose it's hanging on your tie rack in the closet Lane," she replied.

Lane shouted, "Well I'm standing in the closet, looking right at all of my ties, and I don't see it." Azalea replied in a sharp tone of voice, "Well maybe dear, you're just not looking hard enough."

"Wow," Matisse leaned over and whispered to Clay, "Mother sounds a little mad." "You mean angry Matisse," replied Clay, now be quiet, and eat your breakfast; and besides it's none of our business Leah," Lane shouted. "Will you please come up here and locate my tie, before I miss my flight?"

"Lane," Azalea shouted back, Miss Lena the housekeeper and Miss Nettie, the cook, are both off today, so you just have to wait, or wear a different tie." Lane replied. "Why in blazes did you give them the same day off anyway?

Azalea replied, "I didn't, replied Azalea, Have you ever heard of family emergencies Lane? "Of course," replied Lane, "I'm having one right now." From that moment on, whatever it took for her to do so, Azalea would not stop, until she had accomplished her goals.

By the year 1964; Azalea dreams became reality, when her cutting edge designs emerged on the scene, taking the fashion world by storm. Her latest designs, were being sold in all the high-end fashion houses; Azalea once again found herself about to give birth to her fourth child. Darnell was now two years old, and had captured his father's heart. Matisse was now nine, and growing more beautiful with each passing day. Clay now eleven years of age; had entered a private academy that, educated those children of only the most elite high society set in Cherry Blossom, Georgia.

This fourth pregnancy of Azalea's was by far her easiest. She delivered a beautiful baby girl, named Grace Chanel Jenson on August 15th of 1964. Leah was named after the name which Lane so often, had lovingly referred to her mother, Azalea whenever he was in a romantic mood. Azalea had quickly bounced back from giving birth to baby Grace; and was back at the helm of her fashion career more determined than ever; to pursue her own dreams, desires and passions, in her quest for true fulfillment in her life's journey.

Lane was so busy with his own career, that he hardly had time to spend with Azalea, let alone the children. Lane had begun to make money hand over fist, and seemed to never tire of signing a promising business contract, that would lead to him becoming the real estate tycoon he had always hoped to become. He wanted to be the architect, who not only designed tall structures, but owned them.

Lane's humble beginnings and sudden rise to the top of the architectural world; had turned him into a very shrewd businessman, who would not let anything or anyone stand in the way of his achieving his ultimate goal. Lane's lust for money; and power, had clouded his judgment at times. Although, Lane had always loved Azalea, and the children, he had decided a long time ago, that he would never again be poor again.

Lane struggled with the fact that; no matter how hard he tried, he could never forget the many days he went hungry. He could not erase from his mind, being orphaned as a child, and left with his brothers to fend for each other in a cold world. He could not forget the times that he and his older brother Jock, had scrounged for food in garbage cans behind restaurants to eat, so they wouldn't be hungry.

Lane had never shared this fact with Azalea. Lane Jenson had made a promise to himself and to God; that he would never see his children hunger, and that he would make enough money in life to provide for his family, so that they would never be deprived of the finer things that life had to offer. As time went on, the wheeling and dealing over the years; had turned Lane into a tough and sometimes ruthless man in business. Lane Jenson had become a man who saw money as a means to gain great power. Although, there was one area of Lane's life that he could not yield his new found power.

Lane had once again expressed the desire for Azalea to have another child; she had refused to do so repeatedly. The advent of birth control pills in the 60's; had brought about a freedom that Azalea had come to really utilize to her advantage. Azalea felt that she had finally taken back control of her life by having the freedom to choose.

The year was 1969. Matisse is now fourteen years old; and blossoming into the beauty, that Azalea and Shelia had often spoken of her becoming. Matisse was now attending the same high school as Clay. Clay was now sixteen and had only one more year left, before he would graduate from the high school at the Academy of Gifted and Blessed. On Friday evening, Lane told Azalea that he was taking Clay early Saturday morning, for a ride to a construction site where David worked, and that Lane had designed the architecture for. "Leah," Lane said, "I'm taking Clay to the site to see how I got my start." "Lane," Azalea said, "why do you have to take Clay with you?" "He's about to graduate with honors." "Because," replied Lane, "I hope to teach that boy what it takes to be a real man in life." "Azalea, Lane said, "you pamper that boy too much." "It takes more than education to make it in this cutthroat world; it takes guts and graduating from the "school of hard knocks." Azalea replied, "You just make sure my son wears a hard hat." Lane chuckled."

Azalea had chosen this particular private Christian academy, because it expressed how she perceived Clay ever since he had been born. She believed that he would one day become a fine young man, who would achieve great success in the world. Darnell was now six years old and had just entered a private school, called the Academy of the Little Angels. Finally, baby Grace Chanel, turned four years old, and left daily by Azalea in the care of her nanny. She was truly a precious joy to behold Grace Chanel; had become quite a handful to keep up with for her nanny, Mrs. Scott. Mrs. Scott was fifty seven years old, and a grandmother, who just adored baby Leah. Azalea loved her in the interview that was conducted for the position of nanny.

Mrs. Scott's experience caring for her own grandchildren; as well as children other of prominent people in the city of New Orleans, was a big factor in Azalea's decision. Although Lane had expressed some reservations, because of her age, Azalea influence over Lane regarding this decision, ultimately won the argument in favor of her being hired on as a live-in nanny.

Four years ago, following the birth of baby Grace, Azalea had informed Lane that she would be returning to her career as a fashion designer, and would have to employ a leave in nanny if her career was ever to spring back. Lane's love he still had for Azalea, had forced him to agree with her choice. Lane wanted deeply to please Azalea. He felt that marrying her was the best decision he'd ever made in life. Lane Jenson had always considered himself to be a man of integrity. He had always considered himself to be a man of his word. Lane was determined never break his promise he'd made to Papa to provide for Azalea, Matisse, Clay, and any future children they would have. Lane had become obsessed with money and power.

Azalea had always loved writing in her spare time, and was presented with an opportunity she'd hoped would help jumpstart the return of her career. Azalea had been asked by Mrs. Russo, a friend of hers from the Cherry Blossom Garden Society, and publisher of a prominent ladies fashion magazine; to consider writing an article on today's career woman. Azalea was so excited and immediately made the decision to accept the challenge. The article Azalea had written, was entitled, "Women Who Return to Their Careers, After Becoming Moms." The article was so well received by the magazine's readers; that their sales doubled within two months. Azalea was then offered a permanent position to write an article once monthly for the magazine.

The article would inspire women, and prove that it is possible to have it all; a husband, children; as well as successful careers. The success of her writing helped propelled the return of Azalea's fashion career. Lane had designed a private fashion design studio, where Azalea could have privacy to design her fashions while the children were cared for by their nanny, Mrs. Scott. Azalea began getting clients who were requesting that she design bridal gowns, formal gowns, and for their entire weddings parties.

Before very long, Lane purchased a property, in which to build Azalea a fashion house; as well as a seamstress factory warehouse for production of her designs. David's Construction company; was awarded the contract. Azalea hired the best marketing team in Cherry Blossom, who used cutting edge techniques to promote her designs. She hired the best advertising team to promote her new company. Azalea had also hired a publicist; as well as an etiquette coach for her staff. Azalea's goal was to make her fashion designs the "Crème de' le Crème;" that catered to only the "Crème of the Crop." Leah's Divine Fashion Designs; began to build a reputation for the finest couturier gowns in the city.

When Azalea walked into the building of her new design house, she was first greeted by the receptionist, Carol; seated behind the marble desk in the lobby. "Good Morning Madame Leah," said Carol to

Azalea. "It is so very good to see you this fine morning," replied Azalea.

Azalea then walked behind the marble petition, and entered the exclusive Bridal shop, before taking the elevator upstairs to her suite, that was located directly upstairs over the Bridal shop. When she exited the elevator, she was immediately greeted by her newly formed staff, which included administrative office staff, designers, consultants; as well as two seamstresses that had been hired exclusively for any alterations needed on the spot.

"Bonjour; Madame Leah," said everyone "Bonjour;" Azalea replied." Azalea's office staff, as well as her design team had been hand-picked by her personally, and she was assisted by Shelia's input. Azalea felt that this was the only way that she could be sure of designing the finest collections of couture gowns, not only in the city, but perhaps in the country. Azalea private secretary Gigi asked, "Would Madame like a cup of cappuccino and a beignet?" "Merci beau coup Gigi" replied Azalea. I could certainly use a little pick me up.

The offices of Azalea's design house were beautifully designed by Lane, to reflect the Azalea's exquisite taste. Azalea was finally ready to express through her design fashions her true creativity and passion within her.

Azalea and Shelia put their heads together one day, and came up with the idea of a maternity line for expectant career women.

Shelia asked, "Azalea, what would you think about designing a maternity line for working women?" "But Shelia, replied Azalea, we cater to high end fashion. Our designs are formals and exclusives." "Azalea," Shelia replied, "What if you design an Expectant Mother line strictly for career women?" "I see what you mean," replied Azalea; for instance for woman who are attorneys, doctors, or corporate executives." "Exactly," replied Shelia.

"You know something my dear friend," said Azalea, "I believe it's a fantastic; as well as lucrative idea." The idea goes very well with the fact that I am already writing articles on Career woman; who manage to have successful careers; and still lead fulfilling lives as wives, and mothers. It is a great concept, and one that will prove very lucrative for my fashion designing company. Since the line would cater to career woman, we could even do a line that was less expensive and sell to boutiques who would sell the affordable line off the racks for non-career working women." "Right you are," replied Shelia.

Once again, Azalea was right, but the concept had originated with the help of her valued friend, and assistant; Shelia. The orders for maternity fashions that had been, requested by boutiques; increased her sales by fifty percent additional profit. Azalea's only thought now was where do I go from here? She had achieved phenomenal success among rich women; as well as working class woman.

To say that Shelia was an asset to Azalea was an understatement. For every design that the design team submitted to Azalea, Shelia scrutinized it before it even hit Azalea's desk. Shelia was after all the catalyst for Leah's Expectant Mother Career line. Shelia's knowledge of wedding gowns and their fabrics were only surpassed by Azalea herself.

One day while they were relaxing at the spa, Azalea said to Shelia, "Shelia, I owe you so very much." "Shelia replied, "Honey child, you don't owe me a thing." "But Shelia," said Azalea, "I just want you to know, just how much I appreciate your friendship, your ideas, and your loyalty to me." "Look girl," replied Shelia, "just the fact that you treat me to a couple of hours at the spa twice a week is showing your appreciation; not to mention my hefty salary,"

"You something Shelia, said Azalea, "despite the fact that we may not always agree, our friendship endures." Shelia replied;

"I can sometimes be a little obstinate when we're working together Azalea."

"That goes both ways Shelia, because I know that I can also be somewhat difficult when it comes to choosing the designs for our fashion shows. Even when you know your choice idea may be better, you never dispute me, but you are always are patient, which leads me to sometimes see your point of view."

"We've talked about work enough," replied Shelia, "let's talk about babies." "Well as you very well know, replied Azalea, I always talk about juggling family and career; but nevertheless, I have always wanted a nice size family, since I was an only child." "I pray your next is a little girl," replied Shelia "I hope so too, replied Azalea,"

Chapter
13

In 1970, Azalea's hopes, and Shelia's prayers, were both answered; when she went for her doctor's appointment, to find out why she was feeling so tired all the time, and having an unexplained weight gain, she was surprised to learn that she was expecting her fifth child. Azalea then became the perfect model to advertise her maternity line of clothing. She was also the perfect example of the editorials she wrote for the magazine; proving that woman can have it all and be successful at doing it. Azalea was now showing other woman that, when a woman is determined, she could achieve her success, while still not depriving herself of being a wife and mother. The baby was born December 25th, on Christmas morning. Azalea and Lane had decided to name her Lara Crystal Jenson; in memory of Lane's mother; Lara Jenson, who died when he was a little boy.

Azalea's company had begun flourishing like flowers in the springtime. Her designs began setting fashion trends in the formal and bridal gown industry. Her world had been transformed into what she had dreamed of for so long. This was why Azalea felt comfortable, taking some much needed time off and leaving her best friend and now business associate, to run the business. Azalea was now secure in her career, but yearned for the intimate times that she and lane had once shared.

Lane was often away on business trips. He was always seeking the next lucrative business venture; that would finally give him the reassurance of never being poor ever again. He had an insatiable desire to become richer and more powerful. Azalea sometimes wondered if that same insatiable desire for power and riches that Lane possessed, would lead elsewhere.

Azalea had begun to notice for some time now the fact that whenever Lane returned from his business trips, he preferred to unpack his own suitcase. She wondered, what on earth could Lane, possibly feel he had to keep her from finding out about?" Azalea had once even smelled this scent on his collar. Finally Azalea inquired of Lane about it, he told her not to unpack his suitcase anymore, because he didn't like her prying into his company's business. Lane was hurriedly preparing for his business trip, when Azalea woke up that morning. "Good morning darling," said Azalea. "Morning

Leah," replied Lane. Azalea asked, "Going on another business trip?" "Yes," replied Lane; "as a matter of fact I am."

"Oh Lane my darling", she asked; "When will you slow down to enjoy the "fruits of your labors"? "When I feel certain that I have enough; so that my children will never know what it feels like, to ever face hunger, he replied. "Besides," he added, "I still have to build that home I promised you my love," "Oh Lane," Azalea replied; "Can't you see that we love you regardless?" "You needn't buy our love," she replied.

"This has nothing to do with buying love from you or the children," Lane replied; "but rather everything to do with the love and money I never had as a child growing up." "But darling, she replied; "You have everything you could ever want," she continued; "what more could you possibly want?" "You will never understand Leah," he replied; because although you didn't grow up rich, you were never deprived. You were very well provided for as a child."

Lane continued," You always felt loved in your family. My mother died when I and my siblings were very young." "Lane my mother died when I was young also." Lane replied sharply, "Leah, why don't we just drop this conversation, because it's going nowhere."

"Shall I have the cook, Miss Nettie, prepare breakfast for you darling?" Lane replied, "No thanks, because I'm already running late to catch my flight, so I'll just grab a piece of toast and a quick cup of coffee on my way out the door."

Lane gave Azalea a quick kiss, as he rushed out the bedroom, and ran downstairs. "Lane sweetheart," said Azalea, "we never talk like we used to, or spend any quality time together."

"The reason we don't have enough time is because you're so wrapped up in your success, you hardly have time for me or the children," replied Lane. "Darling, replied Azalea, "that is simply not true, and you very well know it," replied Azalea.

"Look, replied Lane, "You wanted a career, and you have it;" "So don't blame me if you feel alone, lonely, neglected, these days; or whatever the case may be," retorted Lane. "I never said that I felt lonely or neglected," replied Azalea. "Well it certainly sounds like it," replied Lane.

"Although I have a successful career; and my beautiful children, I still need to feel your arms wrapped around me Lane," replied Azalea. "I have to go," Lane replied coldly as he left."

Azalea felt as though her idealistic world had begun to crumble down around her. She had begun to feel as though everything she had held near and dear to her heart was slipping away. She became angry with herself, for putting so much faith in a man. She thought to herself, "Why did I trust Lane so?" She then realized that Lane had been welcomed with open arms by Papa. If Papa trusted him, then how could there be any problems that existed with Lane.

What Azalea didn't realize was the fact that Lane Jenson had buried deep inside of him the hard young life he'd had growing up. Lane didn't know where he'd sleep, or what he'd eat sometimes as a boy. This life Lane had a child left he, and his brother to sometimes look for food in garbage cans behind restaurants.

Azalea was seeing for the first time since their marriage, a side of Lane that reminded her of another time when they had a discussion about Lane never attending church with her and the children. This was when they were engaged to be married. Azalea remembered how Lane had put up a steel wall, when it came to sharing his feelings about his childhood. Azalea thought, "Could this be the persona that Lane had hidden, or could this be just the beginning of unveiling a much deeper issue that had been kept hidden from her.

It was now June, 1971, and Azalea

was in full swing as President and CEO of her successful company. She absolutely adored the new Design House that Lane had built for her. Azalea's exclusive fashion design house was comprised of three divisions, located in three different sections of the building, with the upstairs central location designated for Azaleas offices.

The design house; was two stories tall, with a beautiful white arched pergola that sat directly in front of the entrance of Leah's Divine Fashion Design House. Azalea wanted to give every bride to be the feeling that she was arriving at her own wedding.

Once inside the design house, on the first level, you were greeted by a receptionist dressed in one of Azalea's distinctive white dress designs seated behind a beautiful concierge desk in white marble; with a beautiful orchard that sat atop it.

When Azalea first opened Leah's Divine Fashion Design House, she had requested that a delivery be made of fresh orchards by the florist shop once a week. There was also a white marble petition; that divided the beautiful lobby in front from the Bridal Shoppe located directly behind it. The design house was enhanced by the thick and plush white pile carpeting throughout the building. Azalea's offices were located on the second level.

Included on the first level, were the three fashion sub-sections of the design house. The first section, located on the far left of the building, was the maternity section, with fashions designed exclusively for Expectant Career Woman. Located on the far right, was designs tailored for the Executive Career Woman, and located in the center of the building, when you passed the lobby, behind a marble wall, was the Bridal Design Studio.

This was the season that the demand for wedding gowns was at an all-time high. This meant that every Leah bridal consultant; as well as seamstress was needed. Production of Azalea's fashions was trying desperately to keep up with the demand. There were some fashions that received more requests than others. Azalea always catered to each of her clients personally, so as to make them all feel as though they were her favorite.

Azalea loved the prominence she held in the fashion world, but missed the times when she journeyed to get there. She knew that she and Lane were having problems in their marriage, but could not pinpoint the root cause of the problem. She felt as though she needed someone to talk to and share the feelings that she had repressed for some time now.

Azalea did not want seek help from

a psychiatrist, because of her high profile in the community; she could not risk being exposed. After all, she and Lane always looked like the perfect couple whenever they attended social functions among their high society friends and associates.

During the times that Lane was away, Shelia was always there to lend an ear, whenever Azalea felt the need to vent or just talk about her feelings. Shelia would always remind Azalea of the love that she and Lane shared from the beginning. On Friday evening after they had left the fashion house for the weekend; Shelia and Azalea decided to get in some girl time and spend a couple of hours at the spa catching up on their private lives. "Shelia," said Azalea. "I don't know what it could be, but Lane and I are not as close as we used to be." "My goodness," replied Shelia. "Azalea, you and Lane actually have the kind of life that some people dream of having, and never get the chance; so just be happy my friend." "Shelia, I sure hope you know that your advice and wisdom are invaluable to me," replied Azalea; "but I just know that something is terribly wrong."

Shelia could see that Azalea was becoming somewhat agitated, and decided to be more attentive to her best friend. "Azalea," replied Shelia, "What makes you feel that there is a serious problem?" Azalea replied, "Well, for instance, Lane is always traveling on business, more now than ever." Shelia replied, "That's not unusual Azalea, because Lane is extremely successful Azalea, and so are you. Besides, you know very well that goes with the territory. So what else do you have on Lane that makes you feel so suspicious?"

Shelia, he hardly calls me anymore which is something he used to do consistently, just to say "I love you." replied Azalea. Shelia asked, "What else is there?" "Well he's making frequent trips to Hawaii, and when I ask where he'll be staying, he brushes me off, and changes the subject, saying things like, "Look Azalea, I don't book my accommodations, because I have administrative assistants for that. When I arrive at the airport, I'm met by a limousine driver holding a sign with my name on it, and the driver then takes me to my destination hotel."

Azalea said, "Shelia, I think you and I both need to go to the spa very soon." "But Azalea," replied Shelia, "we already visit the spa twice a week for one hour a day." "I mean we'll stay for a full four-hour treatment, my treat" replied Azalea. "I certainly hope that you are not patronizing me my friend," replied Shelia. "Come on now girl," replied Azalea, "you and I both need a break from the rigors of high fashion." Shelia replied, "I suppose I know what you mean. I remember a time when I looked forward to going into a design house just to find a job as a seamstress." "I know girl, that time now seems so long ago," said Azalea. "I know," replied Shelia. "Shelia, do you remember when we both worked at Parkinson's Department store as seamstress," Azalea reminded Shelia. "Of course," replied Shelia, "How could I ever forget? We sewed all day long on those old machines, clothes that were sold right off the racks."

Azalea said, "I can remember when we were so broke, that we put our change together to make it a dollar, so that we could buy and share a hot meal for lunch, instead of a cold sandwich." Shelia laughed and said, "Girl, those really were the good old days." Shelia and Azalea both laughed out loud. "Those were really fun times we shared together," replied Azalea.

Shelia had accomplished her goal of taking Azalea's mind off of her problems with Lane, but she now had thoughts about Lane's suspicious behavior her own self. Thoughts that she was determined to keep quiet for now, but needed to know for certain if her best friend was facing her heart being broken in the future by Lane Jenson, the love of her life.

"Good morning," said Azalea to the children as they rushed downstairs for breakfast. "Mother, where's Daddy, Matisse asked?" "He's on another business trip," replied Azalea. "Father seems to be traveling to Hawaii on business more frequent than ever before," said Clay. "Clay, replied Azalea; "that should come as no surprise you, considering how successful your father is; as well as how he provides for his family. "Please Mom," replied Clay. "You give Father too much credit. How about how successful you are, and how well you provide for us also?"

"Clay, replied Azalea, "There is no denying my success in life, or my financial influence on each of my children's lives, your father is still considered the power on the throne in this marriage publicly, make no mistake about it, I am the source of that power." "I see," replied Clay. I suppose I never thought of it that way before." "Well you just didn't realize it, but that's the way it is, and has been for many years between your father and I, replied Azalea.

When Azalea arrived at her fashion design house that Monday morning, Shelia asked, "How was your weekend?" "Fine," replied Azalea. "How was yours" "Just wonderful, replied Shelia. "David surprised me with a romantic weekend on the Coast of Cherry Blossom; where he proposed to me. Look at the diamond ring he gave me."

"Shelia it's beautiful, replied Azalea. "Why it must have cost a small fortune." "Well of course my David can't yet afford to buy as bigger diamonds as Lane for you Azalea, but he is making some pretty nice money now, and we're already looking to buy a home as soon as we're married," replied Shelia in a snippy tone of voice. "I'm very sorry Shelia if I offended you in any way," replied Azalea "You know that I not only think the world of you, but I also love you like a sister, and you are my dearest friend," replied Azalea. "Shelia replied, I love you too Azalea," as they both hugged each other.

Shelia dabbed her eyes and said, "I sure do know one thing, and that it's certainly no wonder that you and Lane decided to make Cherry Blossom your home; after the two of you were married. It's so beautiful and the two of you can definitely afford it."

"Well, replied Azalea, I really had very little with that decision being made." "Surely you don't regret Lane surprising you with the new home right after your honeymoon," replied Shelia. "Of course not," replied Azalea; "but now, as I look back; I just wish that Lane had afforded me the opportunity to have some input in the decision making process." "Wow my dear friend," replied Shelia. "I knew that the romance between you and Lane was not as strong as it was before, but you act as though the fire has completely gone out." "Oh no Shelia, replied Azalea; "I don't mean to suggest things have reached that level, but these days, Lane seems to have made quite a turn in another direction."

With Lane still away on business, Azalea spent as much time as possible trying to divide her time between career and family. Although she thrived off the excitement of the world of fashion, she absolutely loved and adored her children. In fact, you could say that in Lane's increasing absence, the children were becoming the little joys of her very existence. Her friendship with Shelia was also a tremendous comfort to Azalea.

While at the design shop, Azalea said to Shelia, "What is going on with the seamstress in charge of production of my Enchantment Line of bridal gowns?" "They're actually ahead of schedule Azalea," replied Shelia. Shelia then asked, "What's going on with you my friend?" "I don't know what you mean," replied Azalea. "Look Azalea," replied Shelia, we've been best friends practically our entire lives, and I know when something is bothering you; now

what's the problem?" I'm so sorry Shelia;"
replied Azalea; "I just can't talk about it
now; and I just don't want to speculate."
Shelia replied, "Then I will respect your
wishes," Azalea replied, "I really appreciate
that."

Azalea knew that although Lane had
become very prosperous, he saw education as
the only way for his children to obtain their
own fortunes in life.
Months had passed; the children back in
school and were steady growing. The Jenson
household had suddenly become a haven for
play dates; and weekend sleepovers for the
children's friends.

"Children," said Azalea. "I declare I
never dreamed that I would be a mother to
five children ever." "What are you saying
Mother, Matisse asked?" "Mommy," said
little Darnell," aren't you glad that we're
here?" "Of course Mommy's dear boy," she
replied to little Darnell. "It's just that I was
an only child, and never had so many
children around me, expect when I was at
school or church."

"What about Aunt Shelia," Matisse
asked?" Azalea replied, "Matisse, Aunt Shelia
and I share a very unique bond. We both had
lost our mothers at a very young age; and just
as her grandparents raised her, my Aunt Mae,
sacrificed her life to help my Papa raise me.

Aunt Shelia has been my best friend from the time that she and I first met. We were around five years at the time;" replied Azalea. "That is incredible mother," replied Matisse.

Azalea added, "She has been just like a sister to me my entire life," and "I could not have asked for a better friend or sister." "Mommy," said little Grace Chanel, "Maybe we will all one day meet someone that we will bond with like you and Aunt Shelia." "That's possible, but not probable," replied Azalea.

Little Darnell, who was now nine; asked, "What do you mean Mommy?" "Well my darling Darnell," replied Azalea, "I mean that there are so many of you already, you're not likely to find anyone closer than the bond that exists among the five of you "Although I had no siblings, when I had Clay and Matisse, your Grand Papa would tell them, "If you have one slice of bread, then you'll divide it, he always said." "But Mommy we can't all eat one slice of bread, replied little Gracie." Azalea laughed and replied, that's what we call a metaphor little Gracie.

Little Darnell; the inquisitive Jenson sibling, then asked, "What is a metaphor Mommy? "A metaphor is a figure of speech using other words to describe what you mean." "For example; what I meant was that you will always share if the other doesn't have. So never ever forget that as you all grow older in life." "We won't Mommy, replied little Darnell; as he hugged his mommy before leaving for school that morning. Lane was busy preparing for another trip.

A week later; when Lane returned from his second business trip in two weeks, he was in a much better frame of mind it seem. He had brought home with him, two dozen long stem red roses for Azalea, with a note that read: "With love; your husband Lane." Azalea was pleased with the roses, and relieved to see Lane had an attitude adjustment, but was still baffled by Lane's mood swings.

Trying not to seem inquire too much information about his trip this time, Azalea said cautiously, "I hope your trip was very successful darling, she said." "I'll say it was," replied Lane. "You know baby, we should take a trip back to Hawaii sometime very soon; just the two of us," he added. "I'd really like that darling," replied Azalea.

"I certainly could use a second honeymoon," she replied. Lane said, "How does your calendar look for next month?" "As a matter of fact," replied Azalea; I'm taking time off beginning October 25th "Then we'll take a second honeymoon next month," replied Lane.

Azalea was looking forward to a renewal of their loving relationship that had existed before their success. She knew deep down inside, that Lane still loved her, but the fact that he had actually suggested a second honeymoon, was validation of that love she felt still existed.

Chapter
14
The Spa Day

It was now September, 1972. The wedding season had slowed down until the fall wedding season in October. Azalea and Shelia found themselves with more much needed time to spend at the spa, while the company was being managed by her very professional team.

Azalea and Shelia met for one of those four (4) hour days of pampering at the spa; that they had promised to do some time ago.

When Azalea and Shelia entered the spa, they were greeted by the receptionist, whose name was Candy;

"Good morning Madame Leah, and Miss Shelia." Azalea was more often referred to by her professional name; "Madame Leah," because of her success.

"Good morning to you Candy," replied Azalea. "Good morning Candy," replied Shelia.

Candy said, "Will you ladies please have a seat, and we'll be with you shortly to take you on a fabulous day of relaxation."

"We're so looking forward to it," replied Shelia.

"In the meantime," Candy asked, "would you ladies like a cup of herbal tea, and one of our delicious sugar free fresh baked teacakes?"

"Thank you, replied Azalea, but we've both had a light breakfast of a half grapefruit, toast, and a cup of coffee. " Perhaps later would be better," Shelia added.

It wasn't very long before Azalea and Shelia were escorted to their body massage room to relax in a serene atmosphere, as they listened to soft music playing while being pampered as they unwind. After all their years of friendship, Azalea was still shy about her body. She requested a screen be place between her and Shelia's massage tables for privacy.

"My goodness," said Shelia. "You are still quite the little prude Azalea. "I can't help it Shelia," replied Azalea.

"Have you forgotten how strict my Aunt Mae was?" "Well now that you put it that way girlfriend, I know just what you mean, because my grandmother was the very same way."

"Azalea said, "Do you remember when Aunt Mae told us that babies came from the stork?" "I sure do child, replied Shelia; and do you remember how confused we were after that. "It's no wonder I was so naïve; but not you Shelia, you were smart."

"Azalea girl, I was just fortunate is all. What happened to you could just have very easily happened to me. Your Aunt Mae died when you were only sixteen; but I had my grandmother for years." Azalea replied, "You're the best Shelia; I really mean it."

The masseuse began to skillfully massage each side of Azalea's shoulder's closest to her neck. "Oh boy," Azalea said, "Just what the doctor ordered."

"I know girl, this really relaxes your mind and body," replied Shelia. "I am so glad that you suggested an all-day at the spa," Shelia said.

"I just figured with all that you do for me, you could use a special treat like a day at the spa. It will also relieve any stress you seem to under lately," replied Shelia, I just figured that you could use a day of pampering." Azalea snapped back.

"Azalea," replied Shelia. I really do appreciate your thoughtfulness;" "Don't even mention it girl, because you deserve it," replied Azalea, who was now smiling. "Lord knows, that I have been wound up so tight lately, and all the arguing with Lane hasn't helped one bit.

At that point, the masseuse began using her elbow to knead underneath

Azalea's shoulder blades.

"Ahhhhhh,"whispered Azalea; "this feels so very relaxing."

Just as Shelia was about to reply to Azalea, the masseuse assigned to Shelia, began massaging each side of Shelia's back with her fingertips. "Hummmmm," Shelia moaned, "my back is feeling rejuvenated." Shelia and Azalea both started laughing.

Azalea and Shelia then went into the sauna, to relax a while and chat.

"Do you know what Shelia?" asked Azalea. "No I don't know," replied Shelia, "because I'm not able to read you mind girl."

"Shelia," replied Azalea, "Girl you are something else with that smart talking mouth of yours," Azalea laughed. "Well now look who's talking," replied Shelia. "Why everyone who grew up with us in the town of Sapphire Blue, knows very well that no one has a smarter, not to mention sarcastic mouth than you honey child."

Azalea quickly replied; as she always had, whenever confronted by friend or foe; "Well all I have to say to that girlfriend is, "it takes one to know one." Shelia and Azalea then broke out in a roar of laughter.

"I truly believe that we are joined at the hip," said Azalea. "I just can't say it often enough, replied Shelia; "I just know that it was destiny that we should meet when we did in life; and that we were that were truly meant to be best friends."

Azalea replied, "I can't repeat it enough. "I could not have asked for, nor chosen a better friend than you, Shelia." We may not share the same blood, but we will always be sisters in our hearts." Shelia and Azalea both began crying as they wiped their eyes with the extra towels they had brought into the sauna.

"Hurry Shelia," said Azalea, "you know the time is going by too fast. Let's go the suite where we can enjoy fresh fruit and juices."

Once out of the sauna, they put on their white soft terry robes, and slippers with a towel wrapped around their heads, and headed to the suite to relax.

After what seemed to be the most incredible day of relaxing body massages; with the most aromatic oils, whirlpools baths; with tropical coconut and papaya bath oils added, saunas with the aroma of citrus, skin treatments; that included herbal facial with cucumbers, and manicures; Azalea and Shelia were ready to sat in the comfort of a private spa relaxation suite. The private suite included soft stereo music, the most popular fashion and ladies magazines, a bar attended by a female bartender; fresh fruit, cocktails, that included non-alcoholic mixes, appetizers; fresh juices; such as fresh pineapple, grapefruit, coconut, papaya, strawberry kiwi, orange, and lemonade kept on fresh ice.

Also included were sugar free candies; as well sugar free gum. There were also beautiful stationary for those who wanted to write while being in this peaceful atmosphere. The sofa and loveseat were beautiful and designed for comfort, with soft fluffy throw pillows in each corner of them. There were also two comfortable sofa chairs; as well as two ottoman included for each. Finally, there was bottled spring water in the mini refrigerator.

Azalea and Shelia walked into the suite wearing their white soft thick robes, white fluffy thick slippers, and their hair wrapped in a white hair towel wrap.

"This reminds me of my honeymoon in Hawaii with Lane," said Azalea. Shelia sipping on a coconut and papaya drink said, "Really?" "Yes Shelia, replied Azalea, but I really need to share this with you."

"You know me girl," replied Shelia; "I'm always here for you." "Thank you Shelia," replied Azalea; "I just don't know what I would do without you." "Well let's hope that won't be for some time," replied Shelia.

"Azalea," said Shelia; "Perhaps this can explain Lane's mood swings with you. Azalea replied, "When Lane came back home from his last business trip, he was a very good mood. He even gave me two dozen long stem red roses." "That's a good sign," replied Shelia. "But," replied Azalea, "he literally blew up when I attempted to help him unpack."

Shelia said, "Azalea, That doesn't sound anything like Lane; "What exactly did you do?" "He had decided that he would take me on a second honeymoon to Hawaii, and was all smiles when he was walking to the bathroom to shower, when suddenly he snapped as I was about to open his suitcase."

"Oh no Azalea," Shelia said, as she placed her hand over her mouth; "Not Lane; she said in a muffled voice." Azalea asked; "What is it Shelia?

"It sounds as though Lane is seeing another woman Azalea," Shelia replied. "I love my husband very much Shelia, and he knows it," replied Azalea.

"You know what Shelia, replied Azalea; "Perhaps we should just drop this topic altogether." "Whatever you say Azalea," Shelia replied. "You were the one who brought it up my dear friend, not me." Oh my dearest friend," replied Azalea; "I'm just so afraid." "Lane seems to be turning into someone I no longer recognize sometimes."

But it was Azalea who carried on the conversation. "Shelia," said Azalea; "What has happened to the wonderful man that I met and fell in love with nearly ten years ago?" "Azalea," replied Shelia; "I know that Lane still loves you, but David says that whenever he calls, and gets to talk with Lane, which is pretty rare these days; Lane conversation always go back to his investment portfolio, finances and business matters."

Azalea replied, "That's exactly what I mean Shelia. Lane is like a man possessed with wealth and power. It seems as though he can't relax, and enjoy life anymore.

Shelia replied, "David says that just once, he'd like to take Lane on a fishing trip not in Cherry Blossom, but down home in the country, just outside of Sapphire Blue. David says, For once, that he'd just like to see Lane relax and enjoy life."

Azalea replied, "Shelia, you and David have always been our best friends." "I know that we haven't shown it enough, but we really do appreciate the both of you." "Come on now girl," replied Shelia; "We see each other practically every day at the Fashion House, now don't we?" Tears filled Azalea's eyes, as she replied, "Yes my dear friend, oh yes."

"Well I suppose, that it's time we head on home," said Shelia. "I agree," replied Azalea. "If we don't leave now, I'm afraid I'll fall asleep, and not want to get up until morning;" she laughed. Me too;" replied Shelia with a laugh.

After Lane's return from his trip, he had one week before he and Azalea would be leaving for their second honeymoon. It was a beautiful fall Sunday morning, when Lane and Azalea were awaken by the sounds of the Jenson siblings rushing downstairs to eat breakfast, before they would be leaving for church with their mother; Azalea.

"Children," yelled Azalea; "Stop running down the stairs, before you fall and hurt yourselves." Suddenly the door to the Master bedroom swung open; and Azalea and Lane found themselves staring into the adorable faces of Grace Chanel and Lara Crystal.

Little Gracie was now seven years old, and growing prettier, with each passing day. She had thick hair; that was of a soft grain, and curly. Azalea loved brushing little Gracie Chanel's hair every night before tucking her into bed. Gracie, who was always very spunky, and known for being mischievous at times; decided that she wanted she mother to pick her up in her arms so that she could once again feel the love and nurturing she felt when she was just a toddler.

On this particular night, little Gracie decided to play a game of possum with her mother; Azalea. Little Gracie pretended to be asleep, while lying on the beautiful soft woven rug in front of the television.

"Gracie," said Azalea, "wake-up, so that I can tuck you in bed."

"Oh well my sweet little Gracie," said Azalea; "I suppose I'd better pick you up then." Just as Azalea laid little Gracie's head on the pillow, she noticed that Gracie's eyes were blinking rapidly; indicating that she was not asleep.

Azalea then kissed little Gracie's forehead, and said, "Goodnight, baby Gracie, Mommy loves you so very much"

"Suddenly little Gracie sat straight up in bed and replied, "Goodnight, love you too Mommy." She then hugged Azalea tightly around her neck, as Azalea then laughed; and hugged little Gracie.

Lane who was tired still sleepy and tired from his trip, simply smiled at Gracie and little Lara, as he turned over in the bed. At that moment, little Lara leaped onto the bed between Azalea and Lane, and shouted, "Papa," as she tugged at the covers Lane had pulled over his head.

Suddenly, Lane sat up in bed and said to Azalea, "Did Lara just call me Papa? "She most certainly did," replied Azalea. Lane asked, "Have you been teaching her to call me Papa, Leah?"

"I certainly have not," Azalea replied. "Although;" she added, "I talk about my Papa to the children all the time; and perhaps it's because, I told them that I called my daddy Papa, instead of Father or Daddy."

"I suppose so," replied Lane. Azalea asked, "Is there a problem with baby Lara referring to you as Papa; instead of Daddy?" "Of course not," replied Lane. "It's just that it's rather old-fashioned, don't you think so Leah?"

Azalea then kissed little Gracie and little Lara, and walked them to the door for their Nanny, who was waiting. Azalea then turned around and responded to Lane's question.

"Now," she said; "in response to your question Lane about being called Papa." "I most certainly do not think that it's too old-fashioned." "Have you forgotten that the greatest man that I have ever known, was called Papa by me?"

"I'm very sorry love," Lane replied. "I didn't mean to offend you, believe me Leah." "Oh Lane darling," Azalea replied, I'm sure you didn't. I suppose I just really need some time off that we're about take." "I know love," replied Lane, "It'll really be nice not having to conduct business on a trip for a change." Lane then pulled Azalea into the bed onto the soft white thick featherbed that sat atop their mattress. "Come here my love;" said Lane.

"Lane," replied Azalea with a giggle, "You know very well that I must get ready for church this morning." "Well," replied Lane, "I'm sure that you'll make it up to me on our trip to Hawaii." Azalea remembering her private conversation with Shelia at the spa replied, "Oh darling I am so looking forward to being in Hawaii again with you."

"I can hardly wait to be alone with you again my love," replied Lane. "I know my darling," replied Azalea, "It'll be just like when we first honeymooned."

Azalea thought that Lane was certainly acting different in a very good way. After all, it had been a very long time since he returned from a trip in such a good mood. Azalea decided to cherish those special moments with her husband, who was now acting like the Lane she first married. On Tuesday, October 26th, 1972; while preparing to leave for their trip, Azalea and Lane received a visit from Shelia and David.

"Hi," said Azalea; what a nice surprise to come see us before we leave."

"David and I were married in Cherry Blossom on yesterday," said Shelia. "Shelia; I'm so happy for you both," said Azalea. "Congratulations David;" said Lane.

Azalea smiled as she hugged Shelia. "I hope that the two of you have a wonderful life together." Shelia replied, "I know we will."

Chapter 15

When Lane and Azalea arrived in Hawaii, it was though they were newlyweds again. The only difference was the fact that there were so many wonderful memories this second time around. The beautiful Island of Tropical Isle; was as beautiful as ever, with its' picture risqué white sand beaches along the seashore. The Hotel Aloha appeared to have been renovated, but it still possessed the timeless romance of years ago; when Azalea and Lane stayed there for their first honeymoon. The ocean was as blue as the blue sky. When Azalea and Lane checked in, the same desk clerk that was there for their first honeymoon; was among the courteous staff to greet them.

"Aloha," said the desk clerk. "It is a pleasure to once again welcome you both Mr. and Mrs. Jenson, to the Hotel Aloha" Azalea and Lane smiled, and Azalea replied; "I believe you were here for our first honeymoon. My husband and hope to have as fabulous a time as we had before."

"I remember you both," replied the

desk clerk. "Why yes Mrs. Jenson," replied the desk clerk with a broad smile, you certainly do have an excellent memory." "I knew I was right," replied Azalea; with a victorious grin.

"I remember the fact that your hotel gives a complimentary bottle of champagne to honeymoon couples," Lane said. "I see you also have a most excellent memory Mr. Jenson," the desk clerk replied with a smile.

"Azalea," said Lane, we had better go upstairs to our suite; if we're going to rest before our tour later." "Of course my darling," replied Azalea.

Lane then quickly whisked Azalea into the lobby elevator headed upstairs to their Honeymoon Suite, as the bellman took their luggage up on another elevator.

When they entered the suite, it was even more beautiful, than Azalea had remembered.

"Oh Lane, my darling," said Azalea; "It looks absolutely enchanting." "You know me Leah," replied Lane. "

The suite was decorated with beautiful tropical plants, and flowers that accentuated refined elegance of its beauty. There was sitting atop the bar, a bottle of expensive champagne in a silver ice bucket, with two crystal champagne glasses next to it. Sitting atop the dining table was an immense white basket full of tasty tropical fruit; that included mangos, papayas, kiwi fruit, bananas, pineapples, and even coconuts. Wrapped around the basket, was a very large bow, with a card attached.

"Lane, said Azalea, "Who do you suppose they're from?" Lane replied, "Well let's see my love, as he picked up the card that was attached to the basket, and read:

Dearest Lane and Azalea,
We sincerely hope you two lovebirds; really enjoy your second honeymoon at the Hotel Aloha. Wish we could be there, but this is your special time together to make more romantic memories.
Your Forever Friends,
David and Shelia

"How very thoughtful," said Azalea; "Shelia is such a dear friend to me Lane, I just don't know what I'd do without her," Azalea cried; as a tear rolled down her cheek.

Lane wrapped his strong arms around, and said, "Come on now my love, let's not think about such things." "But, I mean it Lane, replied Azalea; "She's the only sister I've ever known."

"Okay sweetheart," replied Lane, then we're going to enjoy ourselves, like Shelia said in the note." Azalea regained her composure, and said, "You're right my darling." Lane said, "I have a great idea my Leah my love, let's start by popping the cork on this bottle of champagne." Azalea picked up the card and read it, as Lane wrestled with the cork.

Azalea said, "It's from the hotel darling, and it reads:

Aloha, Mr. & Mrs. Jenson:
    We hope you have a very pleasant at the Hotel Aloha; and may your second honeymoon on our beautiful Island of Tropical Isle be filled with fun and excitement.
                    The Hotel Front Desk Staff

Azalea and Lane were each a little tired from their flight, and so after they had toasted their second honeymoon.

Azalea said, "Darling, I'll shower now, so that we can nap before we leave for our tour." "Okay my love, replied Lane; "I catch up on some reading before you come out of the shower." "No you most certainly will not," insisted Azalea.

"Leah," Lane asked; "What in the world has come over you?" Azalea replied, "This is our second honeymoon, and there will be no business on it. Am I making myself perfectly clear?" Lane chuckled and

said, "Yes my love, you certainly are. I see
you still have that feistiness inside of you
Leah. I knew that there was a still fire
burning deep beneath those embers."

Azalea giggled the same girlish way
she did on their first honeymoon. When
Azalea walked past Lane on her way to the
shower, Lane reached out and gave Azalea a
warm embrace and kiss.

"Lane you'd better behave yourself,"
Azalea said as she giggled, and hurried past
Lane. "Leah," replied Lane, "I just can't help,
but to show you how much I love and adore
you, my love."

Azalea said to Lane before closing
the bathroom door, "Well my darling;
tonight promises to be beautiful, with the
stars and moon shinning ever so brightly."
Lane replied "I'm sure looking forward to
watching it from the balcony with you, my
love." Azalea said; I look forward to us re-
capturing the wonderful memories we shared
when we first met."

"Lane lowered the lamp and said,
"Leah my wife, you are as beautiful, as the
night I first made love to you nearly ten years
ago." That night was sheer enchantment, as
Azalea melted in Lane's arms.

The remainder of the trip was filed
with all the fun, and excitement of their first
honeymoon.

Once they had returned home, everything was back to their normal routine. Lane was busy at the firm of Brighton and Brighton, where he and William Brighton's close business relationship, had turned into a close friendship. Azalea was very pleased with the children's progress in school; as well as, their behavior. She was determined to raise them into young men and women who would make their father proud.

Clay who was preparing to graduate, was well on his way to becoming the fine young successful man, that Azalea knew in her heart, that he would always become. Matisse would graduate in a couple of years from college, had developed into a beautiful young woman. The one problem that Azalea had with Matisse, was keeping her from not only spending so much money on shopping, but also spending so much time in the mirror. Matisse certainly was not lacking self-esteem when it came to her looks, and her figure. Clay had even once referred to Matisse as the poster girl for "Vanity." Azalea just wanted to make certain that Matisse realized that looks weren't everything. This at times seemed like a very daunting task, but Azalea was determined nevertheless to teach Matisse humility.

"Matisse," you're going to be late for school, if you don't stop staring at yourself in that mirror."

"Sometimes I really worry about your vanity Matisse," said Azalea. "You're still young and beautiful, but it never seems to be enough for you." "Besides," said Azalea; you have all the time in the world to think about such things." "Oh Mother please," replied Matisse; "enough with the lectures, I hear enough of those at college; and besides, where's your sense of humor,"

Matisse asked? "Besides, weren't you only sixteen years old when you had Clay?" "Azalea snapped back, "Matisse, How dare you speak to me in that tone of voice."

"Mother please," Matisse replied defensively, "Spare me the lecture, I was only joking." "You were not!" "You were deliberately being cruel, and condescending. I won't stand for it one more second. Do you hear me young lady? Have I made myself perfectly clear?" Matisse replied, "Yes Ma'am.

Azalea replied, "I hope we don't have to have this conversation ever again." "Mother," said Matisse; "I apologize for my sarcastic remark." "I never meant to offend you in any way." "You know how much I love and admire your strength, not only as a professional career woman; but also as a wife and mother. I can only hope to one day be as successful and dynamic a woman as you are now."

"Matisse," replied Azalea. "You needn't just hope, but can begin now to structure and build your life upon the foundation that I have laid for you, because of how much I love you," replied Azalea."

"Oh Mother," cried Matisse, as she hugged Azalea. "I love you too."

"You are still my sweet little Matisse, said Azalea. "Mother," Matisse replied; as she began dabbing her eyes, with tissues from the floral box that sat on her vanity. "I'm not a little girl anymore," she said. "I'm well aware of that fact sweetheart, replied Azalea, but you will always be Mother's little girl in her heart." "I know, replied Matisse, "I have to go now mother, after all, I have some studying I need to do at the school library before my first class." Matisse then grabbed her books and rushed out the door.

Azalea mind suddenly flashed back to a time when she'd had these very same conversations with Papa about her not being a child anymore. She now understood Papa a lot better. She now missed the times when Papa would say to her: "I love you Zale, and you is still my child, no matter how old you is." "Good morning mom," said Clay to Azalea as he walked into the kitchen. "Good morning Mother's dear sweet boy, "Azalea replied.

"Mom please, replied Clay; "I'm not a little boy anymore." "I know all too well that you are not a little boy anymore son," Azalea replied. Azalea was being reminded more and more each day by her children, that she truly had been raised by a loving father, and a loving aunt. She now realized that each time Papa referred to her as child or treated her like a little girl, it was just because he loved and cherished her so very much.

Clay had gone out for the football in his sophomore year at the university, and had made the team. Clay had a tall handsome physique much like his stepfather father, Lane Jenson. Those who had known Azalea many years ago; had commented on how much he resembled Lane physically.

Shelia had even gone so far as to say, "Azalea, honey child, if I didn't know any better, I'd believe that Lane Jenson was Clay's biological father." Clay towered over most of the other boys in his class. His statue and agility, made him a perfect fit was the team. In his senior year, Clay decided to try out for the position of team quarterback. Lane had taught Clay to never settle for anything but the best in life. Clay was successful in his quest to secure the lead position on the team. Lane finally seemed proud of Clay accomplishment, and was even more proud, that he would soon be graduating with honors.

"Hey Mom," Clay asked, as he ate his breakfast of bacon, eggs, buttered grits, and sausage biscuits; "when are you returning to your company to oversee things?"

"Very soon Clay, but remember that I have left the company in very good hands; she replied. "You mean Aunt Shelia?" Azalea replied, "Who else would I trust as much as I trust her?" "No one besides Lane I suppose," replied Clay. "Clay," Azalea retorted, "Haven't I told you a thousand times to refer to Lane as Dad or Father?"

"Sure, I would," Clay replied; "but he's not here though just like he usually isn't Mom."

Azalea replied sharply, "Clay, you just watch your tone when you speak to me. Why must you be so insolent all the time? You need to respect your Father, do you hear me?" "But he's not my father," retorted Clay. "He's never really been here for me when I needed him."

"I don't care what you say Clay," replied Azalea. "Lane has always treated you as his biological son, she said. "I'm sorry Mom," replied Clay, "I just don't see it." "I mean I know he spends lots of money on all of us, but I just don't feel the love coming from him that you show us."

"Oh my dear sweet boy," replied Azalea; as she embraced her beloved Clay.

"Lane has always been a loving and devoted husband and father; but he had such a very hard life growing up." "Your father's heart towards the world has hardened because of the indignities he's had to suffer," said Azalea; but I can assure you that he loves his family a great deal. He works so hard that you all will never have to go through what he had to endure as a young boy.

"I know in my heart that what you say is true Mom, I just wish he'd reveal a little more feelings to all of us. Money isn't everything you know," replied Clay. "I suppose not Clay; not when you already have it," Azalea replied. Please try and be just a little more patient with him son," Azalea said. "Sure Momma," Clay replied, "anything for you."

Clay then grabbed his books, and headed to school. Azalea sat in silence, once the children had left for school. She began to reminisce when she and Lane Jenson first met. She thought about the wonderful and exciting times that she and Lane had shared when their love was new. Azalea knew that Lane still loved her, but his lust for money and power, had clouded his passions he once had for her.

Azalea was determined not to let Lane's past, destroy her future with him. Azalea had no idea, that Lane's past was about to change his life; as well as hers, in a way that she nor Lane could have ever expected or thought would be possible

Chapter
16

In 1973, the beautiful home that Lane had promised to build for Azalea; was finally completed. The home sat on twenty acres of land; that stretched along the coast of Savannah. It was the most beautiful beach front home that Azalea could have dreamed of having. It overlooked the ocean, and there were pastel seashells lining the shore near the pier on their property.

Lane had also purchased a yacht which he named *The Azalea Coast.* Lane had acquired a passion for sailing when he became a business associate of William Brighton III. This was why he chose to name his yacht, after the woman who was the love of his life, and the mother of his children, for whom he had great passion.

Azalea through her success, now owned her own coastal land which looked very much like the beach; where they spent their honeymoon. Lane wanted to have a constant reminder of their love, and felt he had achieved it with their new home. Azalea was very pleased to see Lane in a better mood these days.

One day, Lane decided that he wanted Darnell to feel what it was like to work hard as a skilled laborer like he once did; so he took Darnell out to an old building; that was scheduled for demolition. "Daddy," Darnell asked, why are we bringing only one pair of gloves with us?" "Because *you* won't need any son," Lane replied.

Little Darnell replied, "I don't understand Daddy." Lane replied, "Well understand this son; that today; I'm teaching you to become a man, and real men don't need gloves Lane showed Darnell how electricians removed any damaged wiring.

The weather was freezing cold. After nearly an hour had gone by, Darnell's little hands began to tremble. Lane suddenly reached inside of his coat pocket, and handed Darnell, the only pair of gloves.

"Thank you Daddy," said Darnell. "Son, you are turning into quite the little man," replied Lane "I am so very proud of you. I know that at times, I seem so hard on you, almost to the point of being mean; but I do it because, I love you son," said Lane.

"I love you too Daddy," replied little Darnell; "but what will you do now about your hands Daddy?" Lane replied, "Son, I had brought the gloves for your hands all along. I wanted to see just how long you

could endure the cold without them."
Darnell asked, "So how did I do Daddy?"
"You proved that you are coming into your
manhood son. I am very proud of you," Lane
replied. Now let's go home son." Lane then
gave Darnell a hug, revealing a rare side of
his emotions.

By January, 1973; Shelia and David
were expecting their first child. Shelia hoped
for a baby girl, while David had his heart set
on a son. Shelia was always busy, as a bridal
consultant for Azalea's company; as well as
being Azalea's right arm.

One day when Shelia was rushing
around helping organize the largest bridal
fashion show ever, for Leah's Divine Designs
Fashion, she suddenly became dizzy and
nauseous. Shelia, come here and sat for a
while," "said Azalea. "Let me get you a cup
of cold water, you really don't look well."
"I'll be fine," replied Shelia, "I'm three
months pregnant." "Oh my goodness,"
replied Azalea,

"Congratulations Shelia," said
Azalea; "but why didn't you tell me sooner?"
"Well," replied Shelia, "with the fashion
show scheduled for May, I was trying to do
as much as I possibly could, before I needed
any time off."

Azalea asked, "When is the baby
due?" "Not until July, but I've been

experiencing quite a bit of morning sickness." "I remember those mornings," replied Azalea, "It'll pass soon." Shelia replied, "I sure hope so."

Azalea then said to Shelia, "Take the rest of the day off Shelia. It'll be hard, but we'll try and manage without you, my dear friend." "Thank you Azalea," replied Shelia, "I can certainly use it." "You know what," replied Azalea, "Take tomorrow off also Shelia, and visit your doctor, we'll be just fine." "Call me if there is any you need to know," replied Shelia. "You just concentrate on feeling better for that baby," Azalea replied.

In May of 1973, Azalea's hard work had finally paid off in a very big way. Azalea's return; to her passion; fashion designing; was now paying big dividends. Her designs were more popular than ever. She was now producing a signature line of bridal gowns known as Lea's Le Fleur Bridal Collection. Materials and designs of the gowns were made up of primarily French lace, organza ruffles, silks, satins, sheer chiffon, tea lengths, floor lengths, strapless, spaghetti straps, floral lace designs; that emphasized the flowers of springtime. Her designs at her first showing were received with much enthusiasm in the world of high society. Immediately following the spectacular bridal show of her new designs, Azalea heard, "Madame Leah is number one in fashion designing."

"Congratulations Azalea," said Shelia backstage, as she embraced her dearest friend. "You have finally arrived, my strong sister," said Shelia, with joy in her voice for Azalea's success. "You have let nothing stand in your way, Shelia said. "Thank you my dear friend," replied Azalea for sticking with me all these years, and believing with me in my quest for success."

Azalea, amid all of her success, and triumph, still could not shake the feeling, that there was still something more to her existence. There was something else, that would continue to fulfill her life, once the applause, and the bright lights of the runway had faded out.

Azalea said, "Shelia my dearest friend, why do I feel like there's more?" "Azalea," Shelia asked; "What do you mean; what more could there be in life for you; that you have not already achieved"?

"Like I said Shelia, Azalea replied, I just can't explain it, but there is still another piece that is missing." "I'm sure I don't know what it could possibly be Azalea, Shelia replied. "Let's go Shelia," said Azalea, It's time to walk out on the runway, and bask in the glow of our success." "Oh no my friend, said Shelia. "This night belongs to you;" Besides," said Shelia, "I don't want my belly to get in the way," she laughed

Azalea then blew her friend a kiss, as she walked out onto the runway, with bright lights and cameras flashing. Even after giving birth to five children, and now being in her thirties, Azalea's petite figure was as beautiful as ever.

She seemed to captivate the audience, as she strutted proudly up the runway, now flanked by her models. Azalea suddenly turned back and headed towards the backstage, where she gently took Shelia by the hand, and walked back out onto the runway to take a final bow before the shows end.

Immediately following the fashion show, Shelia informed Azalea that she would be taking maternity leave time off to prepare for the birth of the baby. Shelia also had that she needed to spend more time with her husband, David. She did not take her decision to have a baby lightly. She felt as like her biological clock was ticking, and finally decided that it was time she have a baby.

During her time off from work, Shelia had eventually started attending church services on a regular basis with David. It had literally been years since she had attended church.

The turning point in Shelia's life all began one day, while Shelia was shopping for baby clothes. Shelia happened to overhear the sales lady talking to someone who seemed deeply troubled. The sales lady was talking about Jesus Christ. She then told the woman that he would carry all of the troubled woman's burdens, if she would follow him.

Shelia could hear the sales lady tell the woman, that she was not alone in the world, because God loved her, and Jesus Christ, was always right there when you need him. Shelia remembered her grandmother so often praying to the Lord, when she was growing up.

When Shelia went to her next doctor's appointment, she was told that she was in a high risk pregnancy because of her age, which was thirty-five; as well as it being her first pregnancy. Shelia was troubled on her way home, and began to think about the conversation she had heard days earlier concerning the Lord being there when you need him.

Upon arriving home, she gave David the unsettling news about her condition. "David," said Shelia, "The doctor has informed me that I have a high risk pregnancy." "Exactly what does that mean, he asked?" "It means that I could lose the baby if I'm not careful to take all the necessary precautions, and follow the instructions that the doctor has outlined for me."

"My sweet darling Shelia, what have I done to you by insisting you have my baby at this late stage of your life?" "Oh no David, replied Shelia, this was a mutual decision. I love you and wanted for so long to have your baby, but my career kept getting in the way," she replied.

"My darling," said David, I know that you would never admit it, but your loyalty to Azalea was also a factor as well." "I believe that you felt compelled to stick by her side until she had accomplished her dream of reaching the pinnacle of success of the fashion industry." Nevertheless David," replied Shelia, that's water under the bridge, and I don't regret a single minute that I devoted to my dearest friend Azalea."

Shelia began to prayer often for her unborn baby's safety. During this time, Azalea would visit Shelia, and had begun to notice a change in her personality. Azalea attributed the change in Shelia to the pregnancy, but could not shake the feeling that there was a profound change in her friend, that she had never seen in all the years of their friendship. Azalea and Shelia had not seen each other since the fashion show.

When Shelia was rushed to the hospital, to give birth, David called Azalea, who hurried to her friend' Shelia's side. "I have five children David," said Azalea, "but I'm still afraid for my dear friend. What could possibly be taking so long, she asked?" "Shelia didn't want you to know Azalea," replied David; "but the doctors said that this was a high-risk pregnancy, from the very start because of her age." "But," replied Azalea; "She never said a word to me about her condition. "Shelia should have told me David," she said. "Shelia is my best friend. She has always been there for me, through thick and thin."

The baby was born on July 2, 1973. David was told by the doctor, that there were so many complications during the delivery that it was nothing short of a miracle that both his wife and his son survived. "Mr. Roy," said the nurse who assisted in the delivery, "Your wife is fine. You may go in a see her now." "Thank you nurse," said David. "How's my son doing?" The nurse replied with a smile, "Both mother and baby are doing just fine, Mr. Roy."

The entire time your wife was in labor, she continued praying to the Lord for the safety of her and the baby, said the nurse." David replied, "I see." "Your wife is a very devout woman in the faith sir?" David knew that he had noticed a change in his wife, but this was a confirmation that a change had come over her.

"How are you darling," David asked? Both, baby; David Henry Roy and myself; are doing fine," she said with a smile. Shelia had named her son after her husband, and Henry to honor the memory of Hank Stevens, Azalea's Papa, who had treated her like a daughter after her grandparents had died.

"David, "she said, "I know now, that what happened to me was nothing short of a miracle." David asked, "What are you saying darling?

Shelia then began to explain, "During the delivery, my blood pressure had risen to a dangerous level, and I could hear the doctor and nurses saying that they should prepare you for what might happen to us." David asked, "Weren't you even afraid my darling?"

Shelia replied sweetly, "I was afraid in the very beginning, but somehow, my faith was increased when I heard them, and I remembered a conversation I had heard in a store while shopping one day about *Jesus Christ*, and salvation. I then began think about you, and little David. I thought about how much you both needed me. I also thought about the fact that I had never even had a chance to hold my precious baby in my arms."

"It was at this point, when I began to pray: *Lord Jesus* please save me; forgive me of my sins, and make my life brand new. Please come into my heart, and fill me with your divine Holy Spirit."

Shelia continued, "I suddenly began to feel a divine presence in the room next to my bed. I could actually feel a supernatural presence in the room, as he comforted me. I then began to pray, and ask him to spare my life, so that I could raise my baby."

"Suddenly, I heard the nurses tell the doctor, that my blood pressure had stabilized all at once. They all seemed to be amazed at how I was able to deliver a strong healthy baby, and recover so quickly from such a health scare."

David had never seen, or heard Shelia talk in this manner before ever.

"Shelia," said David, "You almost seem like another person." Shelia asked, "What do you mean another person David?" "I don't know exactly how to explain it," David replied. "You just seem different," he added.

"Well I sure hope you know that it is in a good way," she replied. "Definitely in a good way my darling," replied David; as he smiled and leaned over Shelia; and kissed her forehead.

Just at that moment, Azalea walked into Shelia's hospital room carrying a huge fruit basket with a big balloon attached that read, "Congratulations on your New Baby Boy!"

"Azalea," said Shelia, "It's so good to see you again." "How's the fashion design business these days?" "Booming," replied Azalea; "but let's talk about your beautiful baby boy."

"Well I suppose that's my clue to leave," said David. David then hugged Azalea, and said; "Make sure you tell that husband of yours not to be a stranger." "Okay," replied Azalea. "Heck," said David, "I hardly hear from him these days, let alone see him, he added." "I'll make certain to pass along your message to him David, replied Azalea, as David left Shelia's room. "Well, I stopped by the nursery to see the baby, before coming in here to visit with you Shelia," said Azalea. "He is so very fine and healthy." "I am so very pleased that you honored my Papa, by naming him Henry."

"Oh girl," replied Shelia, "I suppose after my grandparents died, I spent as much time as you talking with Mr. Hank, and asking for his wisdom." Azalea replied; "I just wish that I had listened to him more

280

than I did."

"Oh now don't you go talking such nonsense girl," said Shelia. "Just think; if you had thought about it Azalea, Clay and Matisse would be here, and you know how much Mr. Hank loved those two babies." "That is so very true my dear friend," replied Azalea. Shelia always knew how to make her friend feel better, and inspire hope no matter what the situation was.

Shelia then began to tell Azalea of the unusual experience that she had while in labor with baby David.

"Why Shelia," replied Azalea, I have never experienced anything like that, and I've had three babies myself. I know that I should go to church more often, but I just don't seem to have the time I used to anymore."

"Azalea," replied Shelia, "you must make time for the Lord." "Everything that you have now is a blessing from him." Shelia then asked Azalea, "Don't you know, and realize that?" "Oh, Shelia," replied Azalea; "you're starting to sound just like my Aunt Mae." "My friend, replied Shelia, I certainly hope you realize where your help comes from, before it's too late."

"Why look at the time," replied Azalea, as if to change the subject, "I do believe that I'd better be getting on home," as she leaned and kissed Shelia's forehead.

Azalea thought a great deal about her conversation with Shelia. She had not been attending church like she used to before her success. It seemed as though there was never enough time, what with her long days at the design house.

She was always so busy contemplating her next design that would to top the last. Azalea wanted to design a creation that would be so innovative and cutting edge; that it would cause the fashion industry to charter a new course in bridal gowns. Azalea began to think about her best friend, and suddenly the fashion world began to seem very small.

Chapter
17

What Shelia didn't know, was the very night after the last bridal show; her best friend, had come to a realization, that, the road to achieving her goal for success; was far more exciting than the achievement of that goal. She began to understand that there was more to her life than she had originally thought. She suddenly had a revelation that this something went beyond just meeting the right man, and getting married. She suddenly realized that there was something beyond just being a mother of her beautiful children. She suddenly realized that there was more to life than just achieving the goals she had set for herself, and had worked so hard to accomplish.

Finally, Azalea realized that even after achieving her dreams, desires, and passions in life, there was still a void that could not be bed that night next to Lane; who was sound asleep from working so hard at the office, all of these thoughts raced through Azalea's mind. She then closed her eyes, and prayed, "Lord, I ask that you please guide my steps me so that I can someday find true fulfillment in my life's journey; Amen; she said, as she nodded off to sleep.

One month following the fashion show, Azalea was once again pregnant. The gynecologist had revealed to Azalea, that she was expecting twins. Lane Jenson was ecstatic about the news.

"Honey," said Lane after hearing the news; I can hardly wait for my boys to be born Leah; my sweet." "Lane darling, replied Azalea, how do you know that it's going to be two boys, you know it is quite possible, that I'll have two girls," she replied.

"I just can't believe that I'm having two babies at thirty seven years old," replied Azalea. "It's never too late when a man has a wife as fine as you are Leah; my love," replied Lane. "Why Lane," replied Azalea, you haven't referred to me as "your love," in years," said Azalea. "Well," said Lane, "you'd better get used to it." Azalea replied, "I'll enjoy doing so."

"Leah," said Lane, "I know that I haven't been attentive enough with you for quite some time now, but I promise you that all that is about to change now, my love," said Lane.

"I'm forty-two years old now, and

my wife is having a set of twins. I could not be a more proud papa," Lane said. "Why Lane," said Azalea; "Did you just actually refer to yourself as Papa, she laughed? "I know that Papa is smiling down from heaven at that reference"

"Well my love," said Lane. "I must go now," said Lane. "I have a board meeting scheduled for 9:00 am this morning." "Have a nice day sweetheart," said Azalea. "You do the same," Lane said as he kissed Azalea, careful to avoid her now very rounded belly.

On November 28th, 1974, two days before the Thanksgiving holiday; a set of twins; a boy and a girl, were born to Azalea and Lane Jenson. The baby girl was named Janine, and the boy was named for Lane's other younger brother; Justice Jenson.

On the Saturday morning following; two days after the birth of the twins, everyone in the Jenson's household was up bright and early in celebration of the twin's homecoming. The two new baby nurseries Lane had designed for the twins were beautiful. One was designed in beautiful shades of pink, and one in shades of blue. The girl's looked like a princess in pink nursery, filled with beautiful pastel pink chiffons, satins, and organza's that covered the bassinet, crib, and drapes. There were a collection of imported stuffed white and pink stuffed velveteen bunnies, along with white, pink and stuffed bears.

The baby boy, Justice room; looked like a zoo menagerie filled with stuffed animals of every kind from Africa such as, giraffes, tigers, zebras, and elephants. There were subtle shades of beige, browns, forest greens, and burnt orange colors, which decorated the room, which seem like a scene from a fantasy movie.

Lane and Azalea arrived home with the twins, and were greeted by their five other siblings; Clayton who was now twenty one years of age; and had just graduated five months earlier in June of 1974; Magna cum Laude. Clay received a Bachelor of Arts degree in Architectural studies. Lane Jenson had presented Clay with keys to a new car, for his graduation gift. This was the only way that Lane knew how to show love for the children; by spending lots of money on them; which sometimes didn't sit well with Azalea. "Lane you give them too much," she said. "If you spoil them so much, they'll never learn the true value of a dollar." Clay had decided studying architectural designing, would perhaps garner the approval he had always sought from the only father he'd ever known; Lane Jenson.

Matisse; who would be nineteen in July, was about to enter her sophomore year of college at the prestigious St. Hilliard's College for Women. Matisse had graduated from high school with honors. She had received the distinction of class Valedictorian. This was a very high, prestigious honor for Matisse.

Darnell was now eleven, and in sixth grade at the elementary academy. Darnell often spoke of being a great business man just like his father, and designing tall buildings.

Grace Chanel was now nine years old and in second grade. Grace loved drawing fashions, attended etiquette school. Lana Crystal was now four years old and loved trying on beautiful dresses. She would walk with such poise, that Azalea said to Lane one day, "Lana will someday model fashions designed by her sister Grace."

This particular morning, Lane Jenson would exhibit behavior that was most unusual for him. Suddenly, the telephone rang. Matisse, who was nearest the phone, answered it. "Yes, he's here, she replied, whom may I ask is calling?"

"Daddy, said Matisse, "it's a Mr. Red on behalf of one of your important associates; William Brighton." Lane quickly reached the phone; "Hello Mr. Red;" said Lane, "My wife and I, just brought the twins home from the hospital." "What can I do for you?" "Sure, of course I remember Miss Dubois," replied Lane, "Tell Bill Brighton, I'll be there in about thirty minutes to straighten this out."

"Darling, Azalea asked, "What seems to be the problem?" "It's concerning a contract negotiation that Bill Brighton says needs to be wrapped up today." "Well I know you must do, what you must do, darling", said Azalea. "I should be back in about two hours," said Lane.

He then kissed Azalea, and said, "I knew there was a reason I fell in love with you my love," replied Lane Jenson. He then held Azalea in his arms, and kissed her. He then kissed hugged the twins, and the other three younger, children; Darnell, Grace Chanel, and Lana Crystal.

Before leaving, he turned his attention to Matisse and Clayton. "I'm so very proud of the both of you, said Lane." "I love you too Daddy," replied Matisse, as she hugged Lane.

Clayton stood still for a moment; as though in a state of shock from seeing Lane show such emotions to his family. Clayton then said, "You are the only father that I've ever known." "Thank you son, replied Lane Jenson. "That means the world to me, to hear you say that."

Clayton replied, "I know that I don't

always show it Father, but I really do appreciate everything you have ever done for me." "I consider you both to be my best investment yet, Lane replied; as he shook Clayton's hand. I'll see you all very soon."

"Now I must go to meet with Bill Brighton, and the legal team concerning terms of that contract that needs to be finalized."

After several hours had gone by, and Lane was still not home; Azalea became concerned. She knew that Lane often kept long hours, but this was a Saturday, and this was Azalea and the twins, first day home from the hospital.

"Matisse," said Azalea; "I wonder what's keeping your father." "Maybe he went early Christmas shopping for our gifts," replied Matisse. "Matisse," replied Clayton. "Is that all you ever think about is what Father can buy for you?"

"I didn't hear you complaining; when Daddy presented you with the keys to your new red Corvette, as a graduation gift this past June," replied Matisse. "Since my 21st birthday; as well as my graduation were both in June.

Father decided to combine my gifts into one," replied Clayton. "Sure," replied Matisse; you always have all the right answers Mr. Privileged." Clay replied, "Look who's talking, Miss Prissy. Why you're the one who has been spoiled all these years. Father treats you as though you were one of his own." Matisse snapped, "How dare you speak to me like that Clay, Daddy loves all of us the same. He has never played favorites."

Azalea shouted, "That is enough Clay and Matisse. Do you hear me? I will have no more of this. You both need to stop arguing, and saying such mean things to each other, before the children over hear you. "But Mother said Matisse, Clay started it." I don't give care who or how it got started, you both need to stop it right this instance, do you hear me?" Clay and Matisse both responded, "Yes Mother," said Matisse. "Yes Mom," replied Clay. Matisse then rolled her eyes giving Clay a mean look. Clay said; pointing in Matisse's direction, hoping that Azalea would see her making spiteful mean faces, "Look Mom, you see what I mean. Matisse thinks that the entire earth revolves around her. She believes that the moon, the sun and the stars adore her every move on the planet."

"You see what I mean Mother," replied Matisse?" "What do you mean exactly Matisse," replied Azalea. "Clay has always been jealous the closer relationship that I have with Daddy than he does," Matisse replied.

"Enough," I don't want to hear another word from either of you two, replied Azalea, until you can behave like intelligent adults, instead of spoiled little children. It's been several hours since you Father has been gone now, and he hasn't called; and I'm really started to be concerned, said Azalea. "It's not like him not to call when he's running late." "I don't know Mother," Matisse replied, but I'm sure he'll be home very soon. "Mommy," cried little Leah. "Where's Daddy?"

Suddenly the telephone rang. Matisse answered the phone. "Yes, my Mother is right here." "One moment please." "Mother it's for you." They say it's something about Daddy." Azalea reached for the phone, and suddenly felt a cold chill go up her spine. "Yes this is Mrs. Lane Jenson, she said. "Oh no," cried Azalea!". "

Mother," what is it, the children all screamed?" "It's your father children," Azalea said, trying to regain her composure; he's been in an automobile accident." Matisse cried, "Oh no Mother; how is he?" "He's in the hospital right now." Clay asked; "Do you need me to drive you Mother, because I want to help in any way that I can.?" "Yes son, replied Azalea, "I will definitely need you to drive." "Ok Mom," said Clay.

Azalea said, "I have briefed Mrs. Scott on the situation. Mrs. Scott said that she would pray for Lane's speedy recovery, and that God would give the Azalea, and the entire Jenson family the strength needed, to get thru this time of adversity in their lives.

"Matisse and Clay the two of you come with me. Mrs. Scott will watch the other children." "Matisse replied with tears in her eyes, "Of course Mother, Daddy needs us now more than ever." Azalea cried, "Come," she said; "we must hurry." We're right behind you Mother, replied Matisse. "Clay, I'll need you to drive," said Azalea. Matisse and Clay immediately followed. When Azalea arrived at the hospital, she was immediately directed to ICU.

"I want to see him," said Clay. "That's my father in there lying helpless in that bed," Clay said with deep emotion in his voice." "I want to see Daddy too," said Matisse with tears rolling down her cheeks. Oh Daddy," Matisse cried. Azalea said, "Matisse please, you'll make yourself sick. We all need to try and be strong for your father." Matisse continued sobbing, "Daddy has to be pull thru this." Daddy can't die on us," she cried. Lane was the only father Matisse had ever known, and she loved him as though he were her biological dad.

Azalea sat by Lane's side, holding his hand. "My darling" she said, I love you so very much. You must come back to us sweetheart. All my life I have tried to achieve success. I have searched for love. I have retained this burning passion inside of me. "My darling Lane," said Azalea, "I realize that nothing is more important to me than the success of my being a wife to you, and a mother to my seven children. Darling Lane please just wake up for us. We all so desperately need you. I know that over the years, I have forgotten about having faith; the kind of faith that my Aunt Mae taught me about, but I need to grab hold of that faith right now."

Azalea prayed, "Oh Lord, I know that I don't deserve to ask you for any favors, but my Aunt Mae said that if I call on your name, that you would never turn me away. Please help me Lord, and heal my husband?" Azalea had drifted so far away from the foundation of faith that her ancestors had laid for her, but now she need more than ever, to draw from that same faith. This was a trial she had not anticipated in her life. She thought that she had everything under control.

Clay had not been as close to his stepfather, as Azalea would have liked him to be, but she could see the possible impact that Lane had on Clay's life.

Lane at times, seemed to be very hard on Clay, even more so than his biological son, Darnell. Azalea had thought perhaps this was because Lane favored Darnell over Clay, when it was in fact, because Lane had invested so much into Clay, and wanted him to be the son Azalea would be proud of, despite the treatment she had experienced from Clay's father Winston.

As Azalea sat by Lane's bedside keeping a constant visual, she pondered many thoughts. Azalea knew that with each passing minute, she was losing time with the man that she loved so very deeply. Azalea believed Lane to be her soul mate in life.

As Azalea sat with her eyes closed, she started dosing off to sleep, and then heard a voice say, "Mom, you really should go home, and get you some sleep, I'll stay with Father." It was the voice of Clay. "You are a wonderful and very thoughtful son Clayton," replied Azalea.

It was the first time that she had ever referred to Clay as Clayton. She realized that she needed her son more than ever now. Clay was no longer her "little man," but instead had come into his own as a strong young man, who she could depend on during this trying time.

"Thank you so very much son. I really appreciate you and you sister being her for me, as well as for your Father." Lane would be s very proud of you both, said

Azalea. "Don't worry about anything Mom," replied Clay, until Father is back on his feet again, I'll take care of you and my brothers and sisters; as well."

Azalea had not seen this side of Clay, since he was a little boy, before she had met Lane. She now remembered calling him her "Little Man." Azalea appreciated Clay's willingness to be there for the family, but did not want him to sacrifice his education in doing so. "My dearest son Clay, neither Father nor I want you to neglect your education for us."

"I know Mom," Clay replied, "but I already have my Bachelor's Degree in Architectural Design, and I can get the Master's Degree later on, once Father is on has recovered." Azalea interrupted, "You must, and you will complete your education Clayton."

"Matisse," said Azalea; "would you please come with me, so that you can freshen up; as well as take a nap, before we return to relieve your brother Clay." "Of Course Mother," Matisse replied, as she stood up to follow her mother out of the room. "I'm fine Mom," said Clay. "Are you certain that you will be alright left here alone Clay?" Azalea asked. "Of course," replied Clay, "you two just take care of each other, I'll be right here when you both return, "he added. Azalea then left to go home and take a short nap, and also to check on the children. She knew that they were in very good hands with Mrs. Scott, and also the new extra nanny she had recently hired to care exclusively for the twins, Miss Matilda. Azalea still felt that she really needed to hold her twins, and spend some time with the other children, since Lane was now hospitalized.

While Azalea and Matisse, was gone, Clay never left Lane's bedside over their father. Lane may not have conceived them with Azalea, but he sure did raise them with her. Sometimes he seemed so tough with Clay. This was because although Lane never showed it, he believed with a little push in the right direction, that Clay had the makings of a great man inside of him. Lane wanted to make sure that Clay would never disappoint his mother after all her sacrifices made.

While his mother; Azalea, and sister; Matisse, were gone, Clay thought of all the times, since he had first met Lane Jenson. Clay began to remember the very first time as a little boy, that he laid eyes on the tall, strong, and powerful looking statue of a man, Lane Jenson.

Clay remembered how he was forced to give up his seat at the head of the table, where he had always sat directly across from

Papa. This seat was rightly his; he had always been lead to believe, by his mother. Clay had always been referred to as his mother's "little man" in the household; but now had to share the spotlight with this stranger.

It was never Clay's intention to cause any problems between his mother and stepfather; he just wanted to prove to his mother that he loved her. As Clay began to grow into a young man, tensions between he and Lane, seemed to ease; as Clay watched his stepfather provide for his mother.

There was still though, a bit of apprehensiveness on Clay's part, as he observed the amount of time that his mother spent alone, while Lane was earning wealth that they all benefited from. One thing Clay admired about Lane, was the way that he never gave up on goals he set his mind to accomplishment.

When Azalea shared with Clay, the fact that Lane was orphaned as a young boy, Clay immediately began to respect the man that he had one time secretly resented. Now here was that strong powerful man, whom Clay had now grown to love dearly; and proud to call Father, lying helpless in bed. Clay then spoke these words to his father, "Father, you have always met any goal you set, so I know you will come back to your family who loves you."

Once they had eaten, and each taken a relaxing bubble bath and taken a nap, Azalea and Matisse returned to the hospital. Azalea felt very assured that the children; as well as; the twins, were being left in the best care possible. Azalea and Matisse returned to the hospital to relive Clay, and keep a constant vigil by Lane's bed side.

Chapter 18

When Azalea entered Lane's room, she immediately sat next to his bedside, and bowed her head, as she began to pray; "*Lord Jesus,*" she prayed; "Papa is gone, Aunt Mae is gone, and my dearest friend Shelia, now has a baby to care for; which requires a great deal of her time. Now, and Lane is lying here helpless. Lord *Jesus,* she prayed, I have no one else to turn to, but you. I remember when I was a little girl, and my Mama Lucille had died; you sent my sweet Aunt Mae to care for me. I ask you now to help me again. Please raise my husband up so that we can be a family again. Lord, I promise that I will never forget you. Shelia told me about the miracle you performed in her life, and I know you can do the same miracle for Lane. Lord, I ask however; that you would please give me the strength to endure whatever comes. I now believe that regardless as to what may happen; I know that you are able to perform miracles."

Azalea was going through a trial in her life, at this time, and felt that she really needed divine help, but was she really ready to commit her life to Jesus Christ, or was it because she desperately needed divine inspiration that only the Lord could give?

She suddenly felt a light squeeze from Lane's hand. "I love you Leah, please don't cry" Lane whispered. "My darling," replied Azalea; "I knew you would come back, the Lord has answered my prayers," she said.

Azalea quickly ran to the door of the unit where lane was, and called to Matisse and Clay. "Hurry, your father is awake," she cried. Both Matisse and Clay rushed into Lane's hospital intensive care unit room. "Matisse laid her head on her chest, and cried, "Oh Daddy we love and miss you." "Please get well soon."

Clay was a bit more subtle, as he said," "Don't worry father, I'll take care of Mom and the kids, until you're out of here." "I know you will son," Lane whispered. It was the first time that Lane had ever directly addressed Clay as his son. Clay was almost moved to tears, as he choked up and said, "I Love you Father.

"There was suddenly, a loud beeping sound coming from the machines that were attached to Lane's body. *"Beep, Beep, Beep,"* went the heart monitor. "*Code blue, code blue"* a nurse shouted from the nursing station.

Azalea screamed, "Oh no, what's happening? "At that moment Azalea, Matisse, and Clay was rushed out of the room, as a crash cart with paddles was used on Lane in an attempt to save his life. "Mother," screamed Matisse, this just can't be happening." "Clay, cried Azalea, "Please take your sister in the waiting room, while I pray for your father, she said."

Clay complied, as Matisse tried to resist; "No, I won't go Mother, not now, when Daddy needs me most, "she said, as Clay gently escorted her into the waiting room. The loud beeping noise suddenly stopped, and the doctor walked out of the room. "

"Mrs. Jenson, your husband is bleeding internally, and needs immediate surgery," he said. Azalea replied, "I don't understand doctor, what's the problem, you have a copy of my husband's power of attorney; as well as my authorization to perform the surgery?" "I am well aware of all the legal aspects involved, but the problem is that his lab results are back, and they have revealed that your husband has a rare blood disease." Azalea replied, what can we do?"

Dr. Ginseng said, "The only hope he has is to receive bone marrow from a matched donor." Azalea replied, "I'll be tested, and my two oldest children will be tested; as well." The surgeon replied, "His chances are greater with a blood relative match, so we'll test your two children first." "Oh no," replied Azalea, neither of them are his biological children." "We do not have it in supply, and we need to get him prepped for surgery immediately. There's no time to waste," said the doctor.

Perhaps one of his biological children could be a match," said the doctor." Clay walked up to the doctor, and said, "I still want to be tested sir, he is still my father." Matisse had always been afraid of needles; but volunteered to be tested also. Azalea thought that the only other possible match would be Little Darnell.

"Mrs. Jenson," shouted the unit clerk at the nursing desk, "There is a Mr. William Brighton on the telephone for you. He is inquiring about your husband's health status, and we are not at liberty to give out that information; without your authorization." "I'll take the call," said Azalea, as she reached for the receiver. "Hello, Mr. Brighton;" said Azalea. "Hello Mrs. Jenson;" he replied. "How is Lane doing Mrs. Jenson?" Azalea began to weep, "Not very good, Mr. Brighton," she replied.

Azalea could no longer hold in her emotions, as she said, "The surgeon says that he is bleeding internally, and must have surgery now. I'm so very afraid. I just don't know what I would do without him. We had just brought home the twins. They won't ever have known firsthand, what a wonderful father they had; if something happens to him now."

"Don't worry Mrs. Jenson," replied Mr. Brighton, "that's not going to happen." Azalea replied, "How do you know that? How can you be so sure Mr. Brighton?" Bill Brighton replied, "I'm leaving for the hospital right now. I'll be there as soon as possible. Just keep the faith," he said. "I will," replied Azalea.

When the lab tested the blood of Clay and Matisse, neither was a match. Azalea then had her blood tested. It was not a match to donate either. "I'm going to do as Mr. Brighton said, "I'll just keep the faith, she said to Matisse and Clay.

While walking to the chapel, Azalea's thoughts went over her conversation with William Brighton. She thought, "What could he have possibly meant by saying that's never going to happen?" She also wondered why there was so much tension in his voice as he spoke of Lane. Azalea knew that Lane and William Brighton had seemed to form a bond when they had first met; and that they had grown even closer over the years; but William Brighton seemed to have a vested interest in Lane's recovery.

The children's nanny, Mrs. Scott; called the hospital to check up on Lane Jenson's condition. Azalea had just walked out of the chapel, when the unit clerk notified her that she had a call. "You have a call Mrs. Jenson," she said. "Thank you," replied Azalea, as she reached for the phone. The call was from the children's loyal and devoted nanny, Mrs. Scott.

"Hello Mrs. Scott, how are the children?" Azalea asked. "They're doing fine, Mrs. Jenson." "How is Mr. Jenson doing?" "He is about to go into surgery Mrs. Scott; please pray for him," replied Azalea. "I certainly will," replied Mrs. Scott.

"I hope you don't mind Mrs. Jenson, but I already took the liberty of contacting my church Pastor; as well as my Prayer team, of which I belong." "Why Mrs. Scott," replied Azalea; "I had no idea that you were so very devout in the faith. It suddenly dawned on Azalea; that she sounded so very much like Mrs. LeBlanc speaking to Aunt Mae. Azalea realized that she had never given any thought to Mrs. Scott's personal life. She realized that the only thing that mattered to her was the fact that Mrs. Scott was nanny to care for her children in the prominent Jenson's household.

"Why Mrs. Jenson;" replied Mrs. Scott, "I'm a Prayer Warrior for *Jesus Christ*." Whenever there is a need, I kneel and pray," she said. 'If I can't kneel at the time, I just sit or stand; but either way; I know that he hears me." "Oh Mrs. Scott, replied Azalea, will you pray for me too?" "Of course precious child," replied Mrs. Scott. Mrs. Scott then began to pray while on the telephone with Azalea.

"Father *God*, I ask you right now, in the name of your precious son, *Jesus Christ*, that you would extend your mercy towards Mrs. Jenson, and give her all the strength she needs right now to overcome. Dear Lord I pray that you touch Mr. Jenson, with your divine healing resurrection power, and that you will impart your faith in Mrs. Jenson, so that she believes, that you have the power to do anything we ask, when we believe." *Amen*

"Thank you so much Mrs. Scott," said Azalea. "I really hope you know just how much I really value your prayers for my husband; as well as our entire family. I know now that the Lord can answer my prayers, and I now believe that he will. I have even asked him to come into my heart, and I truly believe that he will answer my prayers to heal my husband;" said Azalea. "I know he will.

You just keep the faith," replied Mrs. Scott; as she said goodbye to Azalea.

As soon as Azalea had hung up the telephone after praying with Mrs. Scott for Lane's recovery, she felt a strong hand on her shoulder. There was something so familiar about the touch. It seemed to offer a special comfort to her.

How is he?" When Azalea turned, the deep male voice was that of Mr. William Brighton, and his wife, Candice Brighton. "He's still hanging on, waiting for the right blood match," replied Azalea. Mrs. Jenson you remember my wife Candice?" "Of course, replied Azalea. "How do you do Mrs. Brighton?" "Please just call me Candice," she replied. "Only if you call me Azalea," replied

Azalea said, "I'm just keeping the faith Candice," she added. Look," replied William, "I'll fill you in later, but please let me be tested first." "Of course," replied Azalea. "I pray you are a match." Azalea watched with Matisse and Clay now beside her, as William Brighton headed to the hospital blood bank lab for tests.

Moments later, William Brighton appeared wearing a bright smile. "Azalea," he said; we were a perfect match. "Praise the Lord," shouted Azalea. Mrs. Scott prayed with me, and the Lord has answered our prayers.

William Brighton, then said to Azalea, "Let's all have a seat Azalea," said William Brighton. It is imperative that I share something with you." Benjamin Carlton just made me aware of it, since Lane's accident.

"You see Azalea," said William Brighton; "it's a long story, but your husband; Lane Jenson, is my brother." "Oh my Lord," cried Azalea. "I don't understand. How is this possible?" "Lane's oldest brother was killed," cried Azalea, "and he was separated from his baby brothers, when he ran away from the orphanage." "He and his oldest brother went back for them, but the both of them had already been adopted." In that short time since her prayer, Azalea was already forgetting that God was fully able to do the impossible. "I know it sounds unbelievable, but it's true," replied William Brighton. "I'm so sorry if I seem skeptical," said Azalea, but, I'm still in a state of shock."

Azalea inquired of William Brighton, "How did you find out that Lane was your brother?" "As you well know, my father, William Brighton, Jr. passed away a year ago." "Although my father was aware of this fact, he had asked Mr. Carlton to keep this secret, unless it became a matter of life or death." "I still don't understand," replied Azalea. "How did you find out Lane was your brother?" "When I called Mr. Benjamin Carlton, to notify him of Lane's accident, he then asked me to meet him at his home," "He said it was imperative that he share something with me," William replied.

"Upon my arrival," said William, I was met by Benjamin Carlton's butler, who then directed me to Mr. Carlton's den." When I walked into the den, Mr. Carlton was wearing a smoking jacket and smoking a pipe. The fire was burning bright in the fireplace. Mr. Carlton seemed very relaxed as he pointed towards the tall wingback chair directly across from the one where he was seated." He then said, "Have a seat William;" I have something to tell you; that will change your life."

"I wondered what could have been so important, that it could not wait until after my visit to the hospital." Over the years, William and Lane had formed an unusually close bond. William paused, as though he was becoming chocked up. "Please continue," said Azalea. "I noticed that he was holding some type of document in his hand at the time, replied William."

"I then sat down, and asked, "What is it you wish to tell me Mr. Carlton?" "Read these documents," Mr. Carlton replied. "It was a copy of Lane's birth record, along with a copy of my birth record, as well as a copy of my adoption papers, stamped with a seal from the orphanage. I had the same birth date, but my name was listed as Darnell William Jenson. Lane and I both had the same parents.

"The adoption was to a couple named Mr. & Mrs. William Brighton Jr." "According to Mr. Carlton, my father, William Brighton, Jr.; decided that he and my mother would simply drop my first name Darnell, and just use William, which would make me William Brighton, III, once the adoption was finalized. " "This is astonishing, said Azalea.

Well," replied William; my great grandfather had been for many years, a devoted servant to Mr. Carlton's grandfather. My grandfather and Mr. Carlton go way back as little boys raised on the Carlton Family plantation. When Mr. Carlton's grandfather died, he left in his will, money for grandfather to attend college. When my grandfather died, he had named Mr. Carlton executor of his estate. Over the years, Mr. Carlton and my father, William Brighton, Jr. became confidents; which is why he trusted Mr. Carlton to keep his secret." My father passed away a year ago, but had left instructions to Mr. Carlton, that he reveal the truth of my birth, only in the event of an emergency.

I'm just glad that Lane has at least one of his long lost his brothers back, that he was separated from so long ago after their mother and father died," said Azalea. "Maybe perhaps now there's a chance that Daddy's other brother will surface," said Matisse. "I hope so too Matisse," replied Azalea, "Wouldn't that be wonderful?" "It sure would," replied Clay, but in the meantime, I'm just happy to celebrate the fact that Daddy's close friend, and business associate is our uncle." "I know," replied Matisse. "Imagine that, Mr. William Brighton III; is actually Father's brother; Darnell William Jenson. "I most certainly can imagine it dear sister, because it's now been proven," replied Clay. "Uncle William," Clay continued. "Sure has a really nice ring to it." "It certainly does," replied Matisse. "Just wait until our other siblings, especially Darnell, said Matisse, find out that we have an uncle whom we already know as a friend of Daddy's.

Moments later, the surgeon, Dr. Ginseng appeared. "The surgery is over, he said. " "Your husband should expect a full recovery from the bone marrow he received." "Thank God," said Azalea. We were able to stop the internal bleeding, but your husband sustained a head injury from the accident that required surgery, and is now in a coma."

"Oh no," shouted Azalea. "Please try not to worry Mrs. Jenson." Azalea snapped at the surgeon, "How can you ask me not to worry?" "Mrs. Jenson," Dr. Ginseng replied, "Although your husband came through the surgery fine, he still has some swelling that needs to go down, so we needed to place him in a medically induced coma, until the swelling goes down. The next forty eight hours will be crucial, said the surgeon." "We have done all we can do at this point" "Thank you Dr. Ginseng," replied Azalea. "I didn't mean to speak so harshly to you Dr. Ginseng; but I'm just not accustomed to seeing my husband lying in a hospital bed, totally incapacitated."

Two days seemed like eternity to Azalea and her family. Azalea had decided that she would take a leave of absence from her company, while awaiting Lane's recovery.

In the meantime, Shelia was left in charge of running Leah's Divine Designs Fashion House. Shelia's baby boy, little David, was now over a year old, and David's mother had said that she would be more than happy to care for her first grandson, while Shelia filled in for Azalea. Although Shelia had experienced complications while pregnant with little David, she had made a very impressive recovery in the months that followed his birth. Shelia felt stronger than ever. She had told Azalea to take as much time as she needed to take care of her husband, Lane, until he was fully recovered.

Azalea began to weep softly; as she dabbed her eyes with an embroidered handkerchief, given to her by Aunt Mae. "Mrs. Jenson," the surgeon replied, your husband is a strong fighter, to even come thru the surgery like he has." "Thank you Dr. Ginseng, "replied Azalea; "For giving us the hope for his recovery."

Dr. Ginseng said, "Mrs. Jenson, I have performed many operations, like the one on your husband, and can truthfully say that I have never seen such a fighter." Azalea replied, "Thank you Dr. Ginseng. "I suggest you pray," replied Dr. Ginseng; "because there's nothing else left to do, except wait and pray for his speedy recovery. Dr. Ginseng continued, "Mrs. Jenson, please know that you must have faith," said Dr. Ginseng.

"I can't explain it," said Azalea, "but for some reason, for the first time ever, I am not afraid. I just know that everything is going to work out for our family. I just feel so sure." Before leaving to make his hospital rounds, Dr. Ginseng responded to Azalea's comments, and said; "What you now feel Mrs. Jenson, is known as; faith." Dr. Ginseng then turned and began walking down the hospital corridor. Azalea then said, "That Dr. has truly been a blessing to our family. I now truly believe, and have faith in God that Lane will wake up, and have a complete recovery." After five days had gone by, without Lane recovering, Azalea began feeling discouraged, but continued praying.

Two weeks had passed, since Dr. Ginseng had first informed Lane's family, about his critical condition that existed. For the first time ever, the Thanksgiving holiday was very somber this year around the Jenson's household. Thanksgiving had come and gone, and it was now two weeks before Christmas. Azalea kept a constant vigil at her husband's bedside. William Brighton; Lanes brother, decided that one of the best things to help in Lane's recovery, was to keep him apprised of what the firm had been doing. William would come visit and spend time with his older brother, Lane; while reading some of the firm's latest acquisitions; at least once a week.

Clayton, whom Lane Jenson had adopted as his own, by giving him the name of Jenson, was now an apprentice at his uncle's architectural firm of Brighton and Brighton. The pay wasn't really all that great; but Clayton was finding out that the benefits, not to mention the experience, were valuable assets. Although Lane had set up a trust fund for Clayton, he was not to have control of it, until he had reached the age of twenty (24) four. This was Lane's way of being assured, that Clayton would graduate with a Master's degree in architectural studies, like he himself had. In the meantime, Clayton wanted to prove not just to his father, but also to himself; that he could make it on his own.

Chapter
19

One day, Azalea was sitting in Lane's room in ICU with the drapes open, reading to him, when suddenly; she heard a tap on the window pane. When she looked up, standing in full view, was her best friend Shelia, and her husband David. Azalea beaconed for both of them, to enter Lane's room. Shelia and David both had smiles on their faces.

David held in his arms, a large fruit basket, with a giant balloon attached. The balloon read: "Get Well Soon Lane." Shelia was holding a large bouquet of yellow roses in a beautiful crystal vase. There was a card attached that read: "We love & miss you Lane, so you'd better wakeup soon, Love Your Friends, David and Shelia.

"It is so very good to see the both of you," Azalea said to Shelia and David. "We love you both very much, my friend," replied Shelia. David said, "That's right Azalea, because there is no other place that we would rather be at this time, than here with the two of you." "I really appreciate you both," replied Azalea. As she wiped tears from her eyes, Azalea asked, "How is the baby doing now Shelia?" "Oh Azalea, replied Shelia, he is growing so fast, and just as cute as ever." "My son is handsome," David said; little girls are cute."

"Shelia said to Azalea, "Now isn't that just like a man, to make something so small such an issue?" Azalea and Shelia both giggled, as David just shook his head and said "Lane will you please wake up man, can't you see that I'm outnumbered?" Then David began to laugh.

"Please lower your voices. This is an ICU unit, so you must be quiet," said the ICU nurse, as she entered Lane's room. "I'm very sorry, but I'm afraid that I must ask the three of you to leave the room so that I can check Mr. Jenson's vital signs, and his breathing tube." "Mrs. Jenson," the nurse continued, I'm sure that you could use a little break. The cafeteria is on the ground floor of the building."

"Well," replied Azalea, my son went home to take a nap, and freshen up, but my daughter is still here. She should be back any time now from the gift shop. Shelia said, "Azalea, David and I will both go with you, said Shelia; I'm starving myself David, how about you?" "Sure," replied David, "I hope that they've prepared a variety some type of good meat and potato dishes." "David," replied Shelia with a laugh, "I'll have you know, that we're about to eat in a hospital cafeteria, not a fancy expensive four-star restaurant."

"This is what I mean by missing; Shelia," replied Azalea, "You are always able to cheer me up when I've needed it the most. At that moment, Matisse arrived back from the gift shop.

"Aunt Shelia, Uncle David," Matisse said, as she hugged them both. "It's so good to see the both of you." Shelia replied, "We're glad to see you; as well, my dear niece.

"Matisse darling;" said Azalea, "Your Aunt Shelia, Uncle David and I were waiting for you to return, so that we could go down to the cafeteria."

"What would you like me to bring back for you?" "Thanks mother," replied Matisse. "I'm famished, and would love a burger, fries, and a diet soda."

Shelia said, "I think I'll order me a salad, or a tuna on wheat?" "Me too," replied Azalea. Before leaving Lane's room, Azalea said "Matisse, please do not hesitate to let me know right away, if there are any changes in your Father's condition while I'm downstairs." Matisse replied, "Don't you worry Mother, I will."

After lunch, Azalea, Shelia and

David, were stepping off of the elevator, when suddenly they were met by Matisse, who was crying, and shouting to her mother to hurry.

"Oh Mother, please hurry." Azalea dropped the bag holding Matisse's lunch, as she hurried after Matisse. "Please don't tell me your father is gone Matisse," Azalea shouted." Matisse cried, "You must see for yourself Mother, as she held the door open.

When Azalea walked into Lane's room, she was astonished at what she saw; when the nurse, and Dr. Ginseng stepped aside from obscuring her view of Lane's bed. What she saw next filled her heart with joy. Azalea was amazed at the awesome miracle working power of God. It was one of the most wonderful sights that she could have seen on today.

Not only was her husband Lane Jenson now awake, but he was actually sitting up in bed, sipping water through a straw. "Oh my Lord," Azalea said, as she threw her hands up to her face. "Praise the Lord;" she shouted to the top of her lungs. "The Lord has answered all of our prayers children."

"It's a miracle Mother," Matisse said, "It's a real miracle." Lane said to Azalea," Well don't just stand there woman, can't I at least get a kiss for returning to you and my children?"

"Oh yes, my darling," Azalea replied, as tears of joy rolled down her cheeks. "I love and miss you so very much my darling," she said, as she hugged her husband.

Clayton ran up to the nurse's station; after seeing his sister Matisse crying standing outside his father's room, and asked, "What's going on, is my father alright?"

The nurse replied, "Mr. Jenson, your father is far more than just alright, he has regained consciousness." "What?" Clay shouted, "He's awake?" Clay heard a voice from behind him respond, "Yes son," Azalea said. Your father is truly awake, and has come back to us."

Clay immediately hugged his mother with tears welling up in his eyes. "Can I go in and see him Mother?" "Of course you can my darling son; as soon as the Dr. and nurse complete their examination of him."

Clay said, "Mother you just don't know how much I prayed that Father would wake up and come back to us. I also prayed when he did, that he would be able to recognize each one of us."

"Well," replied Azalea, "I believe that you can be assured that he will recognize you; as well as the rest of your siblings." Matisse said, "Oh Clay," "Isn't it just wonderful news about father?" Clay replied,

"It's the best news yet my dear sister." "

"Clayton, and Matisse," Azalea said enthusiastically, "Your father can see the two of you now," as the nurse and Dr. Ginseng exited the room. Matisse was first to hug, and kiss her father. "Oh Daddy," said Matisse, "I'm so glad you came back to us. I love you and miss you so very much."

"We all did Father," Clay said, as he walked into the room with tears in his eyes. "Well son," said Lane, give your old man a handshake."

Clay could hardly speak, as he ran over to Lane's bed, and hugged his father, as the tears began to flow down his cheeks. Clay had waited many years to have the only man, Lane Jenson; he had always thought of as his father, call him son.

"Father," Clay said, "I just want to apologize for the way that I treated you sometimes. Can you ever forgive me?" "Don't worry about that nonsense now son." replied Lane. "Don't you realize that you have always been, from the moment we met? All that matters now son; is that we are together again as a family."

"I could not be happier than I am right at this moment in time Father," Clay said. "Son," replied Lane, "your mother told me that all of your siblings are doing just fine. I can hardly wait to see them."

"Father," said Clay, I'm now working as an apprentice architect at Brighton and Brighton, until I graduate with my Master of Arts Degree in Architecture, just like you did." "I'm so proud of you son," replied Lane. Clay replied, "Thank you father."

Lane responded, "I always knew that you had it in your heart son, to overcome life's many obstacle Son," said Lane to Clay, "I need to speak with you mother in private now "Will you please call her back into the room for me?"

"Sure Dad," Clay replied. As Clay left the room to call Azalea back in, Lane thought, "That boy finally realizes just how much he means to me, and that I'm his Daddy, and always will be."

When Azalea walked back into her husband's room, she noticed that Lane had a rather somber expression on his face. She wondered what could be serious enough to change the joyous mood he had just experienced at the sight of his family after waking up from a coma.

Lane then asks Azalea to have a seat. "Sit down my love, there's something that's eating me alive inside, that I must share with you. When I first came out of my coma, I had a revelation. I realized that life is fleeting; and that I was blessed to still be alive."

"Oh Lane darling, said Azalea, I'm happy you made it too." Lane replied, "Please don't interrupt me darling," replied Lane. "I must share this with you." "Okay darling," replied Azalea, "I promise that I won't interrupt again." Lane began to share the true story surrounding the hardships that he had endured as a child; as well as a young man.

Lane revealed to Azalea how he and His older brother Jarrett; had run away from the orphanage to try and make a life for their two younger brothers. He shared the hard times that he and Jarrett had, that lead them to scrounge for food scraps out of garbage cans behind restaurants, when they first ran away from the orphanage.

They had both tried very hard to find jobs, but work for unskilled laborers was very scarce at that time period in the country. It was virtually impossible to find a steady job, so they began to do odd jobs, here and there.

Lane told Azalea how his older brother, Jarrett; had been tragically killed while coming to the rescue of Mr. Benjamin Carlton, who later became his benefactor. Lane told Azalea that this was the reason, that he had always been obsessed with making money to secure his family's financial future.

"Leah," my love, said Lane, "I just never wanted our children to ever have to live in poverty, and have to never have to endure the humiliations, and dignities that I had to sometimes as a young boy. This was the only reason, that I was always so hard on Clay. I wanted that boy to make a success of his life, so all your sacrifices that you had made for him would not be in vain." "Oh darling," replied Azalea. "I'm so glad that you have finally opened up to me." There's much more to tell you Leah;" said Lane, as a tear fell down his cheek.

"My darling," said Lane; "Please hear me out before you say a word." Azalea sat down in a chair next to Lane's bed, as she gave him her attention "You now know how hard I had it as both a child; as well as a young man. Believe me my darling Leah, I never meant to hurt you or my children, because of my life growing up. All I ever wanted was to love and provide for my family.

Chapter

20

Divine Destiny

Azalea moved closer to Lane, and began comforting him, as she placed her delicate hand atop his strong hand.

"Leah," said Lane, "Right before you came into my room earlier, Dr. Ginseng, ministered to me about how that the Lord could change my life, if I just received him into my heart."

"I believed the words that he spoke to me, and at that very moment, I made the decision to accept *Jesus Christ* as my Lord and Savior."

"That's wonderful darling," replied Azalea, as she embraced Lane. "I'm afraid there is something else that I must confess to you Leah."

Azalea replied with a beaming and radiant smile, "But darling, I have some really good news for you."

She was referring to the fact, that William Brighton had revealed to her that he was one of Lane's long lost younger brothers; Darnell William Jenson, who had been adopted by the Brighton's as a young boy.

It was as though Azalea didn't want to hear what Lane had to confess. It was as though she already knew. "Please Leah," replied Lane, you must allow me to finish." "Okay darling," Azalea replied."

"Darling," said Lane, "I have a very serious gambling problem. I gambled heavily while on my business trips. It was at a time in my life, that all I could think about was becoming richer than I had ever dreamed of becoming. I had a lust for money and power; that spilled over into my home life, and my marriage, causing great tension."

He told Azalea, of how he had tried to stop a long time ago, but that he would always take a lay-over flight in Nevada, before going on to his business trips in Hawaii. "Darling," said Lane, "I've lost well over half of my wealth.

Azalea threw her delicate feminine hands up to her cheeks, as her big brown eyes widened in dismay. "Oh no," Azalea cried, "How could you do this to me, and your children?"

"Leah please," said Lane, as tears flowed down his cheeks; "I never meant to hurt you."

"But you did Lane, and you have,"

Azalea replied, as she began to sob. "How can I ever trust you again?" "Because I'm being honest with you now Leah," I even thought at one point, that you were being unfaithful to me Lane. I actually believed there was another woman."

"Leah my love," Lane replied. "Don't you know that I would never cheat on you with another woman?"

Azalea replied, "No of course not Lane, but you wouldn't give one thought to gambling away our future, our children's future, and everything we worked so hard to obtain in life"

"Leah please, can't you see that I'm laying it all on the table?" Azalea replied, "You still can't shake off that gambling terminology can you Lane. To tell you the truth Lane, all I see is a man with a guilty conscience clearing it, at the expense of hurting his me and his children."

Lane replied, "Leah I would never deliberately hurt our children. You know I wouldn't. I just need to be delivered from the addiction I had. When I was driving back home to you and the children, it had just begun raining, I started to cry, as I realized just how much I had always loved you. As tears flooded my eyes from the guilt I was feeling,

"Leah, I can remember hearing a

horn blowing, and then the sound of screeching tires, when suddenly, there was a collision, and everything went dark. I don't remember anything after that, except waking up, with the doctor standing over my bed."

Azalea shouted with tears running down her cheeks, "I don't want to hear anymore Lane. You not only betrayed our vows, but you shared what you have done with a total stranger. How could you?" Lane replied,

"I can't explain why, my darling, but for some reason, I began telling him what I had done. All I wanted now was a chance to somehow turn my life around; have your forgiveness for what I had done, and a fresh start at happiness with you, the woman I know that I have always loved."

Azalea replied, "What more are you asking me to endure Lane?" Lane replied, "My sweet Leah, "I know that I don't deserve it my love, but I am asking you for forgiveness with everything I have inside of me."

"Oh Lane," replied Azalea, "I want to forgive you, but I just need some time. This is just too much to take in all at once." "I realize that Leah," replied Lane. "But, one thing is for certain my love; and that is the love I feel for you my sweet Leah is real.

Azalea had just left out of Lane's

room, when she ran into Lane's brother, William, and Dr. Ginseng. "How is he doing, William asked Azalea?" "He's coming along just fine, but Dr. Ginseng would know more about that than I would," said Azalea with a hint of bitterness in her voice.

Dr. Ginseng said, "I'd better check on my patient;" referring to Lane. He then walked away. William asked, "Is everything alright with you sister-in-law?" "Not really, replied Azalea, but I'm a very strong woman, and I have always have been able to overcome any hurdles that life has placed in my way." "I'm quite sure you have," replied William. "I suppose that it's one of the many reasons that my brother loves you so very much." "Well that's debatable," Azalea responded.

William could see that Azalea was in an unusually bad mood for a woman whose husband had just come out of a coma; which is why he quickly changed the subject.

"Did you tell Lane the good news about my being his brother?" "I never had the chance William," she replied. "Besides, I believe it would be better if you do the honors," she replied. "I'll do just that," replied William Brighton, as he walked towards Lane's room.

Dr. Ginseng asked William to please wait a moment, until he finished his examination of Lane. "Could you give me about five more minutes Mr. Brighton?" William replied, "It's actually Jenson, but that's a long story; you see Dr. Ginseng, my brother and I were orphaned and separated as little boys; and didn't know when we initially met, that we were actually long lost Jenson brothers."

Dr. Ginseng replied, "Really, your story ironically enough, sounds much like mine; except, I've never been reunited with my brothers. I'd be interested to hear your story one day." "Sure," replied William; but in the meantime, I have to break some really good news to Lane Jenson."

When William entered Lane's room, Lane was glad to see him. William then began to tell his story to Lane, and finally the words came out of his mouth, "So we're actually brothers Lane."

Needless to say, Lane was overwhelmed by the news. Lane asked, "William, do Leah and my children know?"

William replied, "They most certainly do." Lane responded, "This is incredible news William. Now I see why we bonded so well when we first met." "I know," said William.

"My wife is just as excited as I am, and says that she can hardly wait to have you all over for a family dinner sometime in the near future." Lane replied, "Yes my little brother, by all means, we'll make it a family reunion dinner."

"As you very well have known for some time now Lane," said William, "we never had any children of our own." Lane replied, "I know, and I'm so sorry William." William replied, "Please don't be Lane. Besides, my wife says that she would love to have that big home filled with the sounds of children sometimes."

"That's sound just great to me," replied Lane; "I just hope Leah's feeling up to it."

William then asked, "Why wouldn't she be with all the good news she's had lately Lane?" "Because not all news is good news," Lane replied.

He told William that he regretted the pain he had caused the only woman he ever truly loved, but how he had let lust and greed, for money and power; cloud his judgment to the point of being gambling away over half of his wealth..

Lane finally told William how he had been lead to the *Lord Jesus Christ*, by Dr. Ginseng, and that he hoped Azalea would soon, find it in her heart to forgive him.

After hearing everything Lane had to say, William responded with a hug, and said, "She will, my brother; she will."

William told Lane that he should get some rest, and that there was something urgent he needed to check into, before revealing the results.

Lane prayed earnestly to the Lord, that Azalea would someday forgive him for the pain he had promised he would never cause her. The same pain caused by deception, that she had felt from her past. Lane had come to realize that, although on the surface, he had always seemed to be the one in their marriage who had the power, but it was in fact, Azalea's inner strength that had wielded the greater power that had held their family together over the years. He now prayed that the Lord would place within her the empowerment of forgiveness.

The next several months were very hard for Azalea. Lane had been moved to a new rehab facility to speed up his recovery. Lane had been left with partial mobility after he'd come out of the coma. The doctors had said that with the extensive rehabilitation, that there was every reason to believe, that he would make a full recovery.

Between trying to run a company, visiting Lane, and spending quality time with the children, Azalea began to feel the effects of it all upon her life. Azalea had faced many challenges in her life, but had never felt the weight of them like she had now felt.

It was now December, 1975. The twins; Janine and Justice, were a year old, and as active as ever. Although Azalea found herself tired much of the time, she loved going into their room and playing with them after a day at the fashion design house.

With Shelia having been a business partner, Azalea was able to shorten her time spent running the company. An entire year had gone by since the accident; that had left Lane in a coma.

Lane was now feeling better than ever; but all the trials had taken a toll on Azalea. The day that Lane was being released from the rehab facility, Azalea was there with Clay and Matisse to finally bring their father home.

Lane was already packed and ready to return home. The attendants at the facility had assisted him so that he wouldn't have to wait any longer than necessary to be discharged and leave the facility that had aided in his recovery.

Lane was looking out of the window of his room, when Azalea, Clay and Matisse walked in. "Hello Daddy," said Matisse, "I'm so glad you're finally coming home. We all missed you so."

"Nothing was the same without you Daddy." Lane replied, "Nothing could make me happier than seeing my family, and knowing I will now have time to spend with them; my dearest daughter," replied Lane.

Azalea stood silent, as Clay went to shake his father's hand. Lane then moved Clay's hand aside, as he grabbed him, and gave him an emotional embrace.

"I'm so proud of you son," said Lane. "Clayton," Lane continued; your uncle has filled me in on how well you are doing at the firm, in my absence." Clay replied, "Father I could never take your place, far from it," replied Clayton. "But you will one day my son," replied Lane.

Finally Lane noticed how tired Azalea looked. "Children," Lane said, "May I have a few minutes alone with your mother?"

"Of course," replied Clayton, as he took Matisse by the arm, leading her out of the room. "We'll be seated right here in the visitor waiting lounge next to the rehabilitation therapy station Daddy;" said Matisse smiling.

"Come closer, my Leah," said Lane. As Azalea walked closer towards Lane, he could now see the dark circles around her eyes; that had never been there before. When he looked into her eyes, they were no longer the bright starry eyes of the lovely young woman, with such promise, that he had fell in love with years ago. Lane said, "My dear sweet Leah, what have I done to you?" He sobbed heavily and then he embraced her.

Azalea began to feel for the first time since Lane's confession; her heart began to break, and tears began to flow, as she finally told Lane how much he'd hurt her. Let it all out my dearest, said Lane, as he held on to her for dear life. Azalea told Lane of the bitterness that she had felt towards him, but had decided to hold it in for the sake of the children. The children, whose inheritance Lane Jenson had nearly gambled all away.

Just at that moment, Dr. Ginseng walked into Lane's room. "I'm so sorry, said Dr. Ginseng, "I didn't mean to interrupt a private moment; I'll come back later." "Oh no, replied Azalea, as she grabbed a napkin out of the napkin box, and wiped her tears away."

"I know of someone who will bare all of your grief, and sorrows, and he'll erase all of your tears away; said Dr. Ginseng. All you have to do is surrender your life to him." "Are you speaking of *Jesus Christ*, Azalea asked?" "Yes," replied Dr. Ginseng. Azalea replied, "Lane told me that you had led him to the Lord."

"Believe me darling," said Lane; "my entire outlook on life has changed as a result of *Jesus Christ* becoming Lord of my life, and he'll do the same for you. All you have to do is just ask him into your heart." Azalea replied, "But the hurt runs so deep."

My darling," Lane replied, "*God* is fully able to erase, the pain, bitterness, hurt; and resentment that you now feel, when you accept his son, *Jesus Christ.*" Dr. Ginseng then added, "He will then fill your heart with a joy that is unspeakable."

"My darling," said Azalea to Lane, I now truly believe what Shelia once told me that scripture has said: *"For whosoever shall call upon the name of the Lord; shall be saved,(Romans 10:13)² (KJV) for with the heart man believeth unto righteousness, and with the mouth, confession is made unto salvation.(Romans 10:13)³(KJV)* Azalea suddenly began to weep, as tears streamed down her cheeks, she lifted her hands towards heaven, and she cried:

"Jesus Christ, I humbly confess right now; before you, and witnesses, that I am a sinner. Lord, I ask your forgiveness of my sins, and I now invite you to come into my life, and to be my *Lord,* and my *Savior."* Azalea then began to weep.

Shortly thereafter, she said to Lane, "I can't explain it darling, but something has happened to me. I now feel the same love in my heart for you, that I felt when we first exchanged our wedding vows." "I now forgive you my darling, just as *Jesus Christ* has forgiven me, and gave his life for me," she said. Lane replied, "I will always love you Leah, my love," as he kissed Azalea.

Azalea then embraced Dr. Ginseng. "Thank you Dr. Ginseng," she said. "It was nothing I have done," replied Dr. Ginseng, "but the precious blood of *Jesus Christ* that now covers you." Azalea said to Lane, "I'm going to the nurse's station to find out if your release papers are ready."

On her way to the nurse's station, Azalea spotted William as he was stepping off of the elevator. "Hello William," said Azalea. "Hi Azalea, replied William. "Lane is being released from the hospital today," said Azalea. "I don't know if you are aware of it William, but Lane and I had some problems in the past," she added. "I'm sorry to hear that," replied William.

William and Azalea walked into Lane's room. William had with some type of document in his hand.

"Azalea told me that you were being released today Lane," said William. "I hope I didn't come at an awkward moment." "On the contrary," replied Lane, "your timing could not have been any better, I'm going home today." "That is great news my brother," replied William.

Lane replied, "The Lord has been so good to me, and my family. I truly feel blessed." William then asked to speak to Dr. Ginseng alone. They then stepped out of Lane's room, and stood in the corner of the waiting area, where they were still visible. Azalea saw Dr. Ginseng suddenly sat down in a chair, with a look of astonishment on his face. Dr. Ginseng then stood up, and embraced William. They both smiled, and began walking back towards Lane's room

When Dr. Ginseng and William walked back into Lane's room, William said, "This is all such great news, replied William, and now you are both about to hear and see more wonderful news.

Azalea thought of the scene, that she had just witnessed outside Lane's room; between Dr. Ginseng and William, and wondered what more good news could there in fact be.

William then revealed to everyone, that Dr. Ginseng, was in fact, William and Lane's other brother; Justice Jenson, whom one of the twins had been named after. William said that he felt a bond with Dr. Ginseng, at the hospital, back when they first met.

He said it was the same unusual bond that he had felt with when he and Lane had first met. Dr. Ginseng said, "I could not understand it myself at the time, but I felt it too."

William then said, "It was not until after I had been talking with Dr. Ginseng a while, that I began to notice similarities not only in our facial features, but in our voices; as well."

Lane asked Dr. Ginseng, "Did you know about the investigation too?" Dr. Ginseng replied, "No, I did not, but always thought it rather a really strange coincidence regarding our stories." Azalea said, "My goodness, so it really is true?"

Lane asked, "How can you be sure William?" William replied, "I'm getting to that part now Lane; and I have the documented proof to back it up my brother." Lane and Azalea were so happy; and could hardly wait to tell the children of the news of another wonderful uncle, but had to contain themselves, as William continued.

"It all began about a year ago," said William, when Dr. Ginseng told me that his story was similar to Lane and mine, I decided to hire an investigator to look into his family tree.

The investigator turned up Dr. Ginseng's original birth record; that matched the date, Dr. Ginseng told me he had been born."

William then asked Dr. Ginseng if he could show Lane and Azalea the documents. Dr. Ginseng replied, "Of course, after all we're all family now."

"The investigator was then able to finally turn up the adoption records that had been closed for some time." Dr. Ginseng then added, "It's all true. As it turned out, ironically, I was adopted by a wonderful physician and his lovely wife, who were named Ginseng. I never knew my real last name was in fact, Jenson.

I had always wondered why I didn't resemble either of my parents. When my father died, my mother finally told me the story of my adoption, but said that all she knew about my real name; was that it was very much like my adopted name. That was all I had to go on, and decided that the Lord would someday reunite me with my brothers."

By this time, Matisse and Clay had also entered Lane's room. Clay asked, "Can we join the party too?" Sure son, replied Lane. "Wow," said Matisse, I feel as though I just witnessed my parents first wedding ceremony."

Matisse hugged her mother and father; while Clayton hugged his mother, and shook his father's hand.

"Congratulations Father," said Clayton, "you'd better be sure to treat this lady right." Clay and Matisse, then both laughed. They would never know of their father's gambling problem.

"This is not all," said Lane. "We have just been informed by William, that Dr. Ginseng, who saved my life, is my other long lost brother."

"No way," Clayton replied. Matisse looked at Azalea and, and cried, "Could this really be happening Mother?" "It's true, said Lane.

Lane then said before they walked out of the room; "That's not all the good news we have. Clay asked, "What more is there Father?"

Lane replied, "Your mother has been born again." Matisse asked Azalea, "Are you serious Mother?"

"I have never been more serious about anything in my entire life," replied Azalea. "I now feel as though the weight of the world has been lifted off of my shoulders."

"Well;" replied Matisse, although I'm very happy for you, Mother; I'm still too young to settle down right now."

Azalea replied, "All in *God*'s time Matisse." As the Jenson's leave the facility, Azalea turned to Matisse and said; "As you travel thru life Matisse, and are faced with its' many challenges, you will come to realize, the true fulfillment of life's journey; is spiritual fulfillment, and that; *"Godliness with contentment is great gain." I Timothy 6:6 (KJV)* [4]

When Lane, Azalea, Matisse and Clay arrived home, they were met with all the love and warmth of the Jenson siblings; as well as Shelia, David, and little Hank. Lane had awaiting his arrival, a giant cake, along with a banner and lots of balloons that read "Welcome Home Daddy."

Lane then introduced the Jenson siblings to their both their uncles, William Darnell Brighton, and Dr. Justice Jenson. "This is the best Christmas present we could have," shouted little Darnell, who was now twelve years of age. "It sure is son," replied Lane, "It sure is."

Matisse looked at her mother and said; "Oh no mother, I've forgotten it." Clay replied, "What have you forgotten this time Matisse; your lipstick?" Matisse replied, "Don't be ridiculous." Clay said, "Then will you please enlighten me?"

Matisse replied, "When Mother was lecturing me, as she sometimes does, I forget my beautiful antique compact mirror in Father's room at the facility."

"My dear little sister," Clay replied, "Such vanity; when will you ever change?" I'll have you to know Clay," replied Matisse, "that vanity has nothing whatsoever to do with it."

Clay replied, "Then what does Matisse?" Matisse replied, "The only reason I treasure it so, is because Father gave that mirror to me; as one of my birthday gifts last year."

Clay replied, "Fortunately for you Matisse, Christmas is just around the corner. Right you are, my dear brother, replied Matisse, but nevertheless, I still want the compact he gave me, because I treasure it for its' sentimental value."

Azalea and Lane, both looked at each other, and smiled. "Lane said to Azalea, "It seems to me my love, that you have made quite an impression on our daughter after all." Azalea replied, "It is my hope, that all of our children will come to realize that all they have to do is receive *God's* love through accepting his only begotten son; *Jesus Christ,* as their *Lord* and *Savior.*

Lane had come to realize that no amount of money on this earth, could replace the love of children, Azalea; the jewel of a wife that *God* had blessed, and more importantly, the precious love of his *Lord* and *Savior; Jesus Christ.*

Azalea discovered that it is through our trials and tribulations in life, that we come to realize the true value in that which we hold most dear to our hearts.

Azalea found out that; the true fulfillment in life that she had sought on her life's journey; was always right within her reach. It was never in the monetary value of any objects she owned, or what they were perceived to be. Nor was it in the success that she had aspired to, and was determined to achieve.

Lane and Azalea Jenson both realized that no amount of money could ever pay for the salvation that they had now received from *God;* because the price had already been paid by the suffering and shed blood of *Jesus Christ.*

But he was wounded for our transgressions; he was bruised for our iniquities: the chastisement of our peace was upon him; and with his stripes we are healed. (Isaiah 53:4-12)[5]

Azalea's desire for true fulfillment, had led her to the very thing; that she had tried to run away from her entire life. God had already laid a "foundation of faith," through her ancestors.

It was through her trials and tribulations that she had now been led to *Jesus Christ.* Azalea now had salvation given freely to her by *God*, when she accepted his precious son *Jesus Christ*, as her Lord and Savior.

Through her conversion, she now had a gift that was eternal. … *"But, the gift of God is eternal life through Jesus Christ our Lord."(Romans 6:23)*[6] God's plan for her life, would ultimately lead Azalea to, *"Her Divine Destiny."*

Two years had gone by since Lane's accident. The year was 1977. Lane was forty-five, and Azalea was forty. The time had flown by. Lane and Azalea were no longer that ambitious young man, and determined to achieve success young woman.

Their lives would never be the same after their conversion. They were now both working faithfully in the ministry of helps at their church.

Both desired to help feed the hungry in the community. Azalea also committed to teaching sewing classes once a week at the church center for youth.

Although Azalea and Lane were still prosperous, they did not have the wealth that they once had. Azalea had decided to sell forty-nine percent of her company's stock on the public market, which still gave her fifty-one percent of the company's shares and majority vote on the board.

Her lifelong friend Shelia; was now in charge of the Design House, which gave Azalea more time to devote to her Lane, her family and her ministry.

Azalea and Shelia had met for lunch one autumn day, as they often did at least once a week.

"Hi girl," said Shelia, as she pulled up at the restaurant in her new red sports car. "Hi Shelia," replied Azalea, as she waved to her friend. "Times have really changed haven't they?" said Azalea. "They certainly have," replied Shelia.

They sat and ordered their lunch, as they reminisced about the past.

Shelia had ordered a tuna salad on wheat toast with lettuce and tomatoes. Azalea had ordered a roasted chicken strip spinach salad. Lunch was brief, because Shelia had to be back at the Design House for an important showing.

"I'll see you next week," said Azalea. "I'm hope so," replied Shelia; as she hugged Azalea tightly so as to never let her go.

Azalea said, "Shelia you're squeezing me too tight." "I'm sorry," replied Shelia, but I truly love you like a sister, and really miss our times together." "Don't be silly girl," replied Azalea. "We are sisters in every sense of the word."

"I know replied Shelia, but we have always been there for each other, and I just don't know what we'd do without the other in our lives."

Azalea replied," Well we won't have to worry about that for a long time." Azalea then handed Shelia a handkerchief to wipe her tears.

"Remember what we have always said;" said Azalea, "we'll be together until the Lord calls one of us home." They then hugged once more, and Shelia and Azalea both drove off in their cars headed to their destinations.

Azalea had a quick stop at the market, before returning home. Forty minutes later, Azalea arrived home to find Lane standing in the driveway looking somber.

Azalea stepped out of the car and asked, "Darling what's the matter?"

Lane replied, "Come inside Leah." Azalea replied, "Lane what's going on, you're frightening me?" "Sat down," Lane replied.

"Tell me Lane," Azalea said. "It's Shelia," replied Lane. Azalea asked, "What's happened, what type of game is this Lane?" "It's no game my sweet Leah. Shelia is gone."

Azalea screamed, "You're lying!" Lane replied, "Its true Leah. Shelia had driven to David's job site to pick him up before returning to the Design house. She wanted him to see the layout of the design house, since she was intending to surprise you with renovations.

On the way back to David's job site, I suppose Shelia was rushing to return for her meeting; when her vehicle was struck by a truck killing David instantly. Shelia later died at the hospital."

"Oh no, no, no, my dearest friend, she was like a sister to me Lane, said Azalea as she wept heavily." Lane replied, "I know my darling; as he helped her inside the house to sit down, and regain her composure."

"I want to see her," said Azalea. "But Leah," replied Lane, "she's gone." "You don't understand, replied Azalea, "Shelia is my dearest friend and sister. She needs me more than ever now, and what about little Hank? Both of his grandmothers passed away some time ago.

I'm all he has left in this world." Lane replied, Leah my darling, you must ask the Lord for help right now. "Leah; ask the Lord; he is the only one who is able to see you through these trying times like what you are going thru."

Before Lane could say another word, Azalea prayed; "Lord Jesus, I ask that you give me the wisdom; as well as the strength to endure, and overcome these trial in my life. Lord Jesus make me a vessel to be a blessing to my dearest friend Shelia's baby son; Little Hank. Amen."

When Azalea and Lane arrived at the hospital, they were instructed to wait in a room reserved for families of lost love ones. When they entered, there was a gentleman dressed in a suit and had a briefcase sitting atop a table. "Mrs. Azalea Jenson?" he asked. "Yes," replied Azalea, as she dabbed her tears away."

She asked, "Who are you?" "My name is Phillip Garret, Attorney-at-Law. I have been legal counsel representing the estate of Shelia and David Roy."

"How can we help you," replied Lane. "Well sir," replied Attorney Garrett, Mr. and Mrs. Roy named you both as executors of their estate, in the event they died together. Shelia Roy also left this letter for you. Azalea opened the envelope and began reading;

My Dear Sweet Sister Leah:

You never let me call you Leah before, but now you can't stop me. You are the dearest friend I ever had. You will always be my sister. I have always trusted you with my life, and now I trust you with the life of my precious son, little Hank. Tears began flowing down Azalea's cheeks. Now stop crying girl. You know I hate seeing you sad.

Azalea child, do you remember when we'd argue sometimes, and then cry and make-up? We always said that we'd be best friends until the Lord called one of us home, well I finally bested you at something girl. He called me first. I won. I get the ultimate prize. Well Azalea, I know you never liked goodbyes, so I'll see you one day hopefully far off, so you can raise my son to be a fine young man in life, much like his namesake. Love your forever friend,

Shelia

The namesake she spoke of was Henry (Hank) Stevens; Azalea's Papa. Papa had always loved and treated Shelia like she was a daughter to him. This was why she had honored him, by naming her son David Henry.

Azalea said smiling, through tears streaming down her cheeks, "This is so like you Shelia. You had to have the last word." While Azalea wept, Mr. Garrett opened his briefcase.

Lane handed Azalea his handkerchief to wipe her tears. Mr. Garrett then spoke. "I'm sure you are not aware of how wealthy Mr. and Mrs. Roy were," said Mr. Garrett.

Lane asked, "What do you mean wealthy?" Mr. Garrett replied, "Mr. Jenson, your friends were very rich people.

"Mr. and Mrs. Jenson, they have left you both one third of their estate valued at five-million dollars; the two-thirds being left to their son and only heir, David Henry Roy, naming you both as his legal guardians."
How did Shelia and David accumulate such wealth?" Azalea asked.

"Mr. Jenson was very instrumental in their doing so, the attorney replied. "I'm not quite sure I understand," Azalea replied.

They had both invested in the stock market, based upon the investments you had casually mentioned to Mr. Roy one Christmas, before the two of you were even married Mrs. Jenson. "Apparently it was at the last Christmas dinner we had when Papa was still alive," said Azalea to Lane.

"Yes my darling," replied Lane, but although I seldom spent time with David like I used to, whenever we talked on the phone, I would discuss my investment portfolio with him." Azalea replied, "Then darling, he must have said something. I mean you must have had some type of clue from him."

Lane replied, "I can remember one time, David asked me what stocks I would consider most lucrative, and I remember mentioning those companies William had made investments in, but I told David if he really wanted to invest, try companies that were floundering now from the recession, but would later turn around when the economy stabilizes. I also told him to always "buy low," and "sell high."

I never gave it a second thought after that. I mean David Roy was never really the type of guy to take any financial risks."

Mr. Garrett replied, "Well apparently he and his wife both were, and they have rewarded you handsomely for your advice. What I was told by the both of them; is that when Mrs. Roy became an associate of yours Mrs. Jenson, and shared in the company's profits, she then invested in the stock market.

Azalea said, "Shelia never let on how wealthy she and David had become, not even to me her best friend." Mr. Garrett replied, "She had once told me that she loved giving, and that she had treasures stored up in heaven, that were far more valuable than an thing on this earth. She even had me set up a trust for feeding the homeless. She loved giving to charities. She also had me set up a trust for her son." Azalea replied, "This is incredible!" Lane said, "Unbelievable!"

Azalea said, "Shelia always looked out for me, even now from heaven. I don't know how I'll go on without her." Lane said you will my darling for little Hank's sake." Just at that moment, little Hank's nanny walked in holding the hand of little Hank who was now three years old.

He ran up to Azalea, as she picked him up and hugged him tightly." "Auntie Zalee please," said little Hank," you're squeezing me too hard."

Azalea looked at little Hank, as she remembered those were some her last words to his mother Shelia, and chuckled. "I'm sorry little Hank, I just love you so very much."

Azalea and Lane both raised David Henry Roy; who would later study at the Seminary, earning a Master Degree in Theology. He would later earn his Doctorate Degree in Theology becoming Pastor of the newly formed Mt. Bless Pentecostal Church.

Meeting Shelia was pre-destined by God. Once Azalea surrendered her life to Jesus Christ, her search for purpose and fulfillment, had led her on the path that God had originally ordained for her life; a path that ultimately led to *"Her Divine Destiny."*

THE END

"PRAISE the LORD!"
"THANK YOU JESUS!"

Author's Bio

Desiree Evans
Christian Author/Writer/Novelist

I surrendered my life to Jesus Christ in 1984, and the Savior delivered me from both; depression and alcohol addiction right at the time of my conversion. I thank the Lord God Almighty, that through the shed blood of his precious son, Jesus Christ; by the power of his Holy Spirit, he delivered and set me free. I am so over joyed to testify of his grace and mercy he has shown me. I thank him for pouring his anointing upon me as a Prayer Warrior, and Servant of Jesus Christ.

The Lord has blessed me to graduate with an Associate of Science Degree in Criminal Justice in 2008. I have recently completed my undergraduate studies with a Bachelor of Science Degree in Criminal Justice from Ashworth College. The Lord blessed me to graduate from Lakewood College with a graduate certificate in Mediation and Conflict Resolution; and have the distinction of becoming a member of the National Association of Certified Mediators. I am an elected member of Delta Epsilon Tau International Honor Society. I am also a wife, mother, and grandmother. My hobbies include writing, and I love baking, and decorating cupcakes.

ENDNOTES

---

[1] Ephesians 2:8,9 (James, Original Copyright 1611) (KJV) emphasis mine

[2] Romans 10:13 (James, Original Copyright 1611) (KJV) emphasis mine

[3] Romans 10:10 (James, Original Copyright 1611) (KJV) emphasis mine

[4] 1 Timothy 6:6 (James, Original Copyright 1611) (KJV) emphasis mine

[5] Isaiah 53:4-12 (James, Original Copyright 1611) (KJV) emphasis mine

[6] Romans 6:23 (James, Original Copyright 1611)

Bibliography

James, K. (Original Copyright 1611). *The Holy Bible/ the King James Version (KJV)*. United States of America.

Made in the USA
Charleston, SC
24 October 2012